UNPLUGGED AND UNPOPULAR

AN ONI PRESS PUBLICATION

UNPLUGGED

AND

AN ONI PRESS PUBLICATION

UNPOPULAR

WRITTEN BY
MAT HEAGERTY

ILLUSTRATED BY
TINTIN PANTOJA

COLORED BY
MIKE AMANTE

LETTERED BY
HASSAN OTSMANE-ELHAOU

COVER ILLUSTRATED BY
TINTIN PANTOJA
WITH **MIKE AMANTE**

LOGO DESIGNED BY
RICKY DELUCCO

BOOK DESIGNED BY
ANGIE KNOWLES

EDITED BY
ROBIN HERRERA

PUBLISHED BY ONI PRESS, INC.

JOE NOZEMACK founder & chief financial officer
JAMES LUCAS JONES publisher
SARAH GAYDOS editor in chief
CHARLIE CHU v.p. of creative & business development
BRAD ROOKS director of operations
MARGOT WOOD director of sales
AMBER O'NEILL special projects manager
TROY LOOK director of design & production
KATE Z. STONE senior graphic designer
SONJA SYNAK graphic designer
ANGIE KNOWLES digital prepress lead
ROBIN HERRERA senior editor
ARI YARWOOD senior editor
MICHELLE NGUYEN executive assistant
JUNG LEE logistics coordinator

ONI PRESS

ONIPRESS.COM
FACEBOOK.COM/ONIPRESS
TWITTER.COM/ONIPRESS
ONIPRESS.TUMBLR.COM
INSTAGRAM.COM/ONIPRESS

FIRST EDITION: OCTOBER 2019

HARDCOVER ISBN 978-1-62010-680-8
PAPERBACK ISBN 978-1-62010-669-3
EISBN 978-1-62010-670-9

PRINTED IN CHINA.

LIBRARY OF CONGRESS CONTROL NUMBER: 2019934120

1 2 3 4 5 6 7 8 9 10

CHAPTER ONE

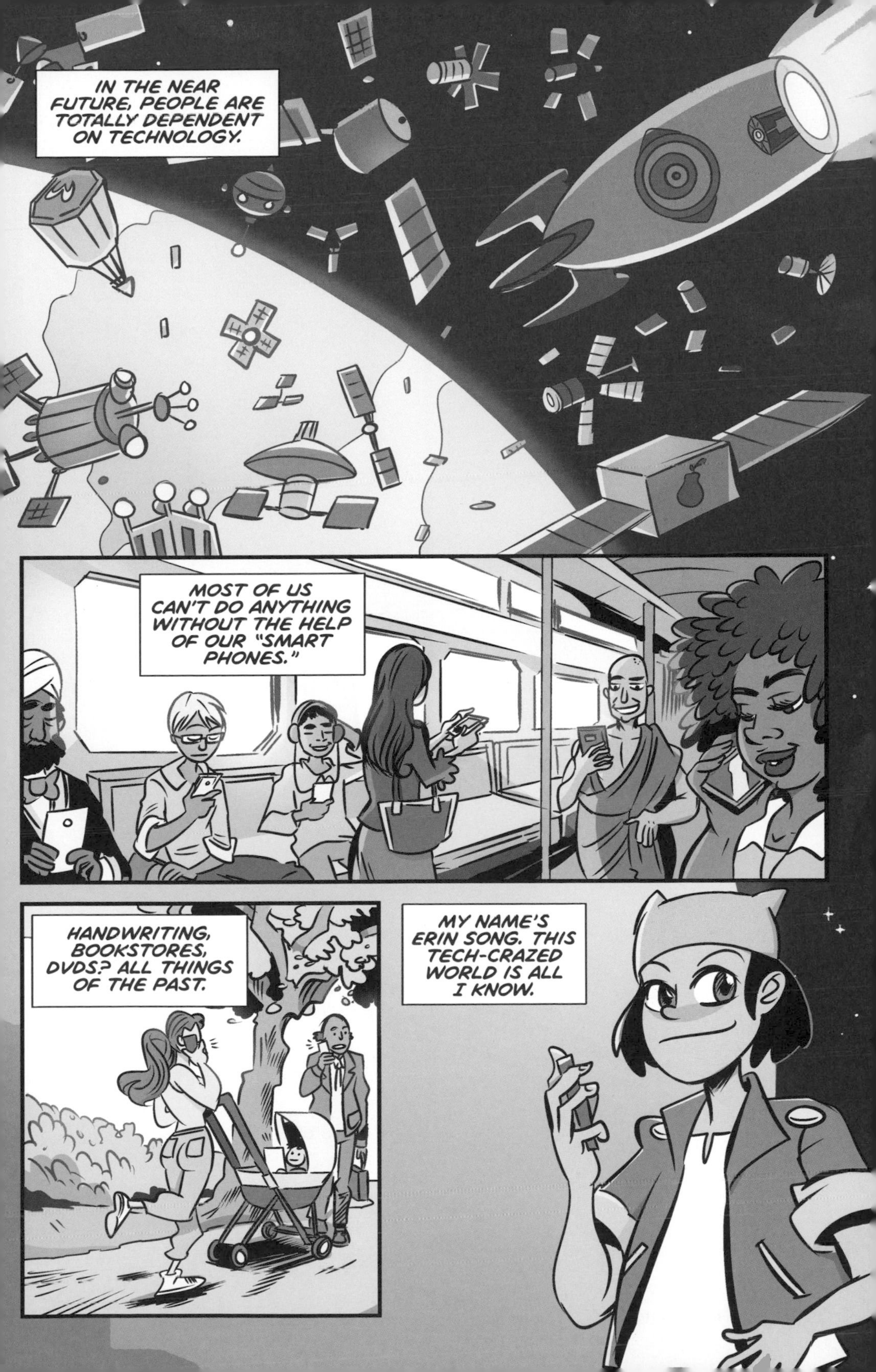
IN THE NEAR FUTURE, PEOPLE ARE TOTALLY DEPENDENT ON TECHNOLOGY.
MOST OF US CAN'T DO ANYTHING WITHOUT THE HELP OF OUR "SMART PHONES."
HANDWRITING, BOOKSTORES, DVDS? ALL THINGS OF THE PAST.
MY NAME'S ERIN SONG. THIS TECH-CRAZED WORLD IS ALL I KNOW.

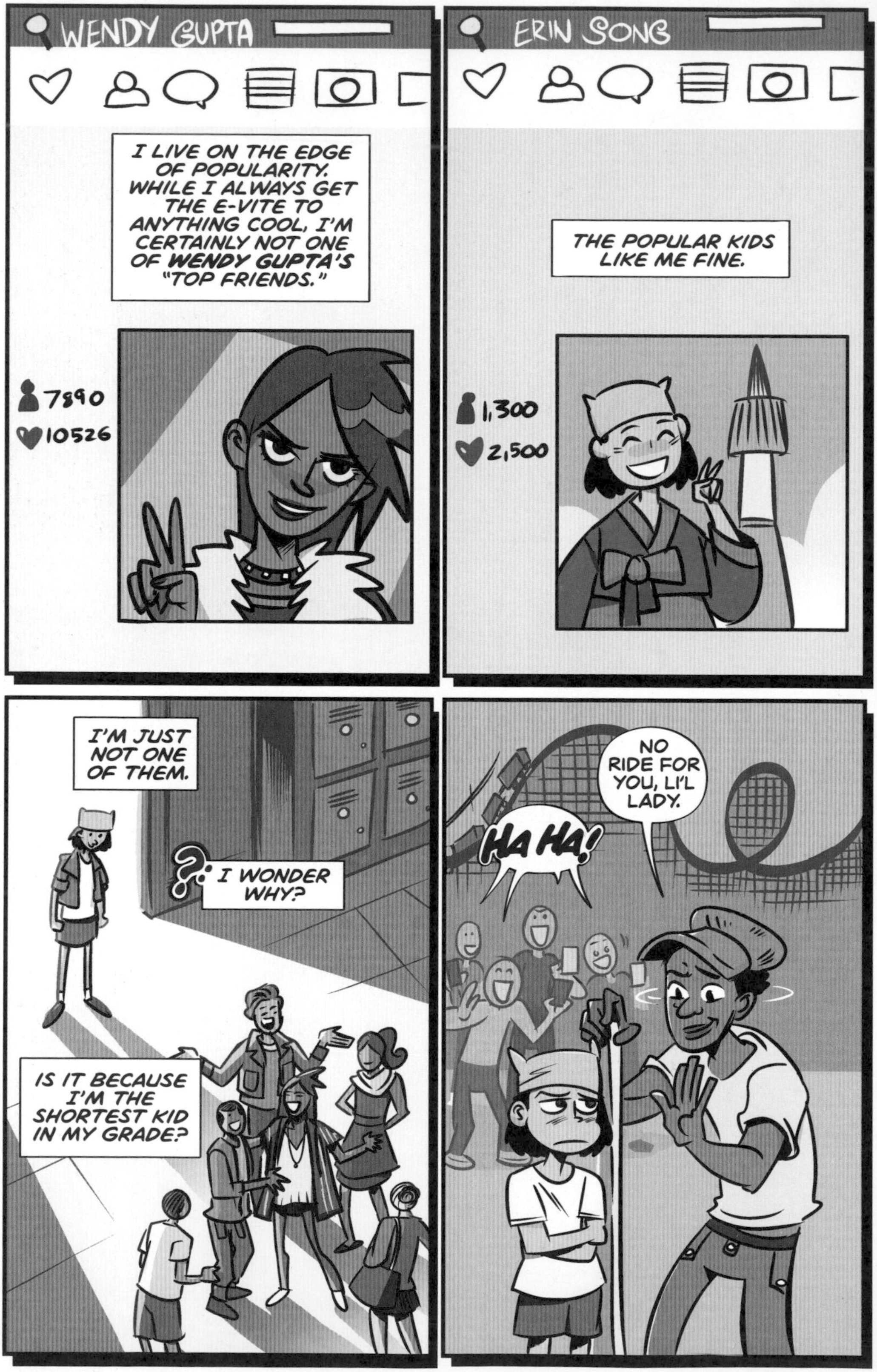
WENDY GUPTA
I LIVE ON THE EDGE OF POPULARITY. WHILE I ALWAYS GET THE E-VITE TO ANYTHING COOL, I'M CERTAINLY NOT ONE OF WENDY GUPTA'S "TOP FRIENDS."
7890
10526
ERIN SONG
THE POPULAR KIDS LIKE ME FINE.
1,300
2,500
I'M JUST NOT ONE OF THEM.
I WONDER WHY?
IS IT BECAUSE I'M THE SHORTEST KID IN MY GRADE?
NO RIDE FOR YOU, LI'L LADY.
HA HA!

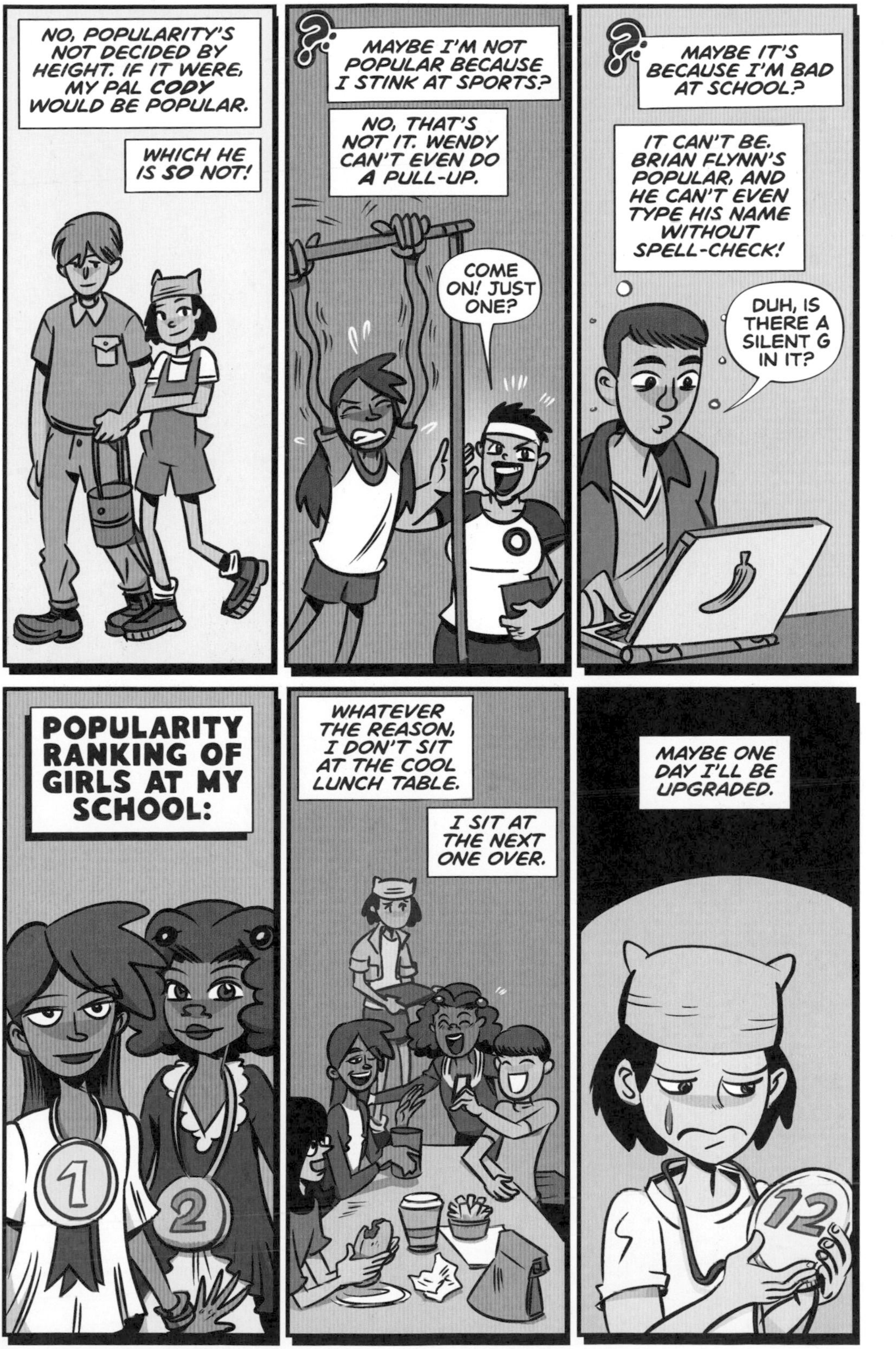
NO, POPULARITY'S NOT DECIDED BY HEIGHT. IF IT WERE, MY PAL CODY WOULD BE POPULAR.
WHICH HE IS SO NOT!
MAYBE I'M NOT POPULAR BECAUSE I STINK AT SPORTS?
NO, THAT'S NOT IT. WENDY CAN'T EVEN DO A PULL-UP.
COME ON! JUST ONE?
MAYBE IT'S BECAUSE I'M BAD AT SCHOOL?
IT CAN'T BE. BRIAN FLYNN'S POPULAR, AND HE CAN'T EVEN TYPE HIS NAME WITHOUT SPELL-CHECK!
DUH, IS THERE A SILENT G IN IT?
POPULARITY RANKING OF GIRLS AT MY SCHOOL:
1
2
WHATEVER THE REASON, I DON'T SIT AT THE COOL LUNCH TABLE.
I SIT AT THE NEXT ONE OVER.
MAYBE ONE DAY I'LL BE UPGRADED.
12

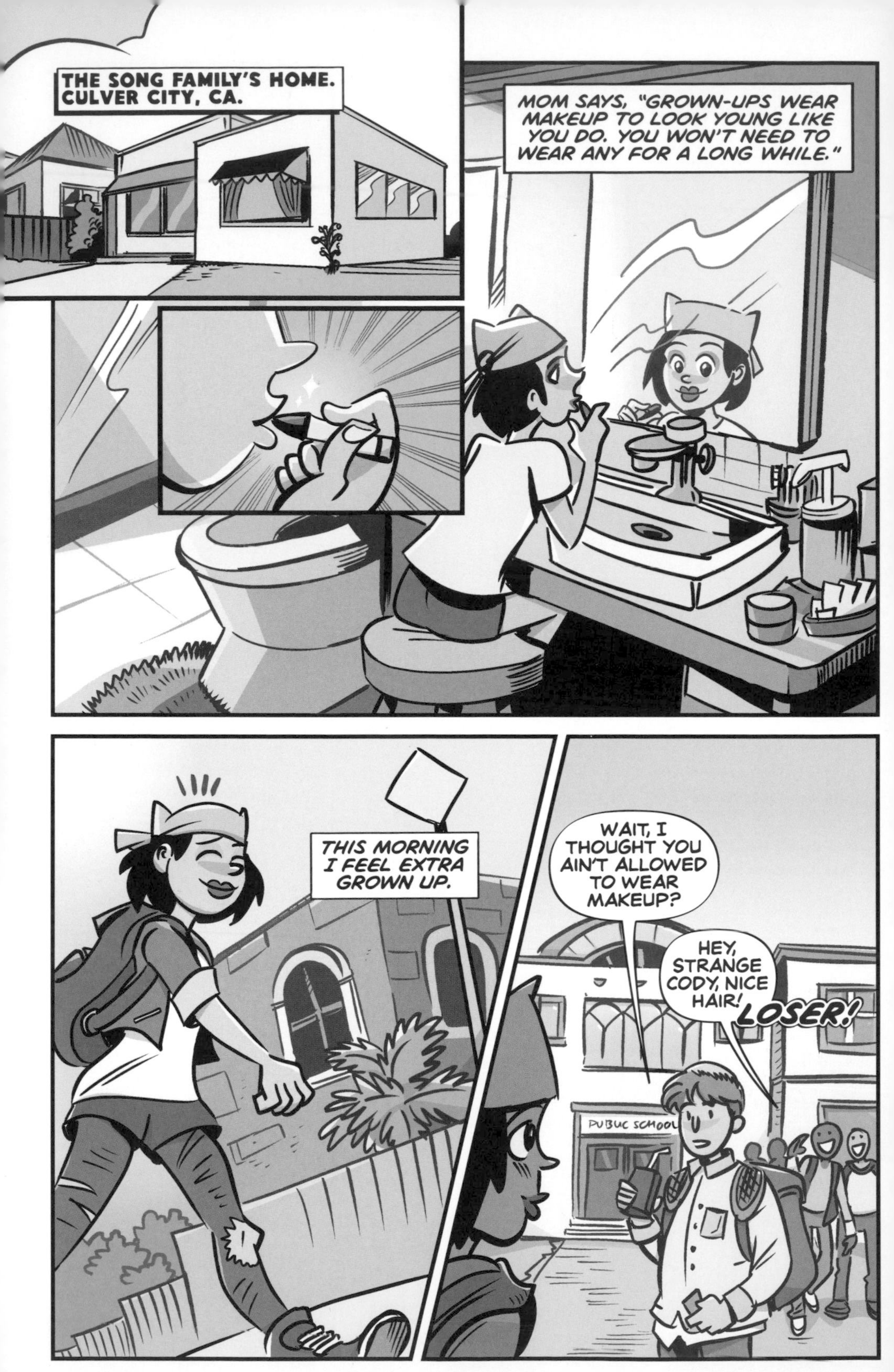
THE SONG FAMILY'S HOME.
CULVER CITY, CA.
MOM SAYS, "GROWN-UPS WEAR MAKEUP TO LOOK YOUNG LIKE YOU DO. YOU WON'T NEED TO WEAR ANY FOR A LONG WHILE."
THIS MORNING I FEEL EXTRA GROWN UP.
WAIT, I THOUGHT YOU AIN'T ALLOWED TO WEAR MAKEUP?
HEY, STRANGE CODY, NICE HAIR!
LOSER!
PUBLIC SCHOOL

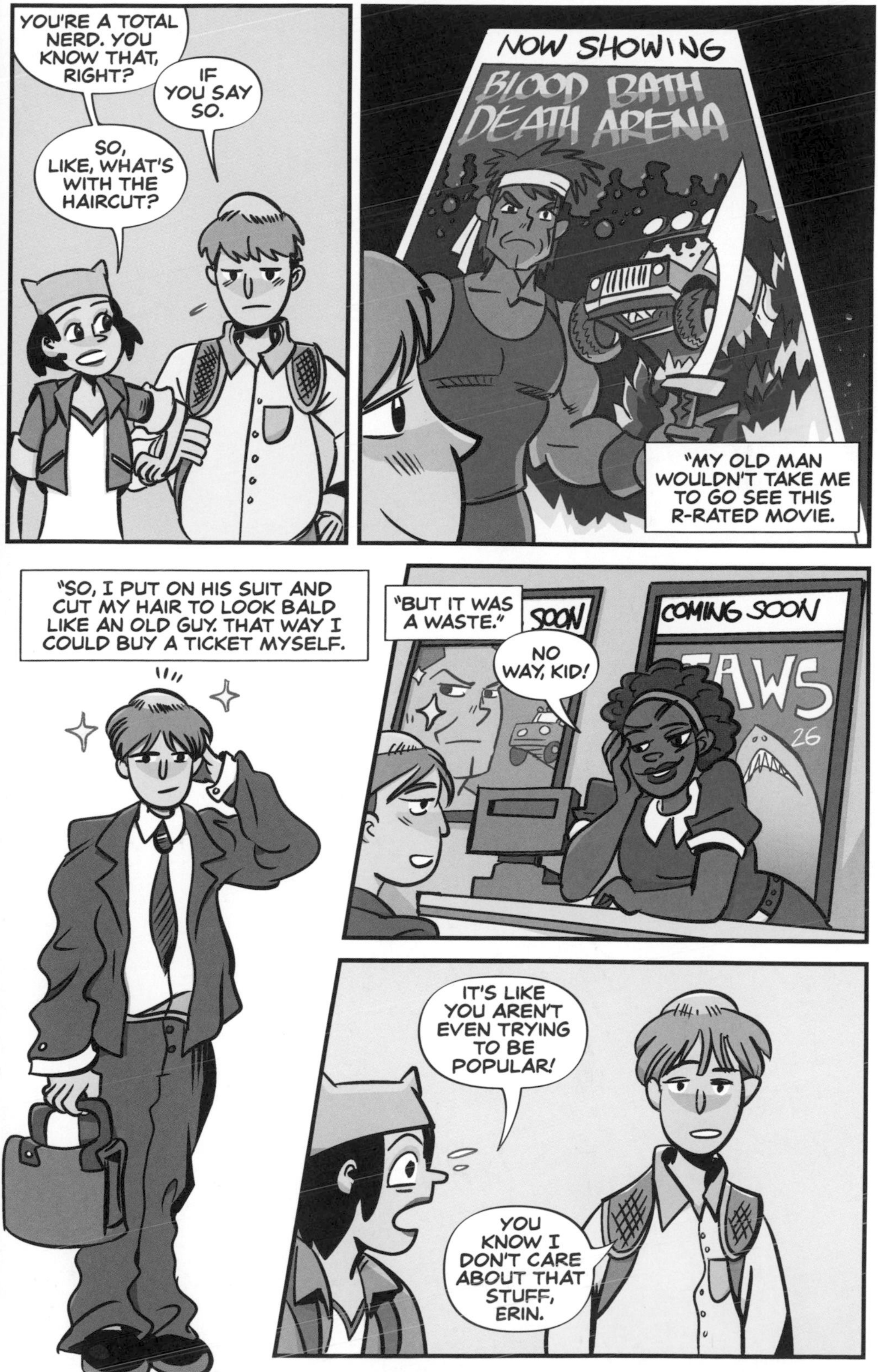
YOU'RE A TOTAL NERD. YOU KNOW THAT, RIGHT?
IF YOU SAY SO.
SO, LIKE, WHAT'S WITH THE HAIRCUT?
NOW SHOWING
BLOOD BATH DEATH ARENA
"MY OLD MAN WOULDN'T TAKE ME TO GO SEE THIS R-RATED MOVIE.
"SO, I PUT ON HIS SUIT AND CUT MY HAIR TO LOOK BALD LIKE AN OLD GUY. THAT WAY I COULD BUY A TICKET MYSELF.
"BUT IT WAS A WASTE."
SOON
COMING SOON
NO WAY, KID!
JAWS
26
IT'S LIKE YOU AREN'T EVEN TRYING TO BE POPULAR!
YOU KNOW I DON'T CARE ABOUT THAT STUFF, ERIN.

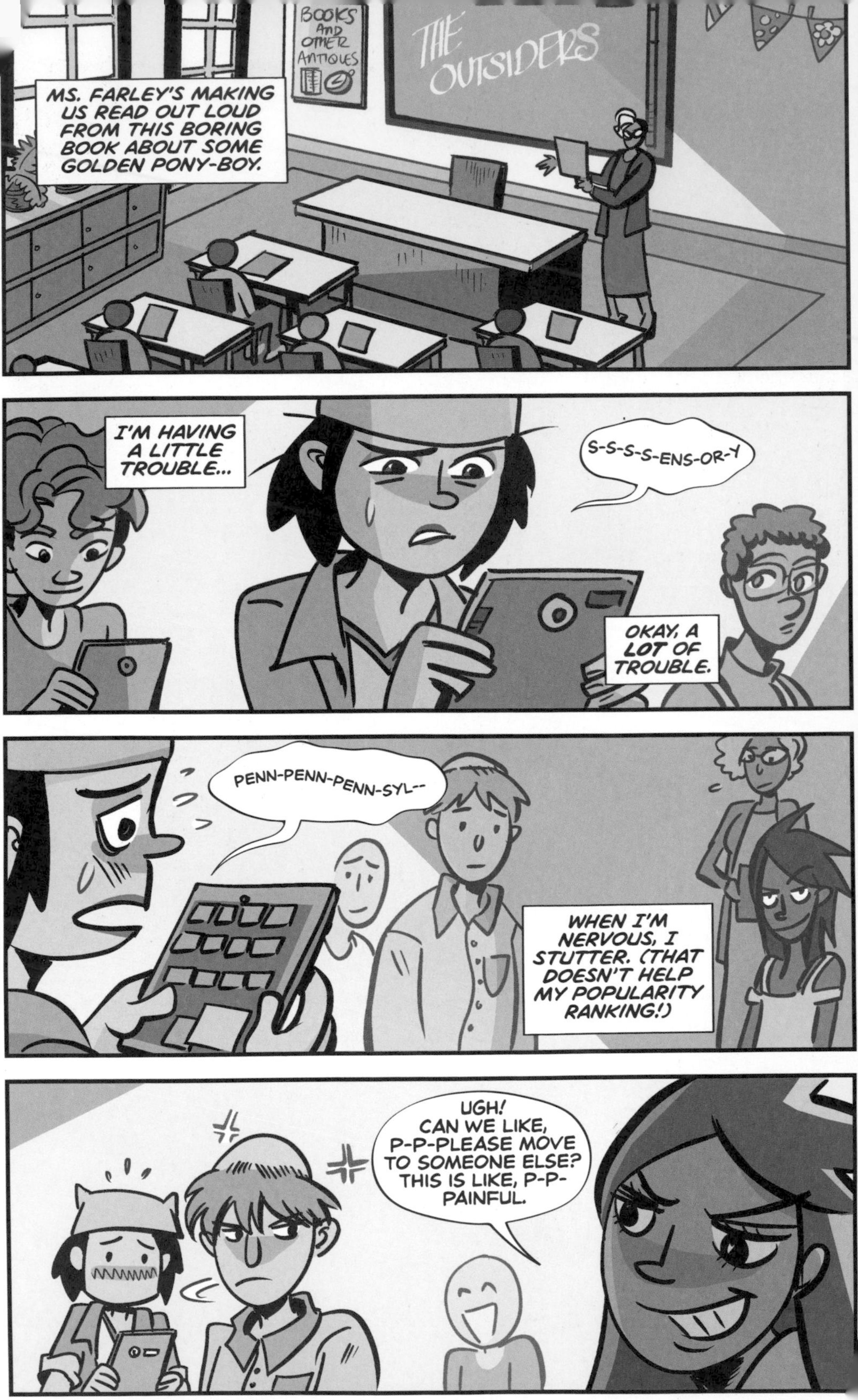
BOOKS AND OTHER ANTIQUES
THE OUTSIDERS
MS. FARLEY'S MAKING US READ OUT LOUD FROM THIS BORING BOOK ABOUT SOME GOLDEN PONY-BOY.
I'M HAVING A LITTLE TROUBLE...
S-S-S-S-ENS-OR-Y
OKAY, A LOT OF TROUBLE.
PENN-PENN-PENN-SYL--
WHEN I'M NERVOUS, I STUTTER. (THAT DOESN'T HELP MY POPULARITY RANKING!)
UGH! CAN WE LIKE, P-P-PLEASE MOVE TO SOMEONE ELSE? THIS IS LIKE, P-P-PAINFUL.

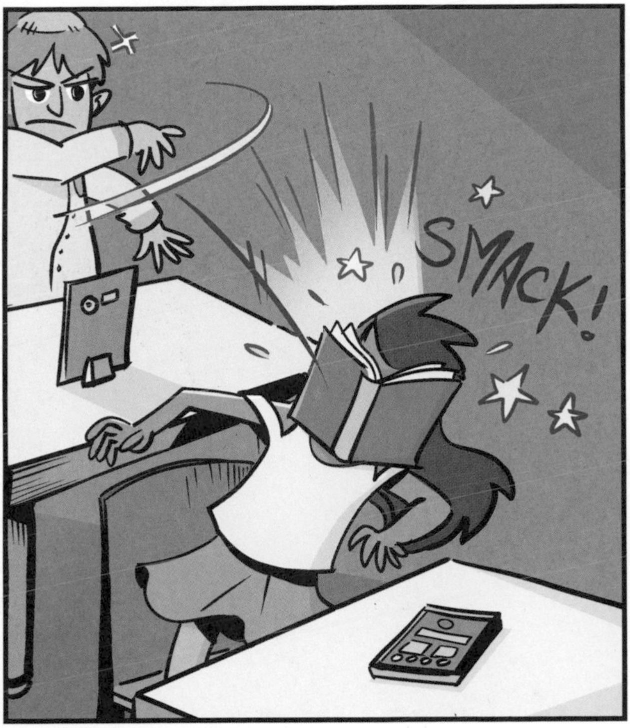
SMACK!

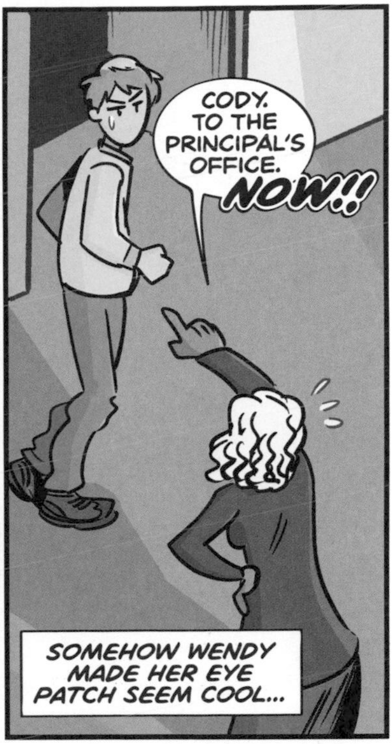
CODY. TO THE PRINCIPAL'S OFFICE. NOW!!
SOMEHOW WENDY MADE HER EYE PATCH SEEM COOL...

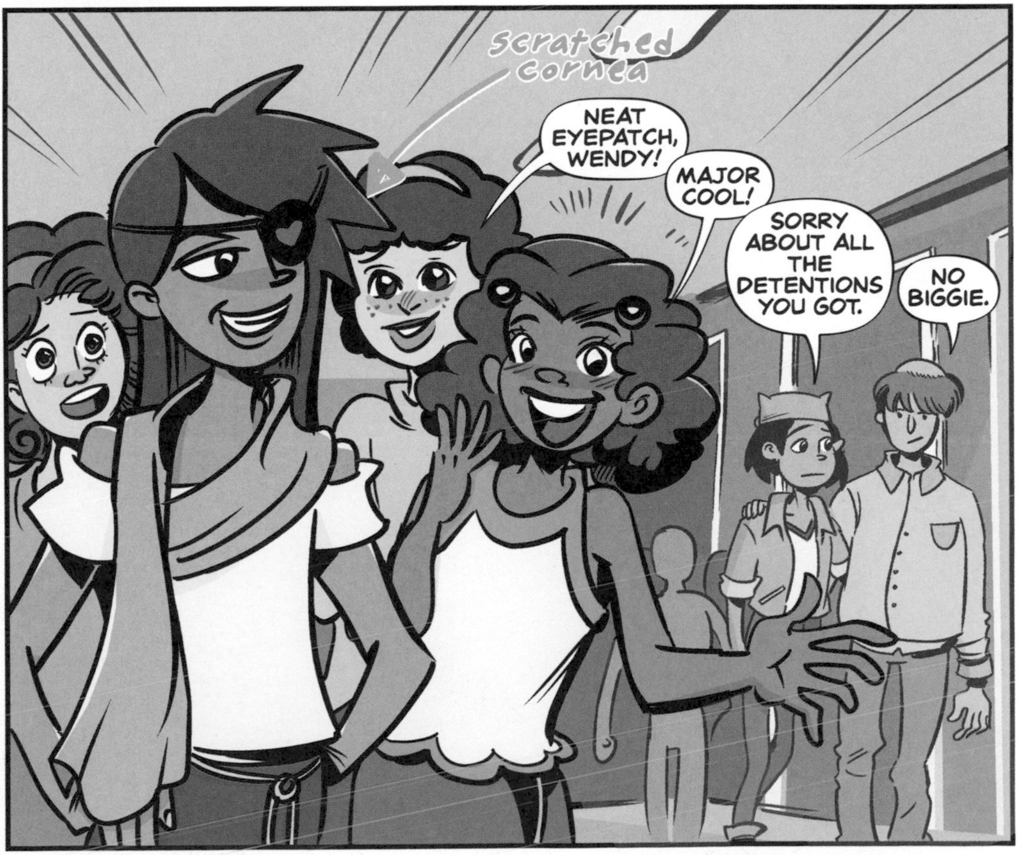
scratched cornea
NEAT EYEPATCH, WENDY!
MAJOR COOL!
SORRY ABOUT ALL THE DETENTIONS YOU GOT.
NO BIGGIE.

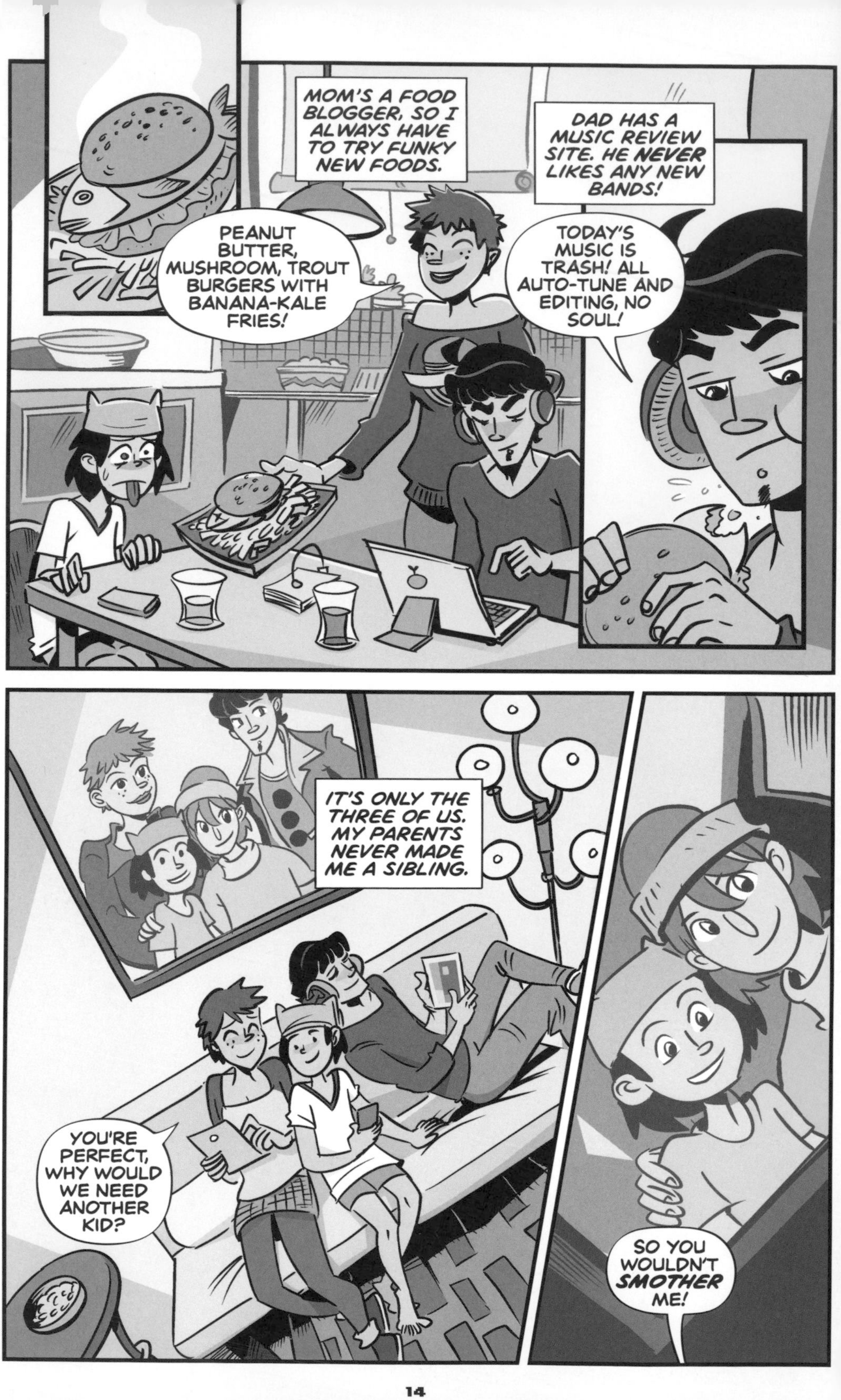
MOM'S A FOOD BLOGGER, SO I ALWAYS HAVE TO TRY FUNKY NEW FOODS.
PEANUT BUTTER, MUSHROOM, TROUT BURGERS WITH BANANA-KALE FRIES!
DAD HAS A MUSIC REVIEW SITE. HE NEVER LIKES ANY NEW BANDS!
TODAY'S MUSIC IS TRASH! ALL AUTO-TUNE AND EDITING, NO SOUL!
IT'S ONLY THE THREE OF US. MY PARENTS NEVER MADE ME A SIBLING.
YOU'RE PERFECT, WHY WOULD WE NEED ANOTHER KID?
SO YOU WOULDN'T SMOTHER ME!

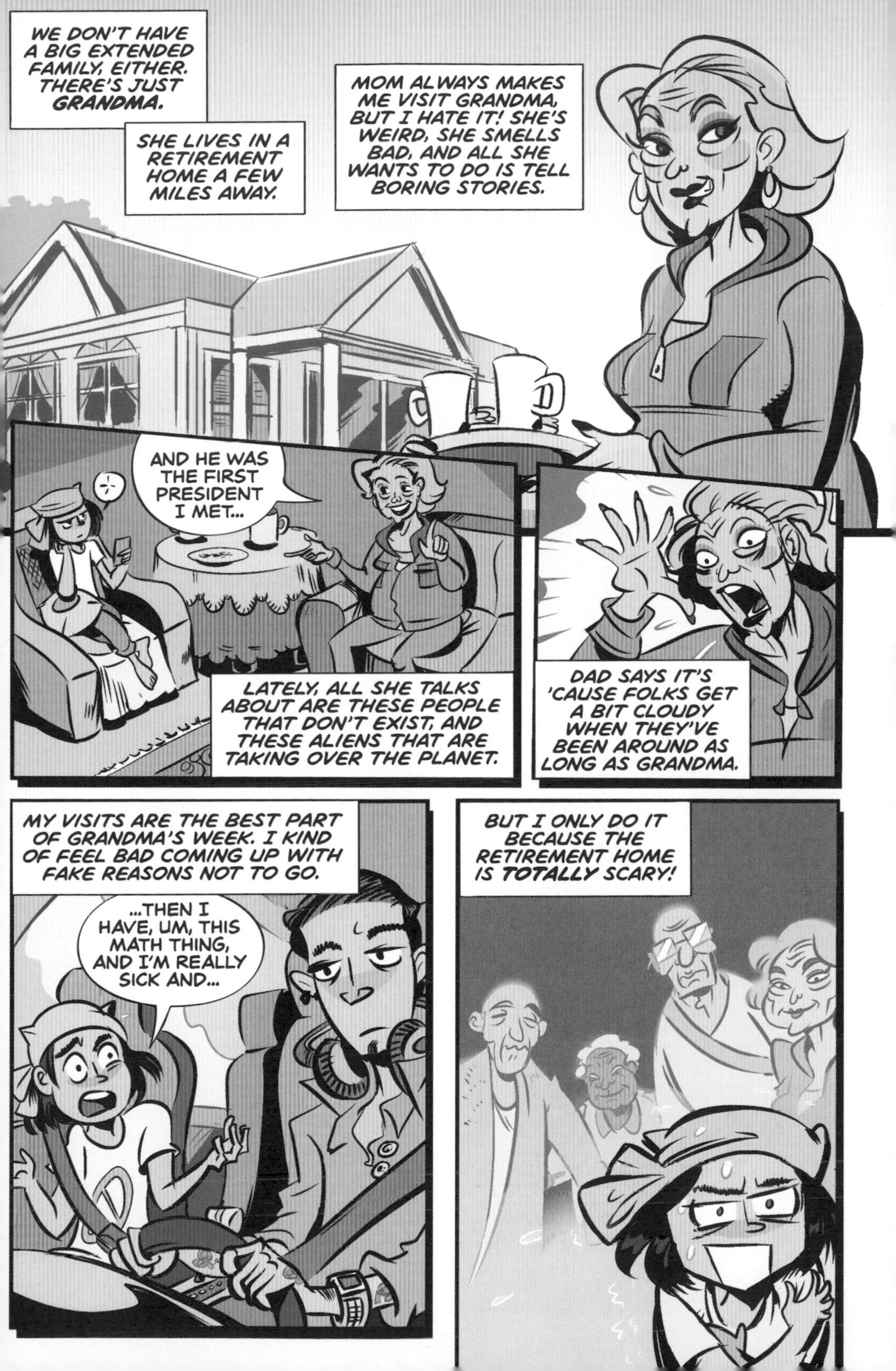
WE DON'T HAVE A BIG EXTENDED FAMILY, EITHER. THERE'S JUST GRANDMA.
SHE LIVES IN A RETIREMENT HOME A FEW MILES AWAY.
MOM ALWAYS MAKES ME VISIT GRANDMA, BUT I HATE IT! SHE'S WEIRD, SHE SMELLS BAD, AND ALL SHE WANTS TO DO IS TELL BORING STORIES.
AND HE WAS THE FIRST PRESIDENT I MET...
LATELY, ALL SHE TALKS ABOUT ARE THESE PEOPLE THAT DON'T EXIST, AND THESE ALIENS THAT ARE TAKING OVER THE PLANET.
DAD SAYS IT'S 'CAUSE FOLKS GET A BIT CLOUDY WHEN THEY'VE BEEN AROUND AS LONG AS GRANDMA.
MY VISITS ARE THE BEST PART OF GRANDMA'S WEEK. I KIND OF FEEL BAD COMING UP WITH FAKE REASONS NOT TO GO.
...THEN I HAVE, UM, THIS MATH THING, AND I'M REALLY SICK AND...
BUT I ONLY DO IT BECAUSE THE RETIREMENT HOME IS TOTALLY SCARY!

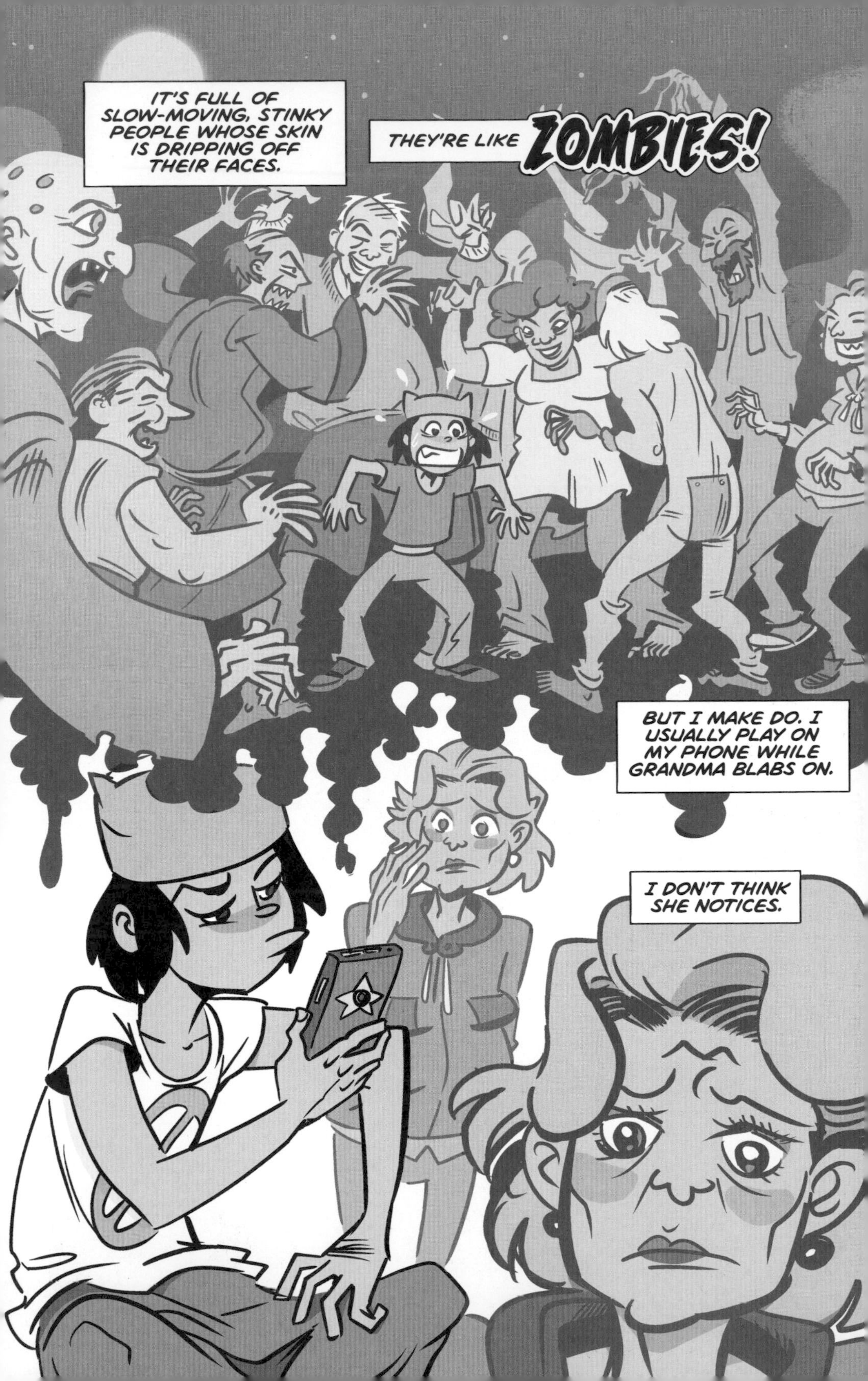
IT'S FULL OF SLOW-MOVING, STINKY PEOPLE WHOSE SKIN IS DRIPPING OFF THEIR FACES.
THEY'RE LIKE ZOMBIES!
BUT I MAKE DO. I USUALLY PLAY ON MY PHONE WHILE GRANDMA BLABS ON.
I DON'T THINK SHE NOTICES.

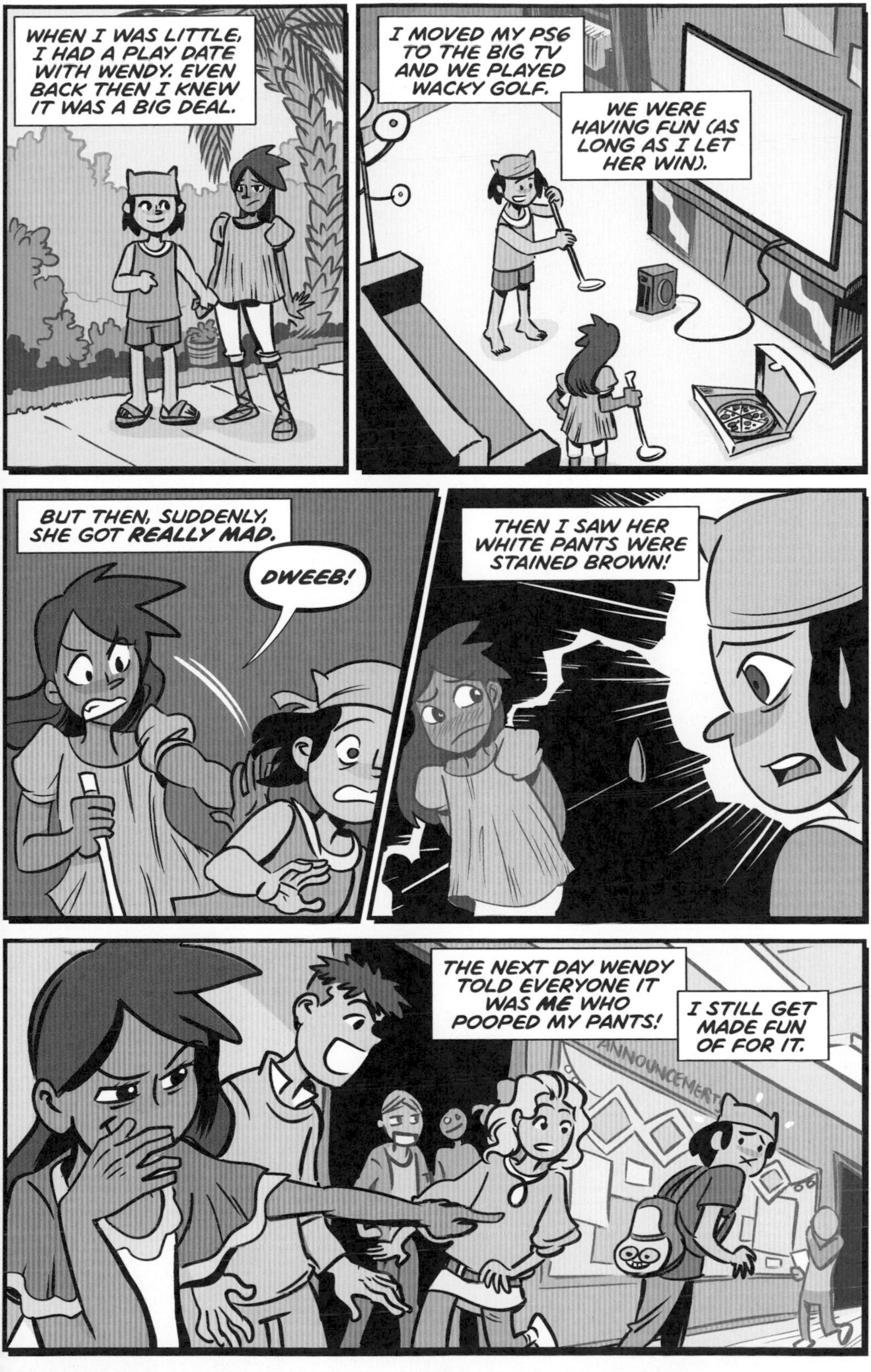
WHEN I WAS LITTLE, I HAD A PLAY DATE WITH WENDY. EVEN BACK THEN I KNEW IT WAS A BIG DEAL.
I MOVED MY PS6 TO THE BIG TV AND WE PLAYED WACKY GOLF.
WE WERE HAVING FUN (AS LONG AS I LET HER WIN).
BUT THEN, SUDDENLY, SHE GOT REALLY MAD.
DWEEB!
THEN I SAW HER WHITE PANTS WERE STAINED BROWN!
THE NEXT DAY WENDY TOLD EVERYONE IT WAS ME WHO POOPED MY PANTS!
I STILL GET MADE FUN OF FOR IT.
ANNOUNCEMENTS

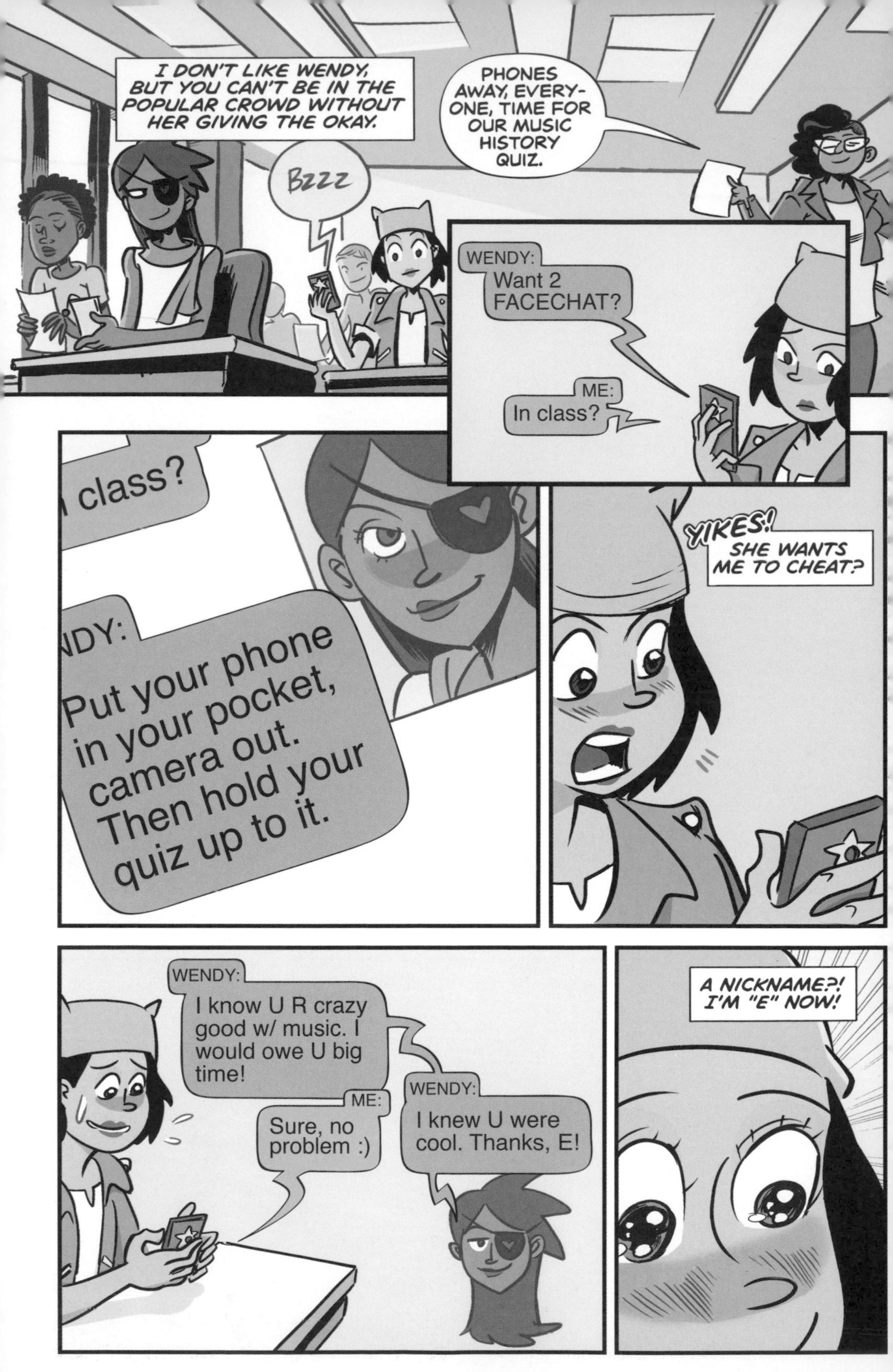

I DON'T LIKE WENDY, BUT YOU CAN'T BE IN THE POPULAR CROWD WITHOUT HER GIVING THE OKAY.
BZZZ
PHONES AWAY, EVERY-ONE, TIME FOR OUR MUSIC HISTORY QUIZ.
WENDY:
Want 2 FACECHAT?
ME:
In class?
class?
DY:
Put your phone in your pocket, camera out. Then hold your quiz up to it.
YIKES! SHE WANTS ME TO CHEAT?
WENDY:
I know U R crazy good w/ music. I would owe U big time!
ME:
Sure, no problem :)
WENDY:
I knew U were cool. Thanks, E!
A NICKNAME?! I'M "E" NOW!

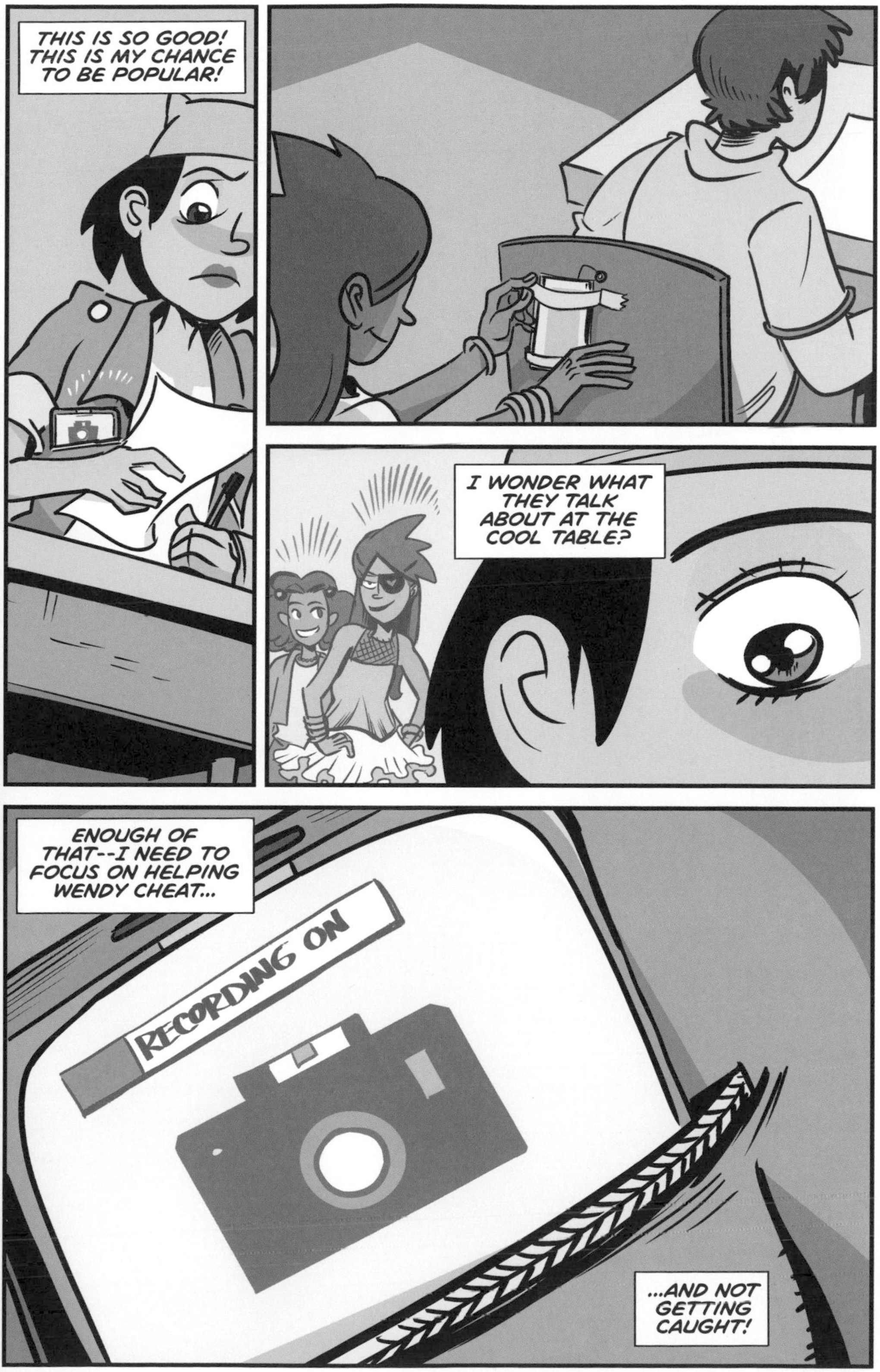
THIS IS SO GOOD! THIS IS MY CHANCE TO BE POPULAR!
I WONDER WHAT THEY TALK ABOUT AT THE COOL TABLE?
ENOUGH OF THAT--I NEED TO FOCUS ON HELPING WENDY CHEAT...
RECORDING ON
...AND NOT GETTING CAUGHT!

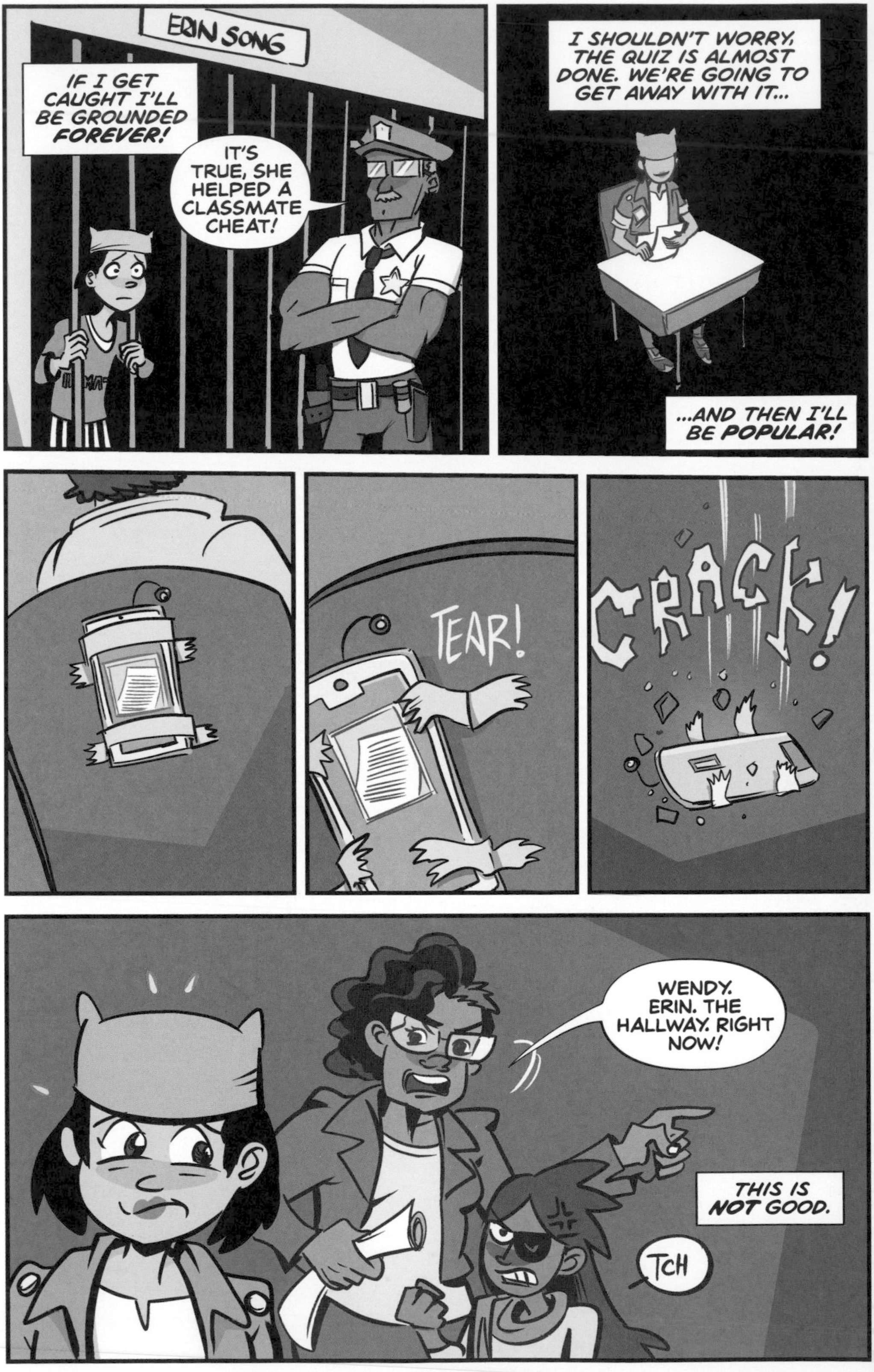
ERIN SONG
IF I GET CAUGHT I'LL BE GROUNDED FOREVER!
IT'S TRUE, SHE HELPED A CLASSMATE CHEAT!
I SHOULDN'T WORRY, THE QUIZ IS ALMOST DONE. WE'RE GOING TO GET AWAY WITH IT...
...AND THEN I'LL BE POPULAR!
TEAR!
CRACK!
WENDY. ERIN. THE HALLWAY. RIGHT NOW!
THIS IS NOT GOOD.
TCH

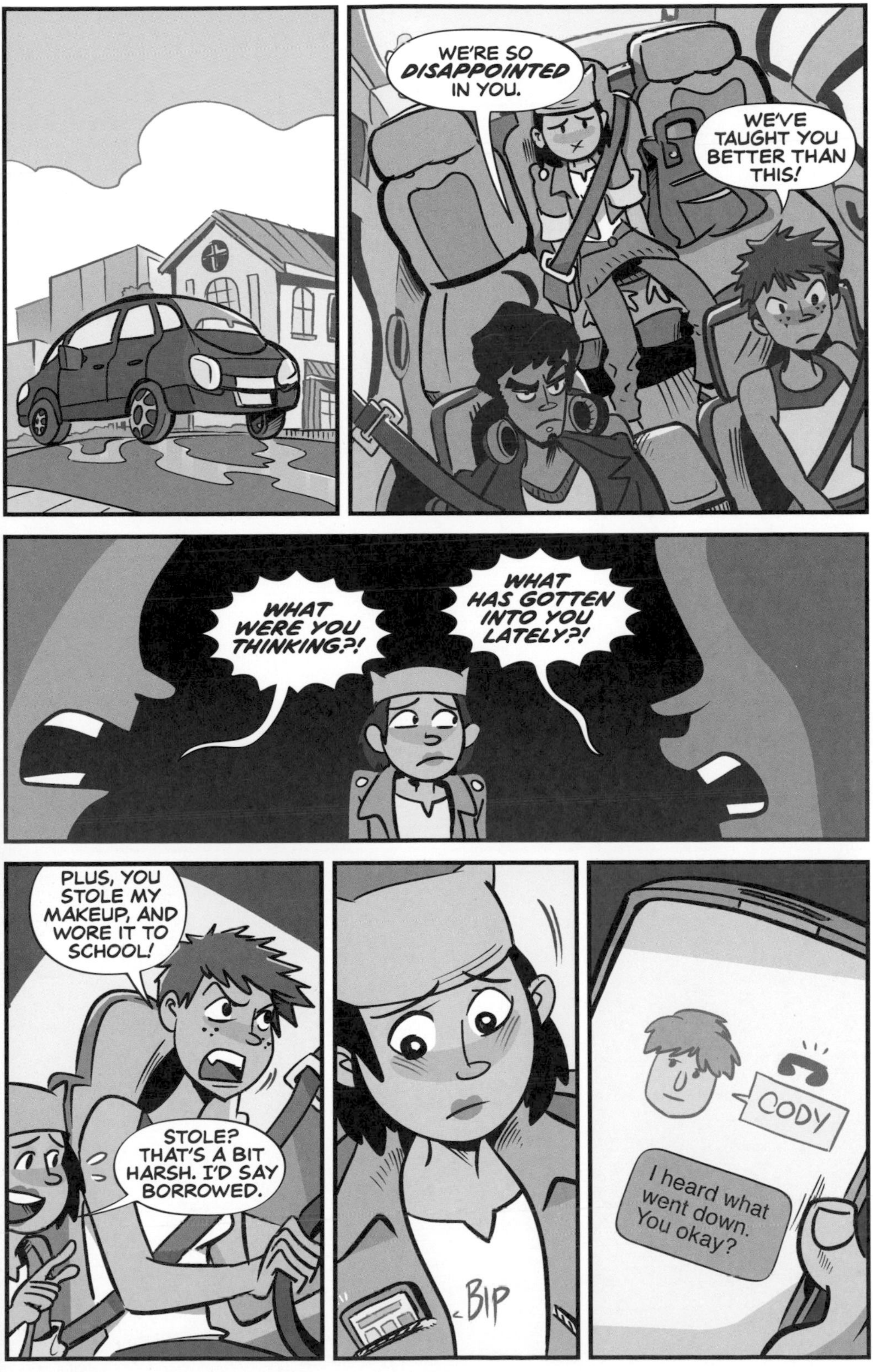
WE'RE SO DISAPPOINTED IN YOU.
WE'VE TAUGHT YOU BETTER THAN THIS!
WHAT WERE YOU THINKING?!
WHAT HAS GOTTEN INTO YOU LATELY?!
PLUS, YOU STOLE MY MAKEUP, AND WORE IT TO SCHOOL!
STOLE? THAT'S A BIT HARSH. I'D SAY BORROWED.
BIP
CODY
I heard what went down. You okay?

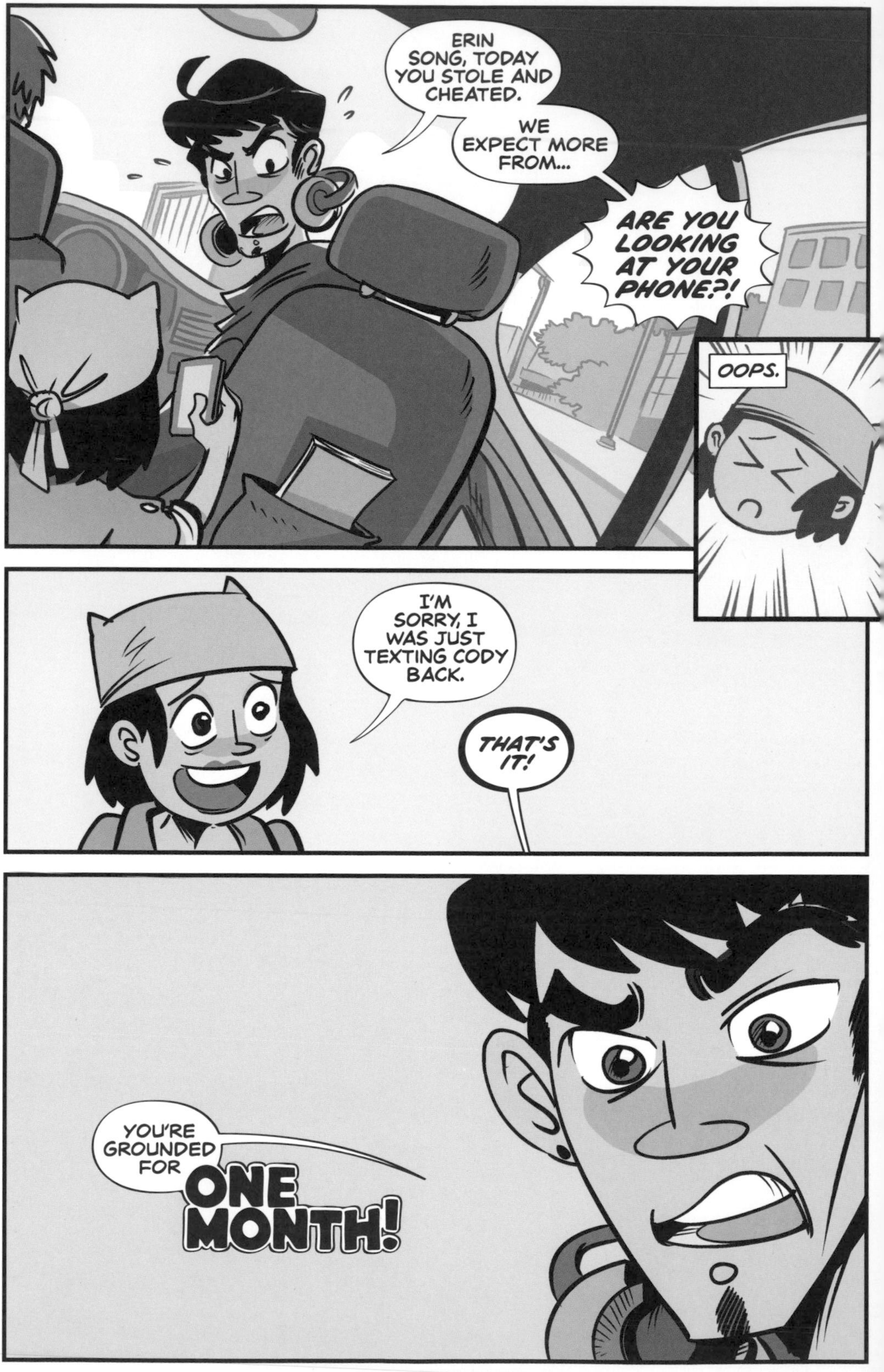
ERIN SONG, TODAY YOU STOLE AND CHEATED.
WE EXPECT MORE FROM...
ARE YOU LOOKING AT YOUR PHONE?!
OOPS.
I'M SORRY, I WAS JUST TEXTING CODY BACK.
THAT'S IT!
YOU'RE GROUNDED FOR ONE MONTH!

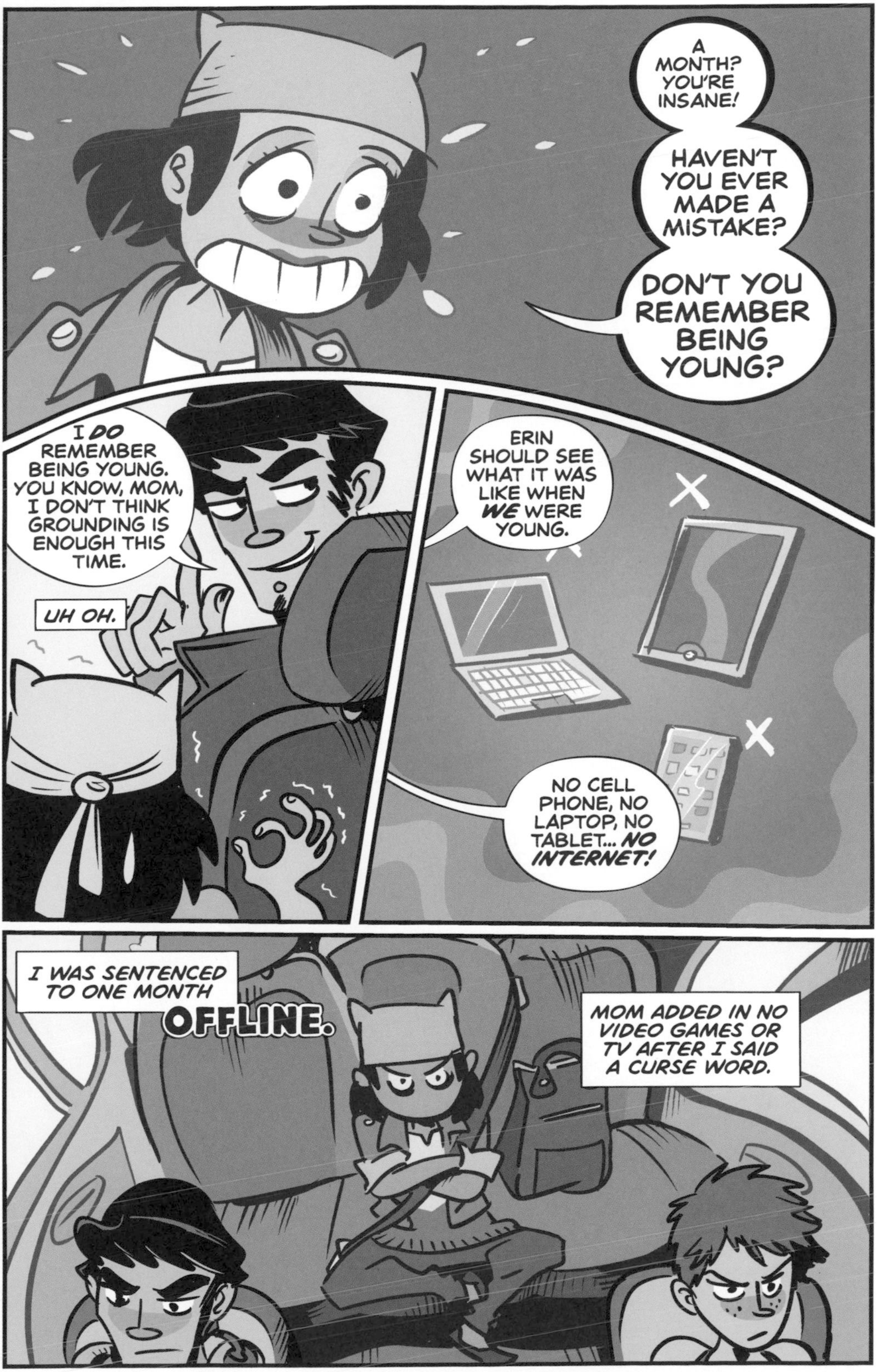
A MONTH? YOU'RE INSANE!
HAVEN'T YOU EVER MADE A MISTAKE?
DON'T YOU REMEMBER BEING YOUNG?
I DO REMEMBER BEING YOUNG. YOU KNOW, MOM, I DON'T THINK GROUNDING IS ENOUGH THIS TIME.
UH OH.
ERIN SHOULD SEE WHAT IT WAS LIKE WHEN WE WERE YOUNG.
NO CELL PHONE, NO LAPTOP, NO TABLET... NO INTERNET!
I WAS SENTENCED TO ONE MONTH OFFLINE.
MOM ADDED IN NO VIDEO GAMES OR TV AFTER I SAID A CURSE WORD.

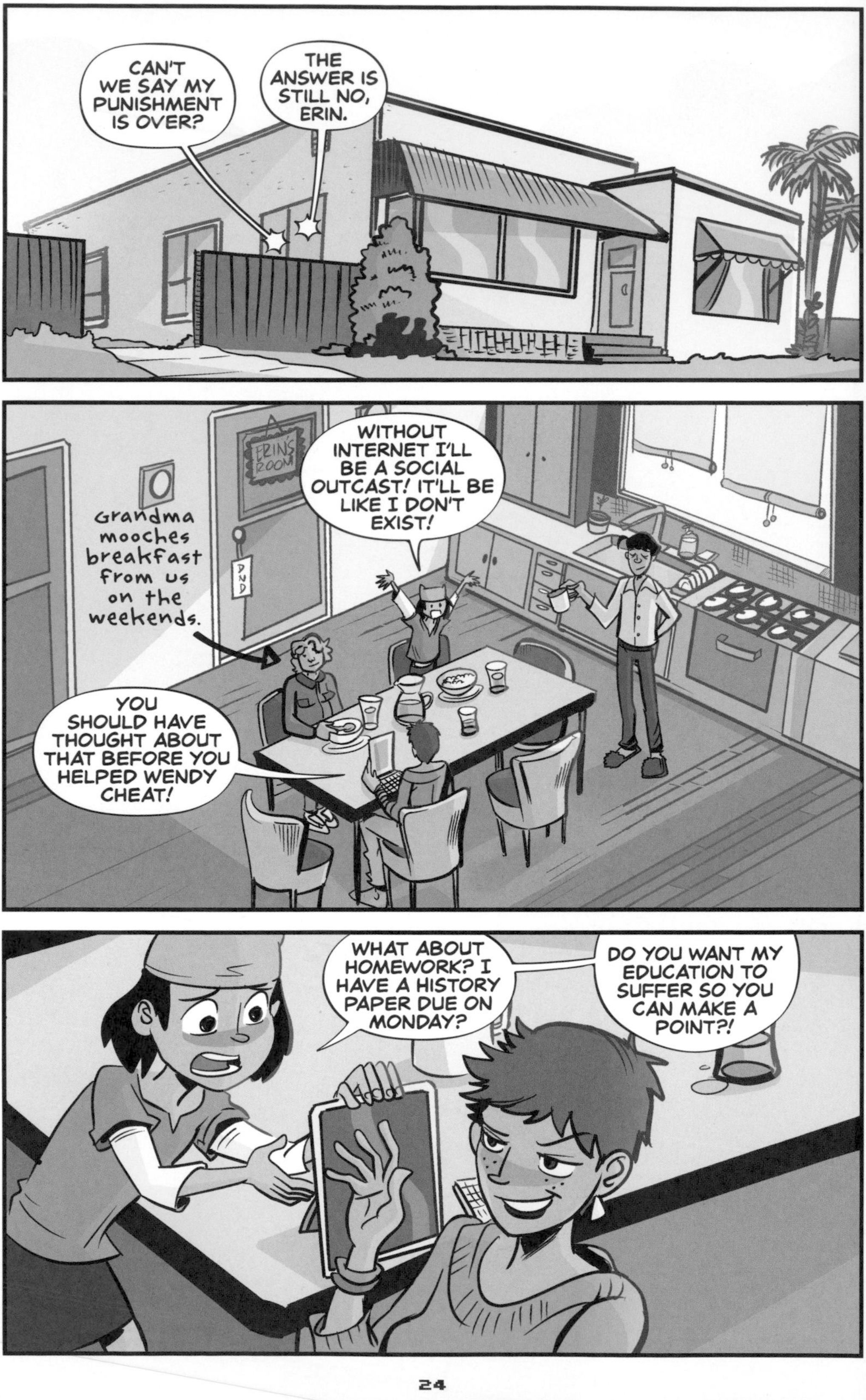
CAN'T WE SAY MY PUNISHMENT IS OVER?
THE ANSWER IS STILL NO, ERIN.
ERIN'S ROOM
DND
Grandma mooches breakfast from us on the weekends.
WITHOUT INTERNET I'LL BE A SOCIAL OUTCAST! IT'LL BE LIKE I DON'T EXIST!
YOU SHOULD HAVE THOUGHT ABOUT THAT BEFORE YOU HELPED WENDY CHEAT!
WHAT ABOUT HOMEWORK? I HAVE A HISTORY PAPER DUE ON MONDAY?
DO YOU WANT MY EDUCATION TO SUFFER SO YOU CAN MAKE A POINT?!

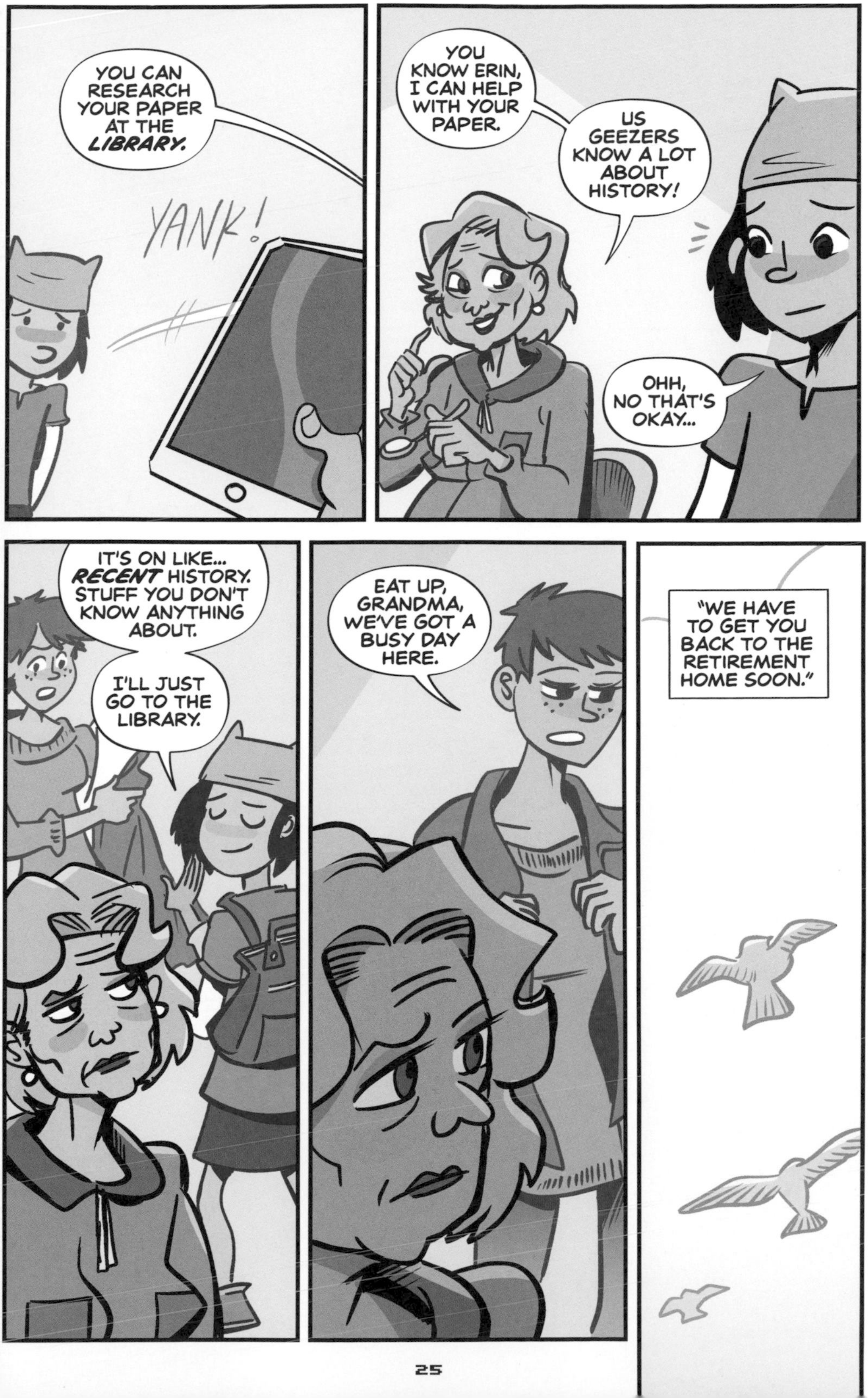
YOU CAN RESEARCH YOUR PAPER AT THE LIBRARY.
YANK!
YOU KNOW ERIN, I CAN HELP WITH YOUR PAPER.
US GEEZERS KNOW A LOT ABOUT HISTORY!
OHH, NO THAT'S OKAY...
IT'S ON LIKE... RECENT HISTORY. STUFF YOU DON'T KNOW ANYTHING ABOUT.
I'LL JUST GO TO THE LIBRARY.
EAT UP, GRANDMA, WE'VE GOT A BUSY DAY HERE.
"WE HAVE TO GET YOU BACK TO THE RETIREMENT HOME SOON."

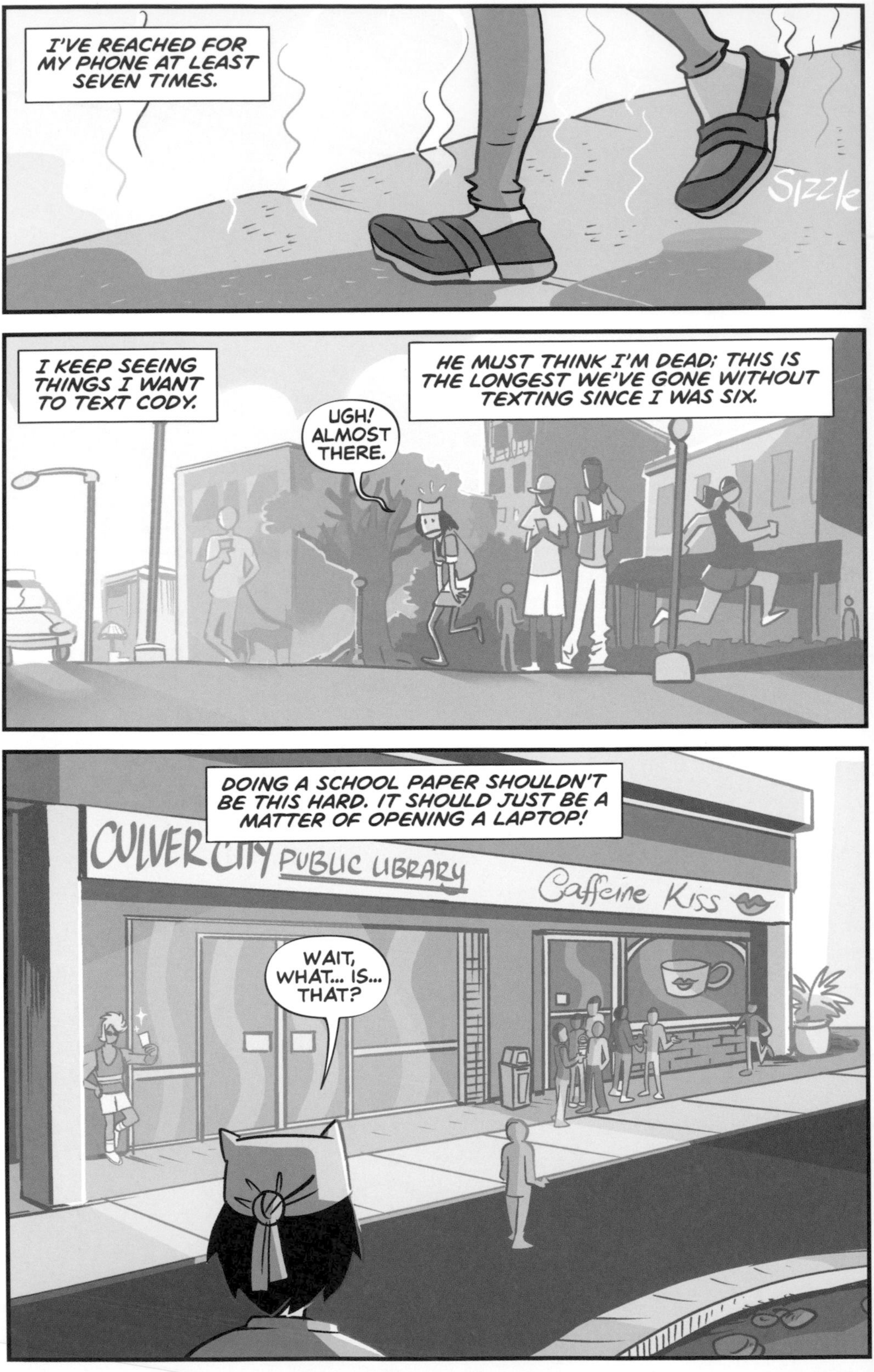

I'VE REACHED FOR MY PHONE AT LEAST SEVEN TIMES.
SIZZLE
I KEEP SEEING THINGS I WANT TO TEXT CODY.
UGH! ALMOST THERE.
HE MUST THINK I'M DEAD; THIS IS THE LONGEST WE'VE GONE WITHOUT TEXTING SINCE I WAS SIX.
DOING A SCHOOL PAPER SHOULDN'T BE THIS HARD. IT SHOULD JUST BE A MATTER OF OPENING A LAPTOP!
CULVER CITY PUBLIC LIBRARY
Caffeine Kiss
WAIT, WHAT... IS... THAT?

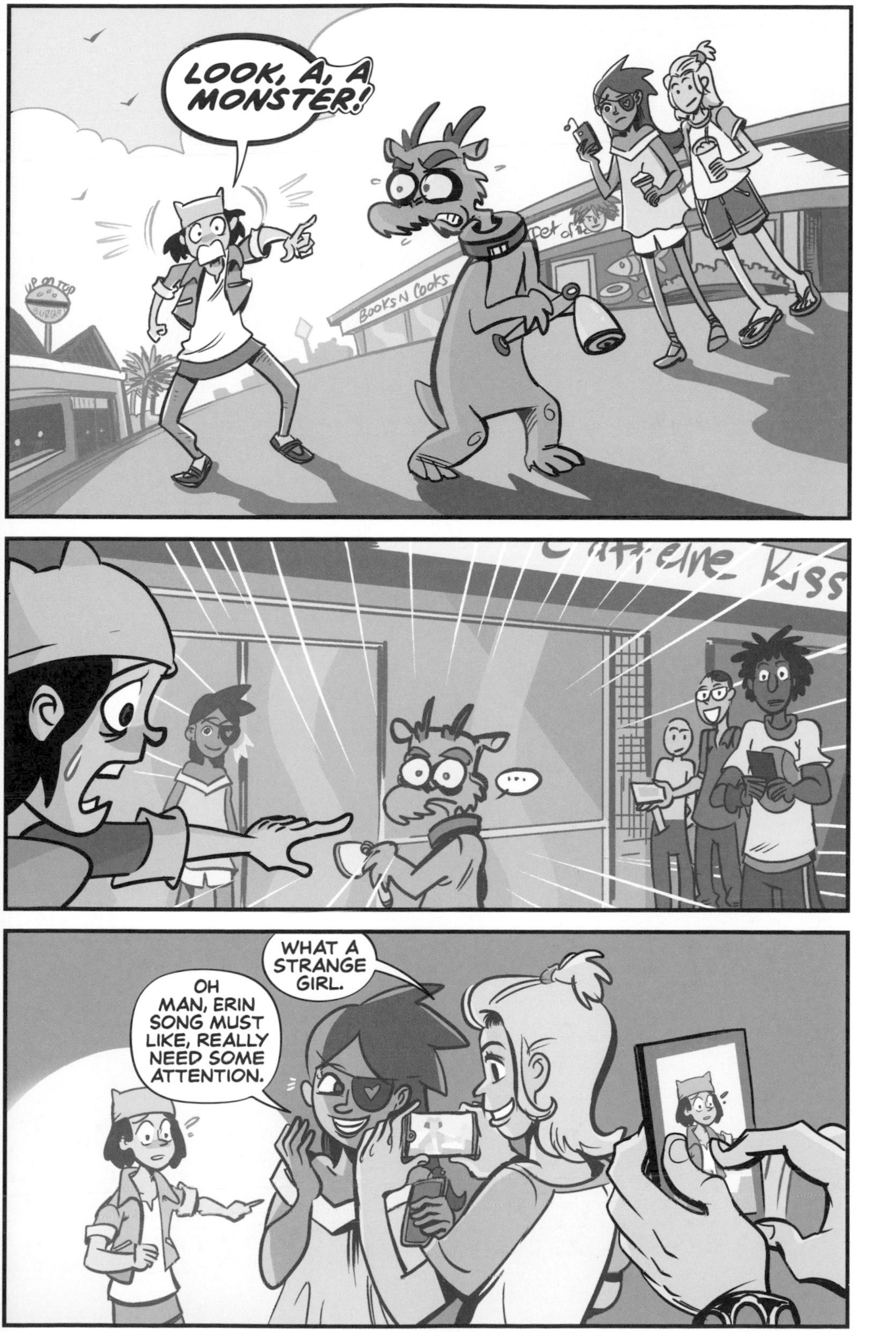
LOOK, A, A MONSTER!
BOOKS N COOKS
...
WHAT A STRANGE GIRL.
OH MAN, ERIN SONG MUST LIKE, REALLY NEED SOME ATTENTION.

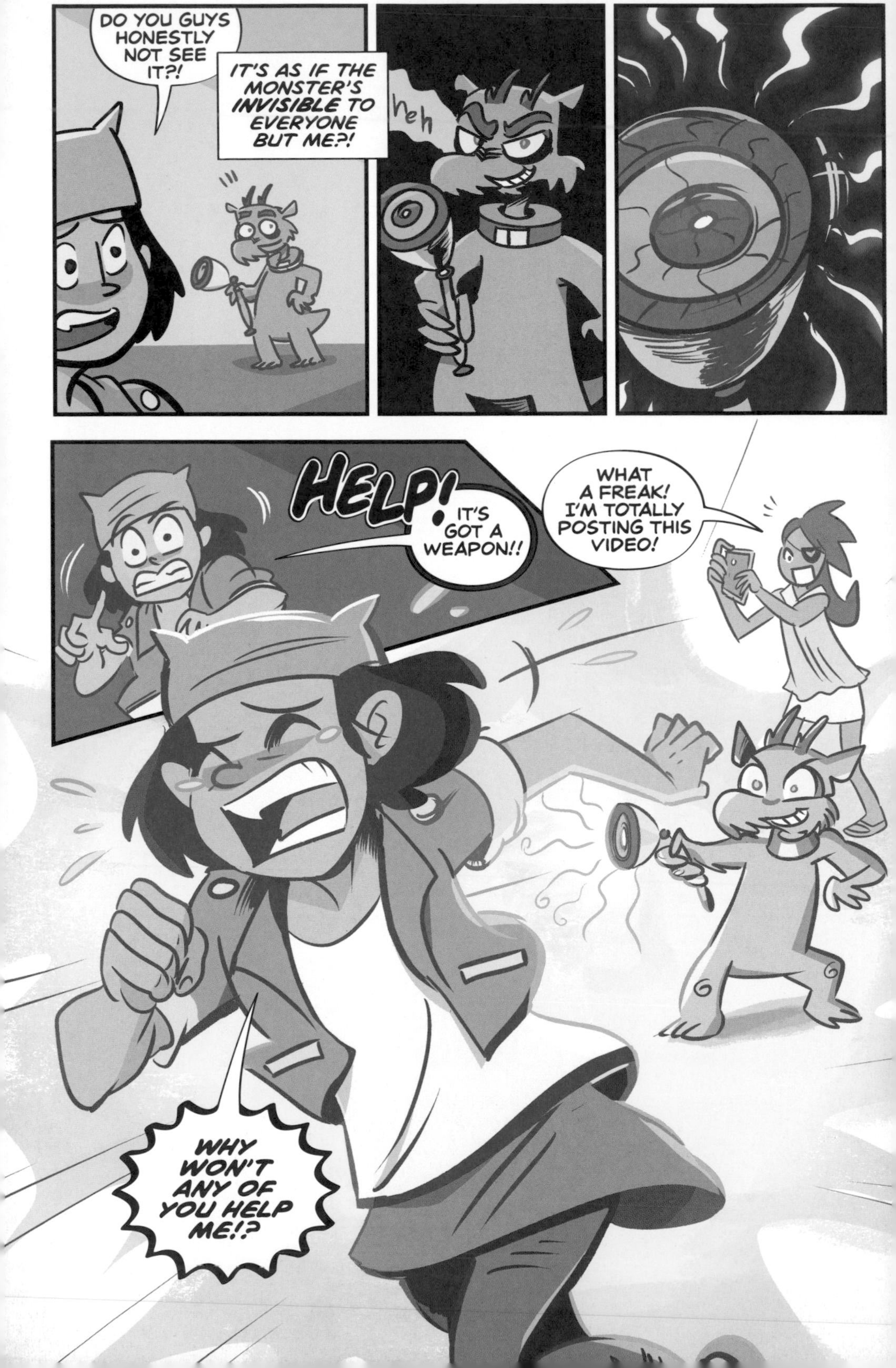
DO YOU GUYS HONESTLY NOT SEE IT?!
IT'S AS IF THE MONSTER'S INVISIBLE TO EVERYONE BUT ME?!
heh
HELP!
IT'S GOT A WEAPON!!
WHAT A FREAK! I'M TOTALLY POSTING THIS VIDEO!
WHY WON'T ANY OF YOU HELP ME!?

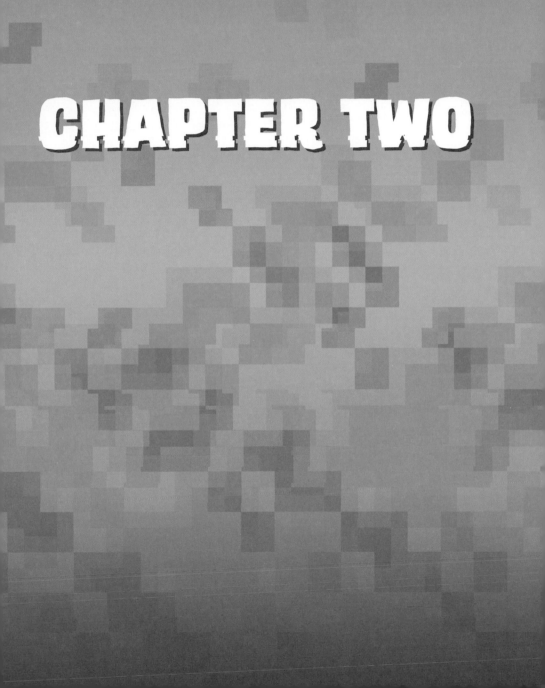

CHAPTER TWO

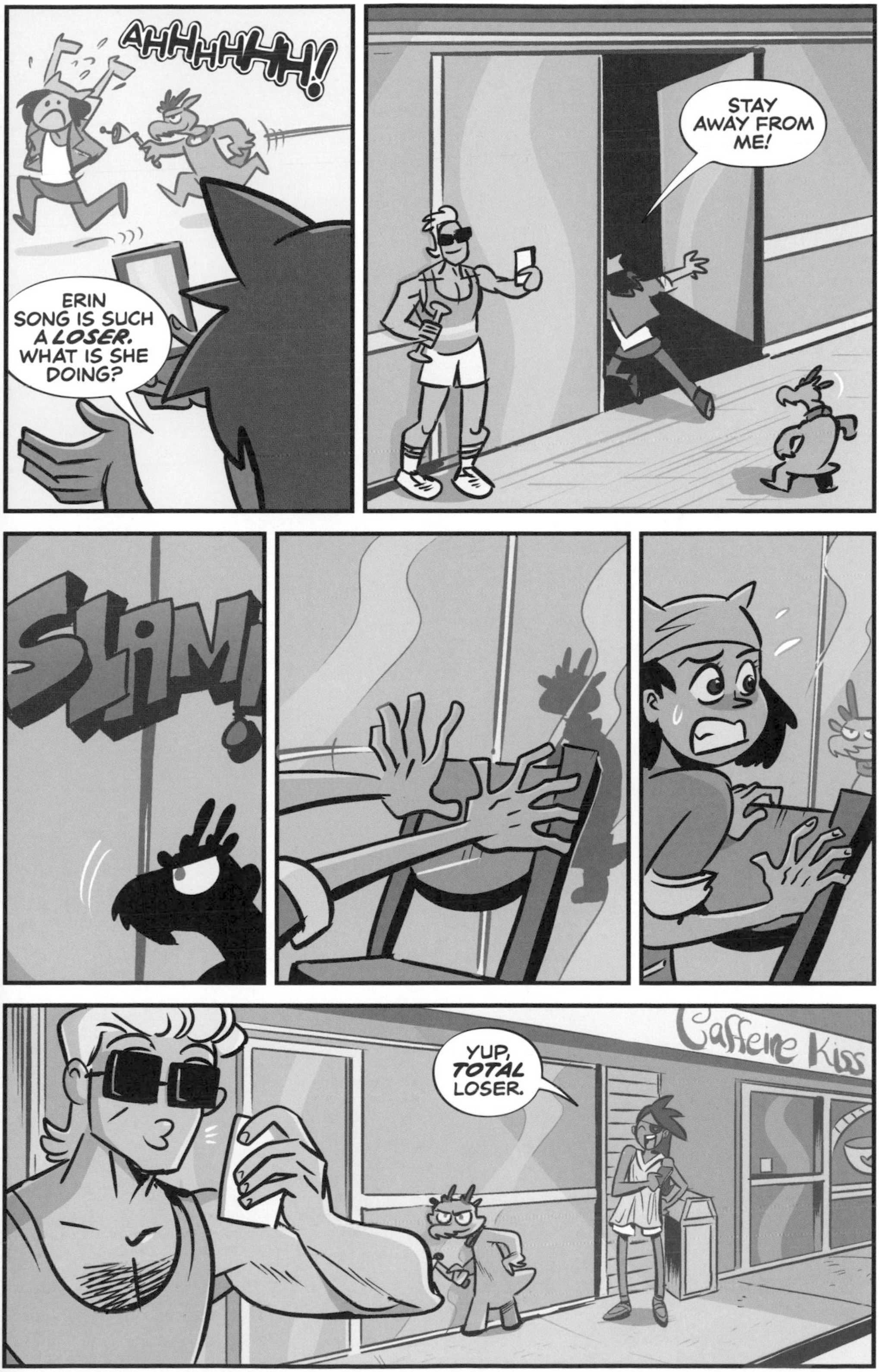

AHHHHHHH!
ERIN SONG IS SUCH A *LOSER.* WHAT IS SHE DOING?
STAY AWAY FROM ME!
SLAM!
YUP, *TOTAL* LOSER.
Caffeine Kiss

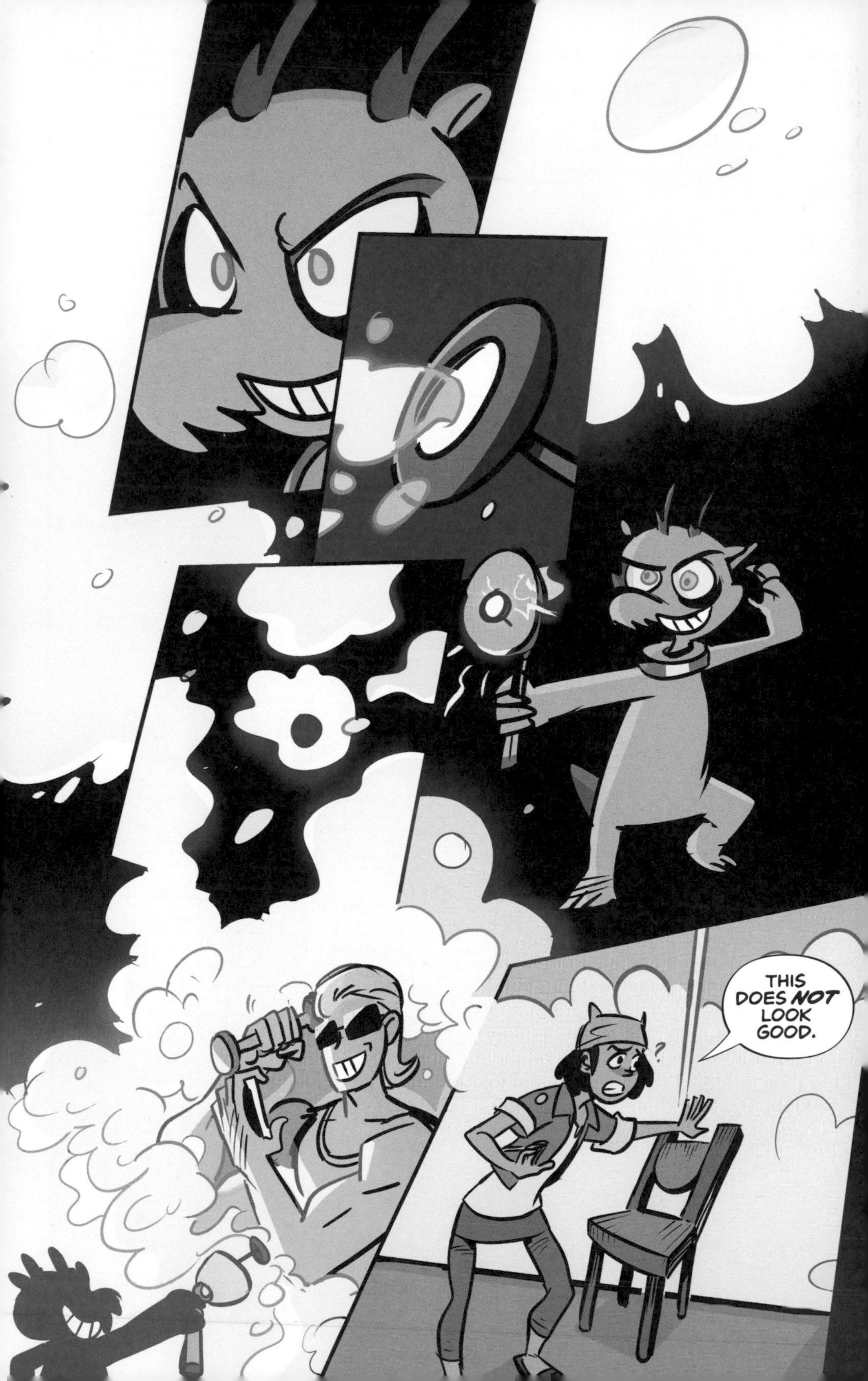
THIS DOES NOT LOOK GOOD.

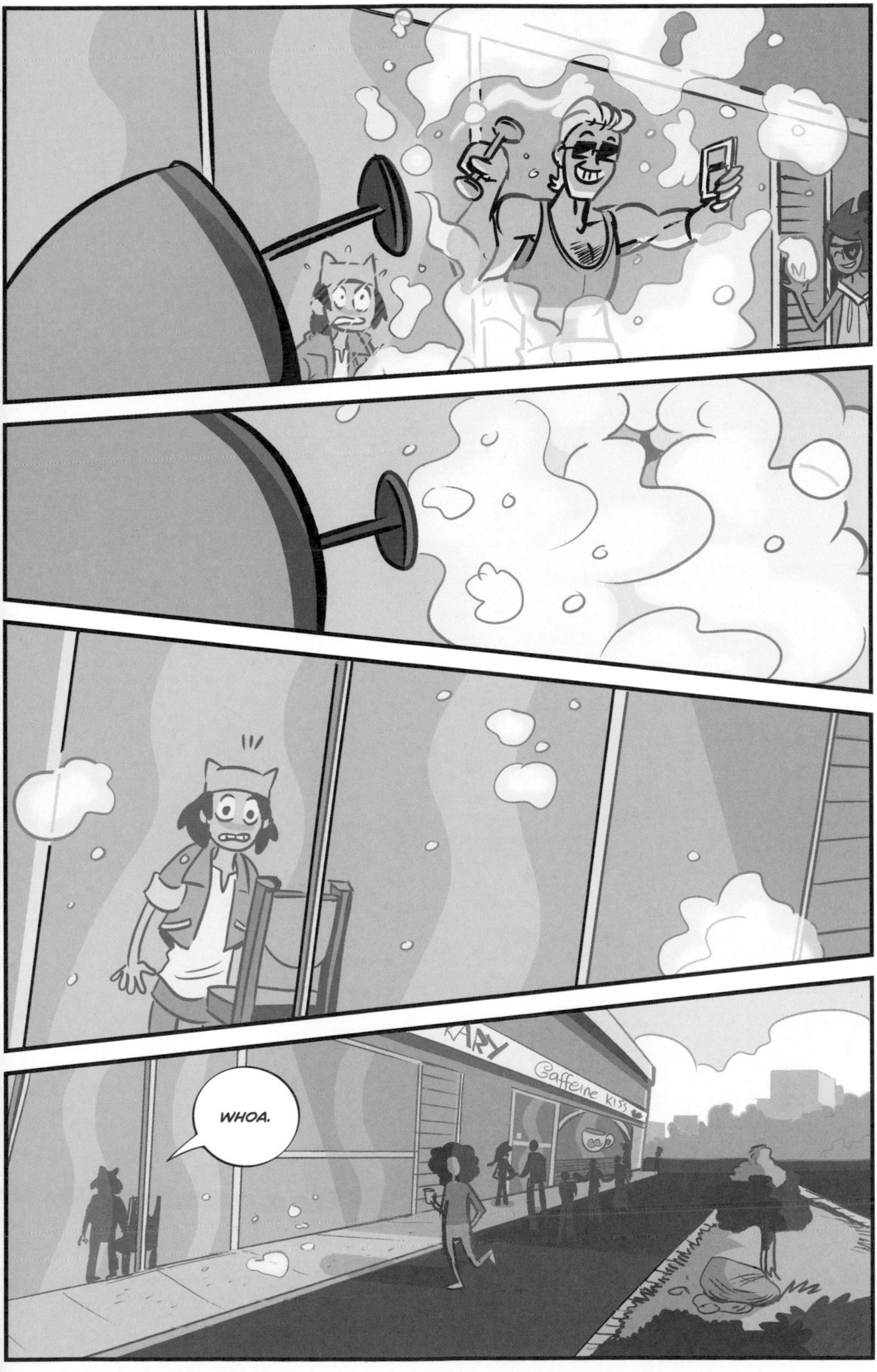
WHOA.
Caffeine Kiss
ARY

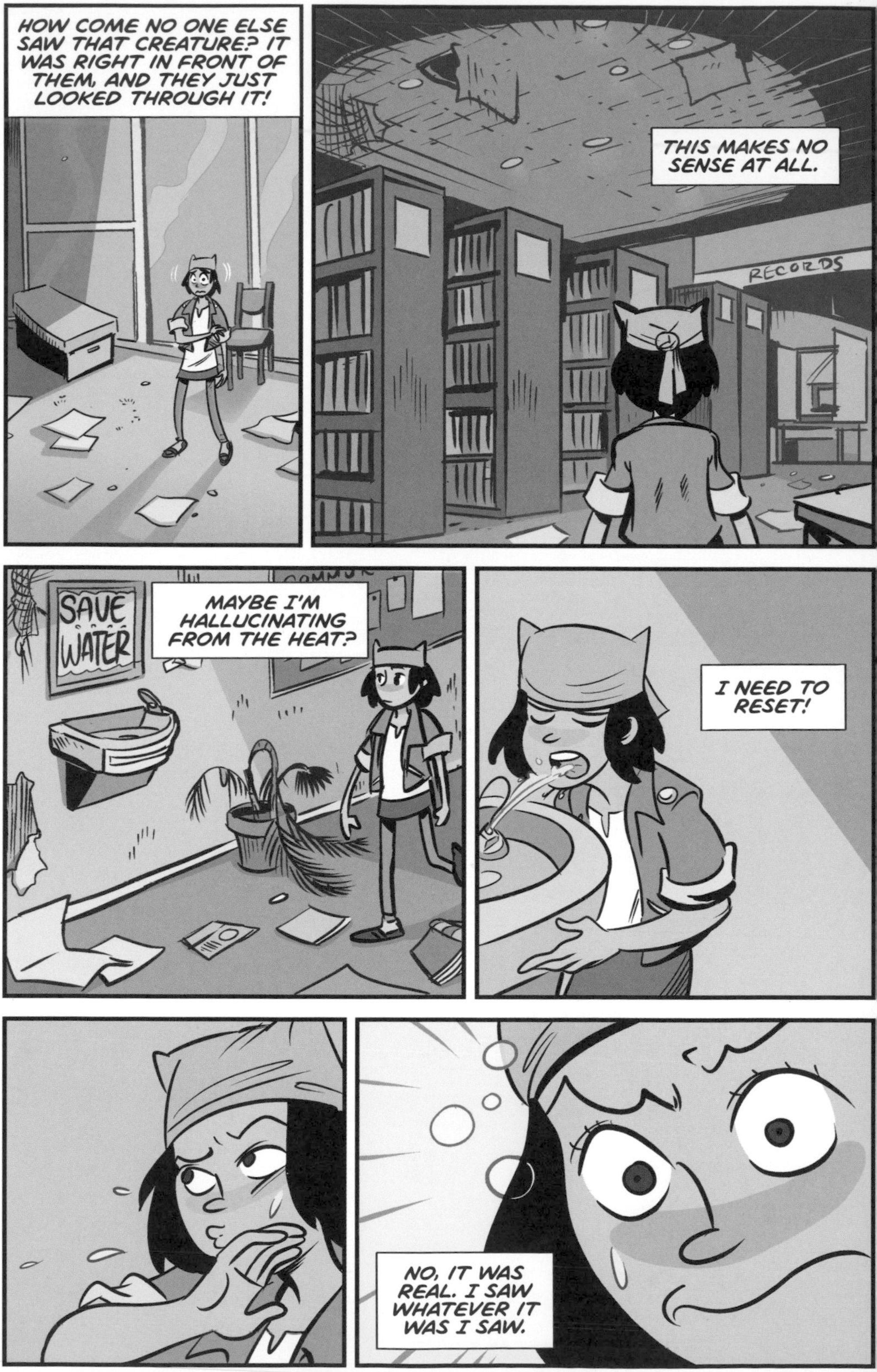
HOW COME NO ONE ELSE SAW THAT CREATURE? IT WAS RIGHT IN FRONT OF THEM, AND THEY JUST LOOKED THROUGH IT!
THIS MAKES NO SENSE AT ALL.
RECORDS
SAVE WATER
MAYBE I'M HALLUCINATING FROM THE HEAT?
I NEED TO RESET!
NO, IT WAS REAL. I SAW WHATEVER IT WAS I SAW.

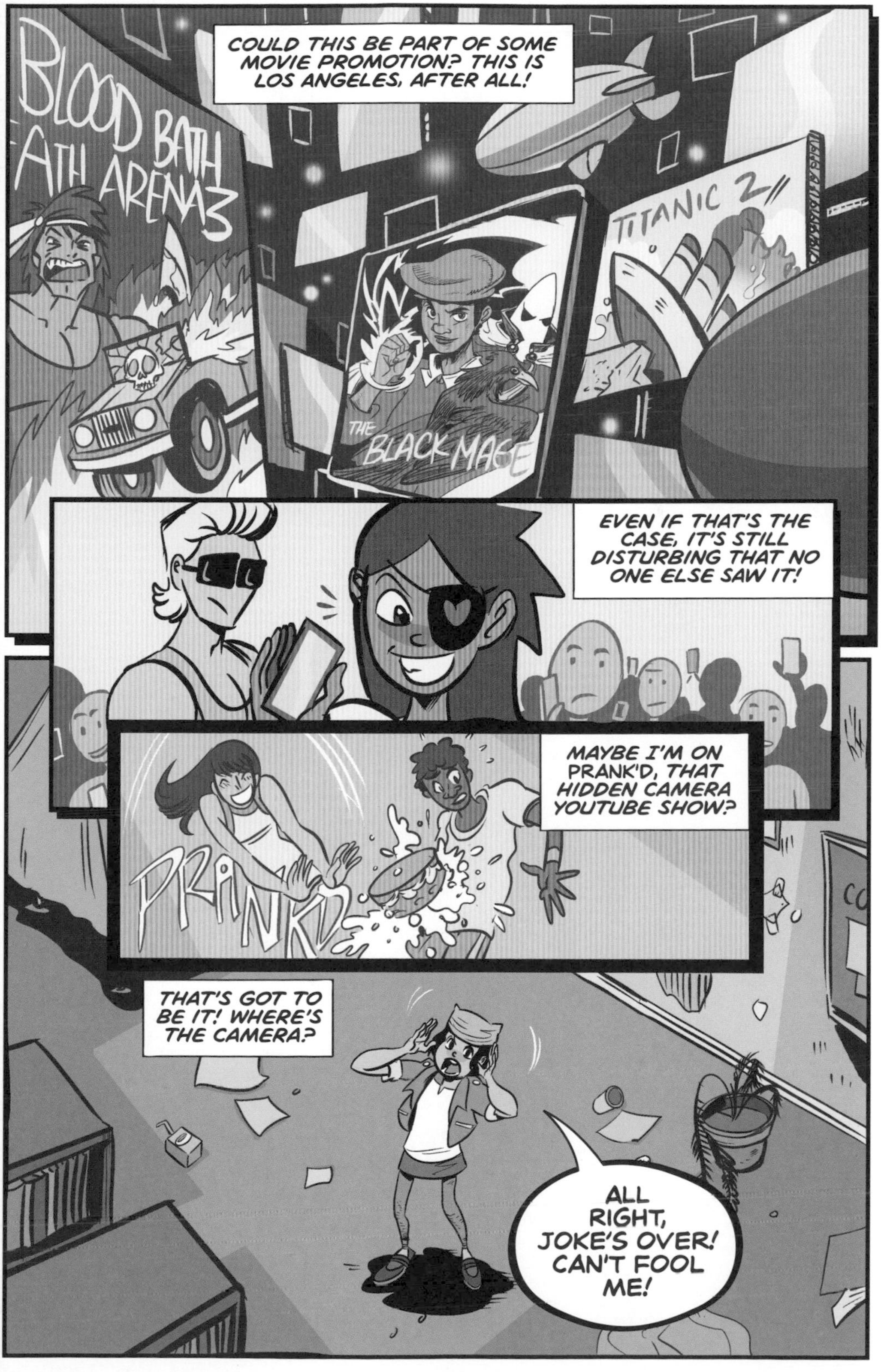
COULD THIS BE PART OF SOME MOVIE PROMOTION? THIS IS LOS ANGELES, AFTER ALL!
BLOOD BATH ARENA 3
TITANIC 2
THE BLACK MAGE
EVEN IF THAT'S THE CASE, IT'S STILL DISTURBING THAT NO ONE ELSE SAW IT!
MAYBE I'M ON PRANK'D, THAT HIDDEN CAMERA YOUTUBE SHOW?
PRANK'D
THAT'S GOT TO BE IT! WHERE'S THE CAMERA?
ALL RIGHT, JOKE'S OVER! CAN'T FOOL ME!

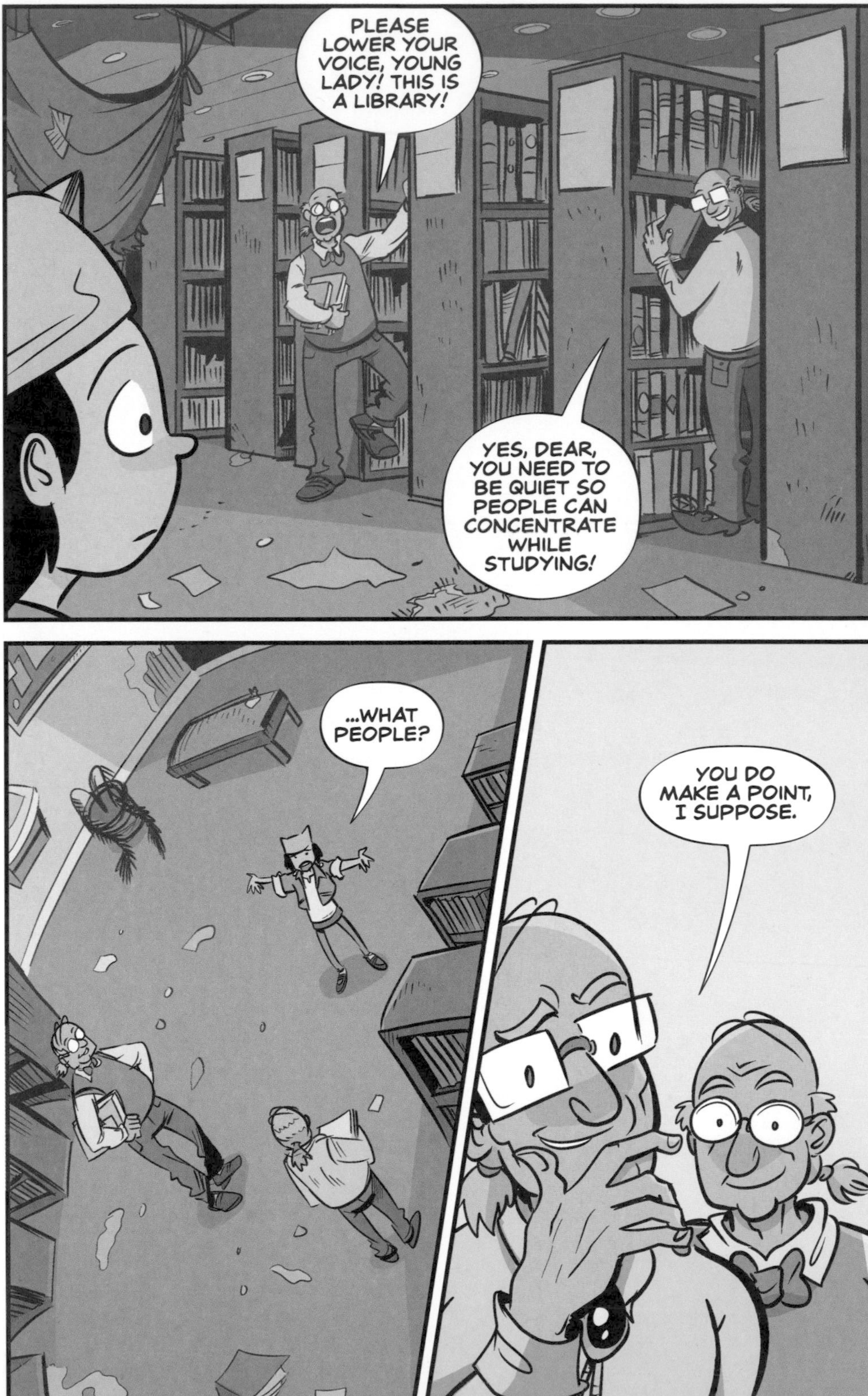
PLEASE LOWER YOUR VOICE, YOUNG LADY! THIS IS A LIBRARY!
YES, DEAR, YOU NEED TO BE QUIET SO PEOPLE CAN CONCENTRATE WHILE STUDYING!
...WHAT PEOPLE?
YOU DO MAKE A POINT, I SUPPOSE.

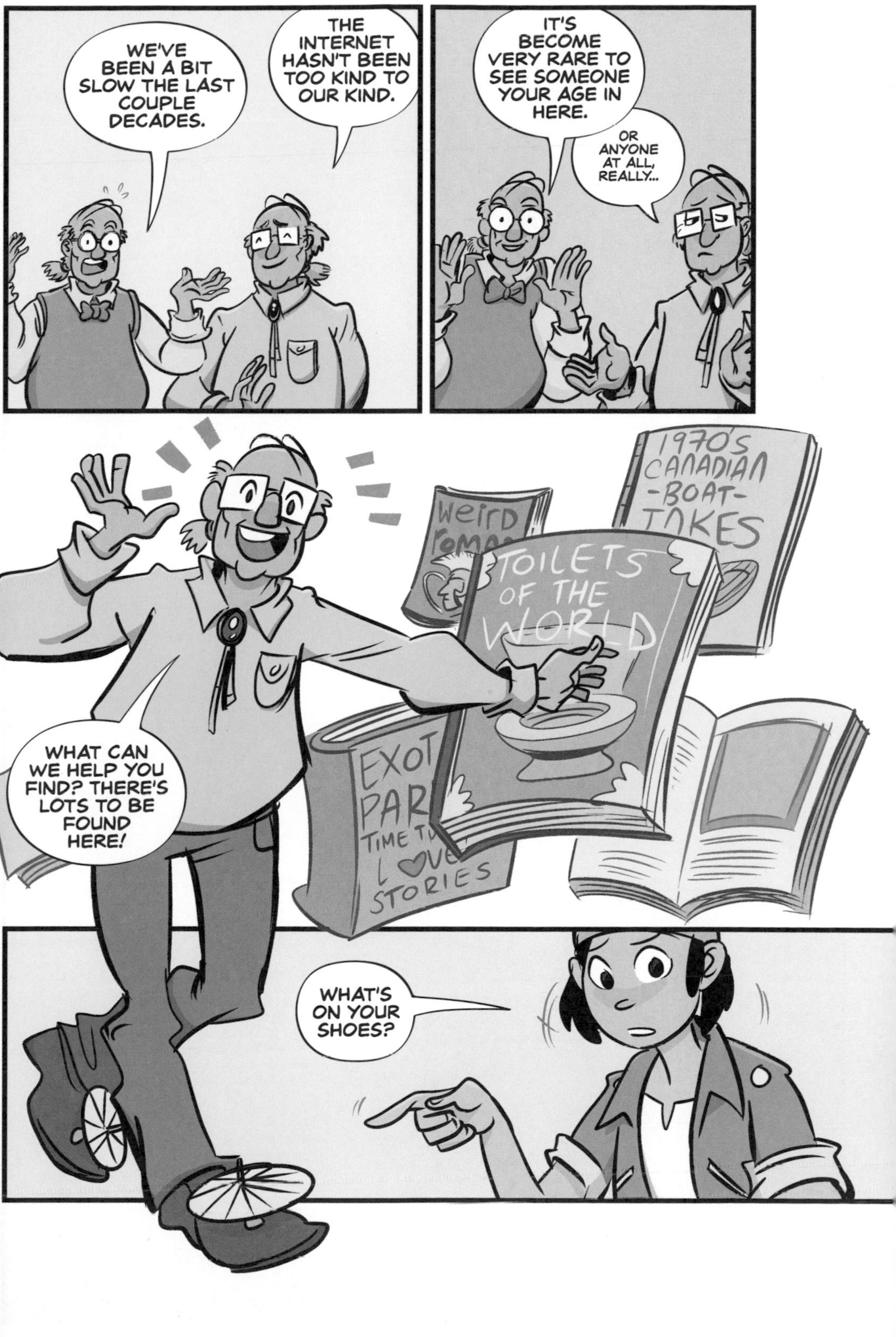

WE'VE BEEN A BIT SLOW THE LAST COUPLE DECADES.
THE INTERNET HASN'T BEEN TOO KIND TO OUR KIND.
IT'S BECOME VERY RARE TO SEE SOMEONE YOUR AGE IN HERE.
OR ANYONE AT ALL, REALLY...
1970'S CANADIAN -BOAT- TAKES
WEIRD ROMA
TOILETS OF THE WORLD
WHAT CAN WE HELP YOU FIND? THERE'S LOTS TO BE FOUND HERE!
EXOT PAR TIME TU LOVE STORIES
WHAT'S ON YOUR SHOES?

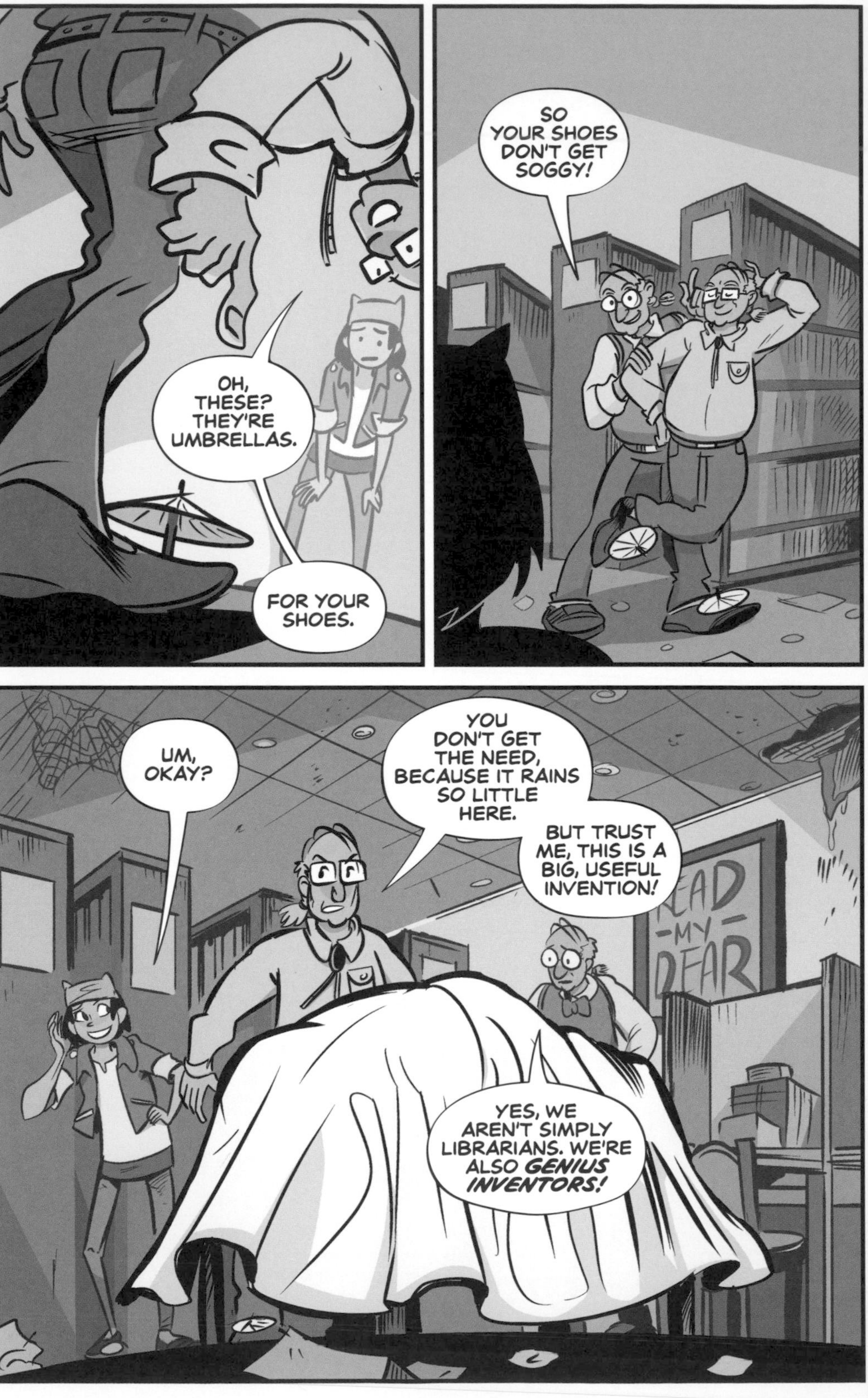
OH, THESE? THEY'RE UMBRELLAS.
FOR YOUR SHOES.
SO YOUR SHOES DON'T GET SOGGY!
UM, OKAY?
YOU DON'T GET THE NEED, BECAUSE IT RAINS SO LITTLE HERE.
BUT TRUST ME, THIS IS A BIG, USEFUL INVENTION!
READ MY DEAR
YES, WE AREN'T SIMPLY LIBRARIANS. WE'RE ALSO ***GENIUS INVENTORS!***

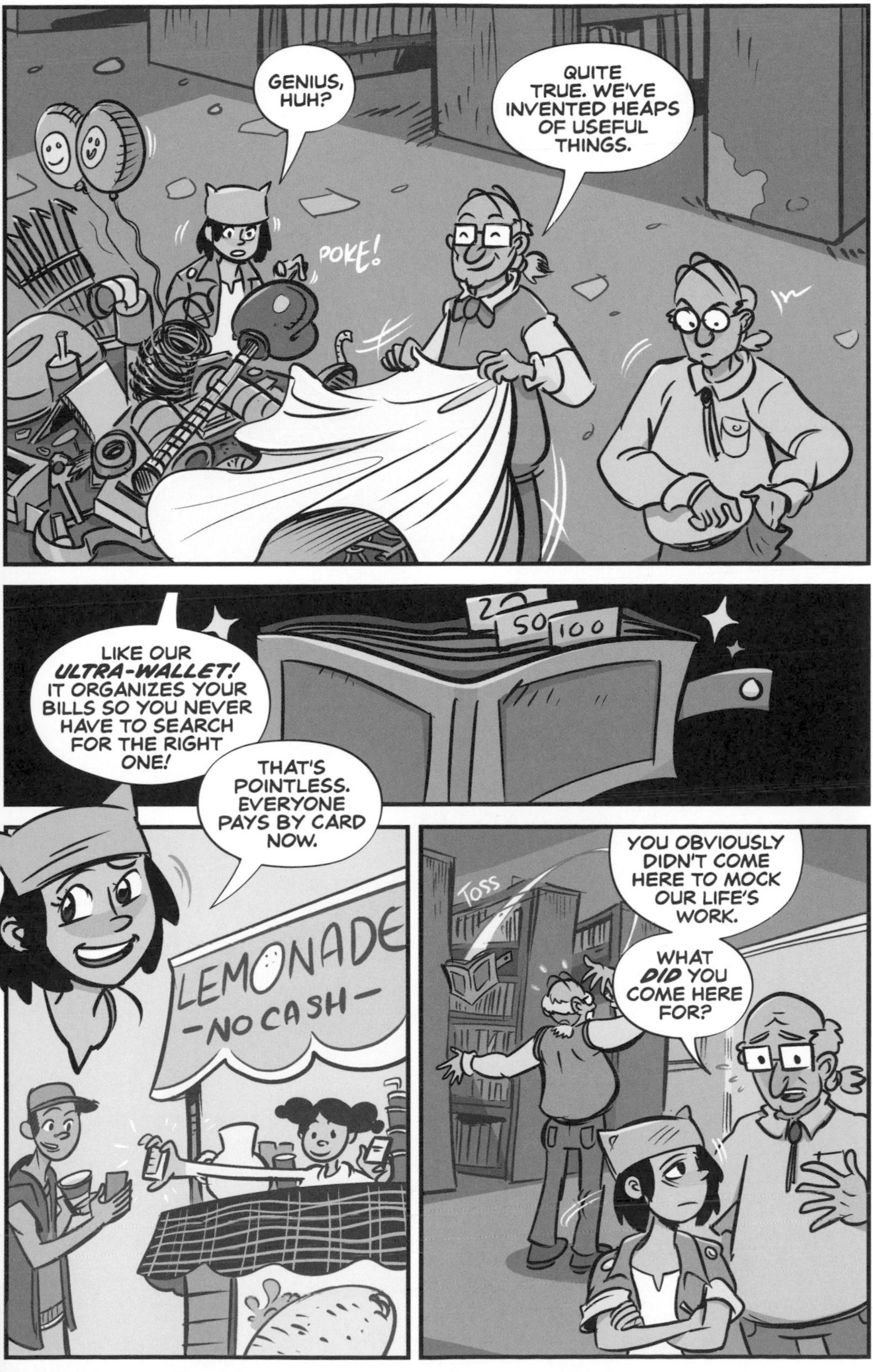
GENIUS, HUH?
QUITE TRUE. WE'VE INVENTED HEAPS OF USEFUL THINGS.
POKE!
LIKE OUR ULTRA-WALLET! IT ORGANIZES YOUR BILLS SO YOU NEVER HAVE TO SEARCH FOR THE RIGHT ONE!
20
50
100
THAT'S POINTLESS. EVERYONE PAYS BY CARD NOW.
LEMONADE
-NO CASH-
TOSS
YOU OBVIOUSLY DIDN'T COME HERE TO MOCK OUR LIFE'S WORK.
WHAT DID YOU COME HERE FOR?

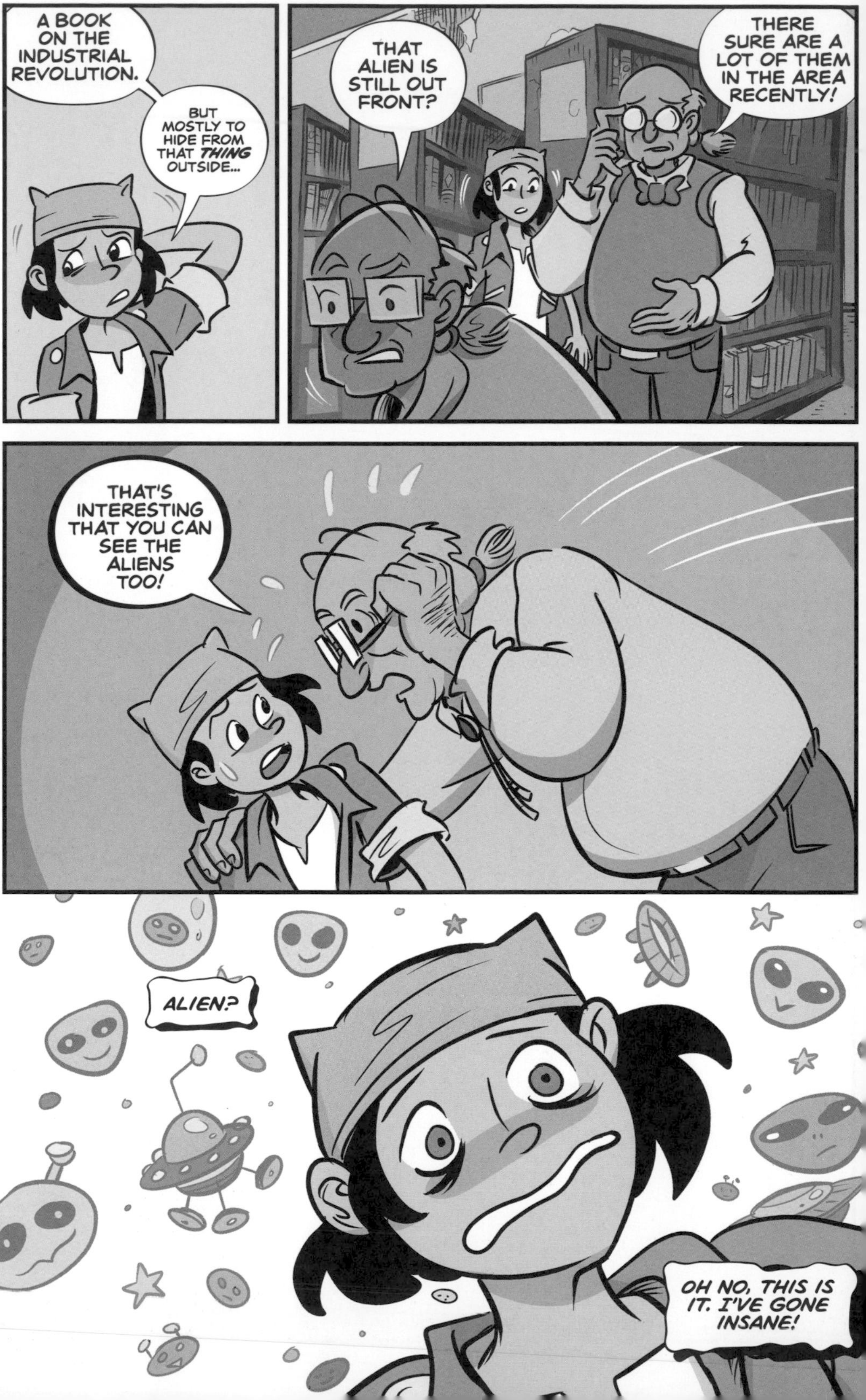
A BOOK ON THE INDUSTRIAL REVOLUTION.
BUT MOSTLY TO HIDE FROM THAT *THING* OUTSIDE...
THAT ALIEN IS STILL OUT FRONT?
THERE SURE ARE A LOT OF THEM IN THE AREA RECENTLY!
THAT'S INTERESTING THAT YOU CAN SEE THE ALIENS TOO!
ALIEN?
OH NO, THIS IS IT. I'VE GONE INSANE!

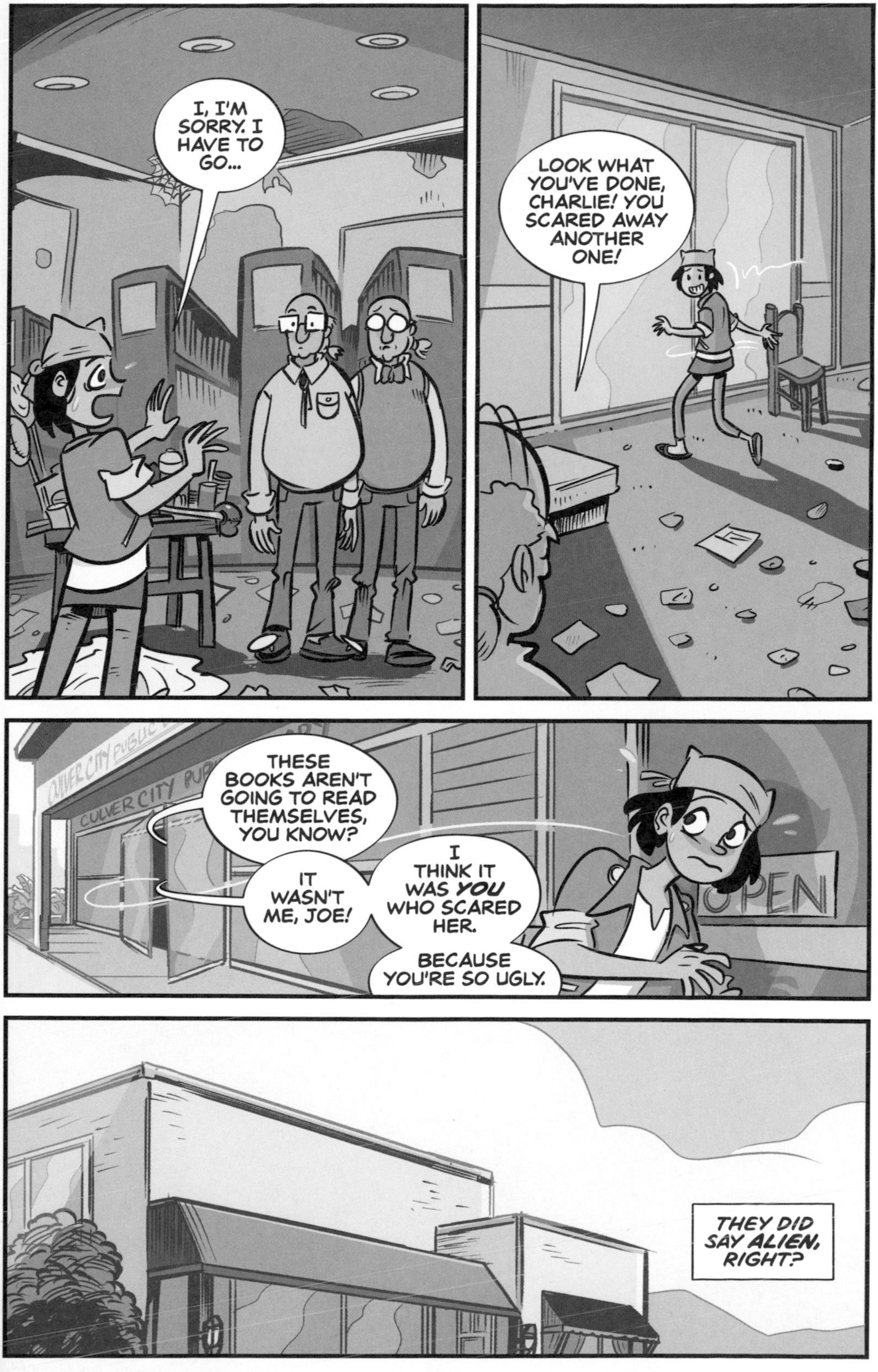
I, I'M SORRY. I HAVE TO GO...
LOOK WHAT YOU'VE DONE, CHARLIE! YOU SCARED AWAY ANOTHER ONE!
CULVER CITY PUBLIC
CULVER CITY PUB
CULVER CITY
THESE BOOKS AREN'T GOING TO READ THEMSELVES, YOU KNOW?
IT WASN'T ME, JOE!
I THINK IT WAS *YOU* WHO SCARED HER.
BECAUSE YOU'RE SO UGLY.
OPEN
THEY DID SAY ***ALIEN,*** *RIGHT?*

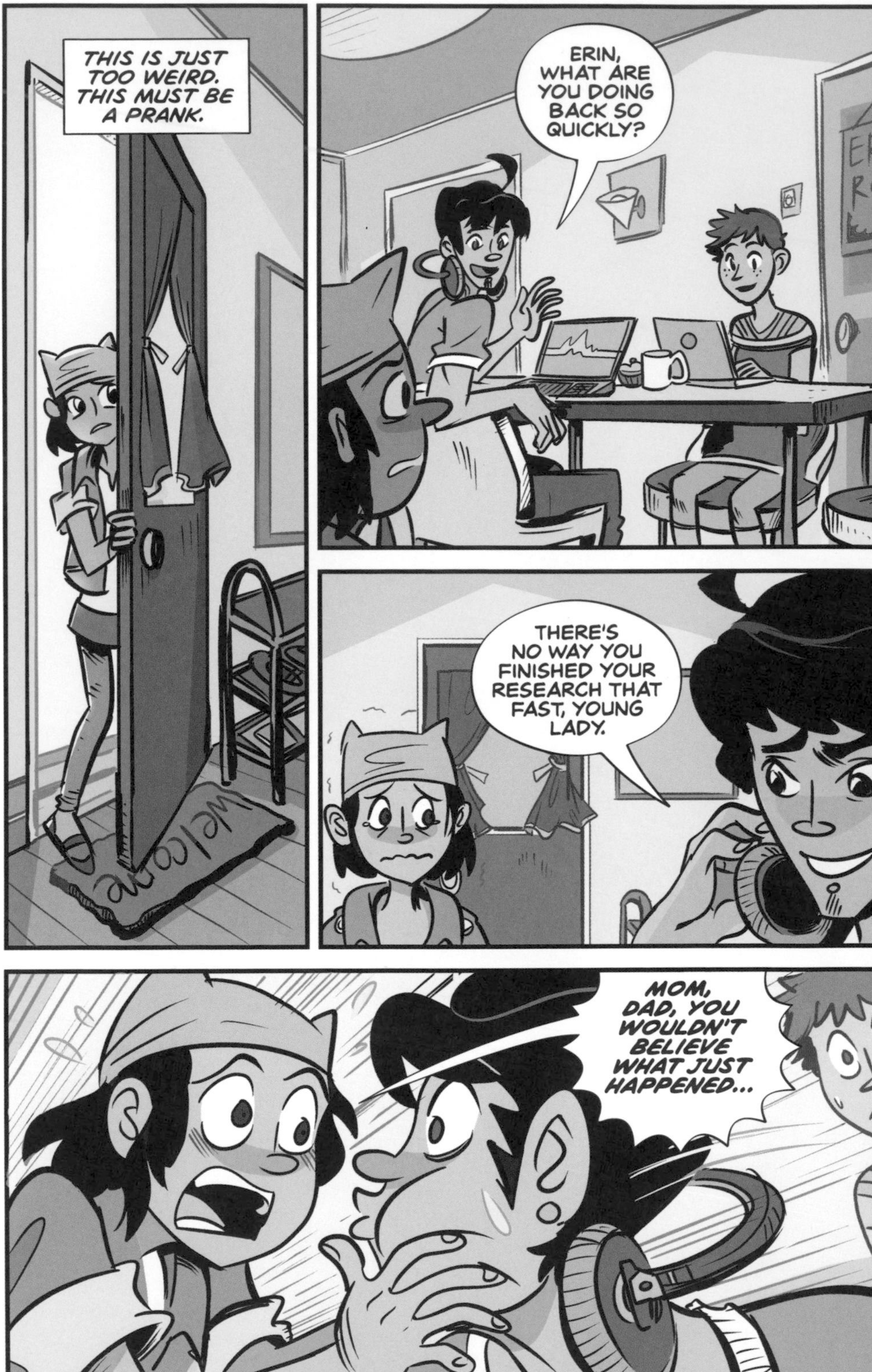
THIS IS JUST TOO WEIRD. THIS MUST BE A PRANK.
ERIN, WHAT ARE YOU DOING BACK SO QUICKLY?
ERIN ROO
THERE'S NO WAY YOU FINISHED YOUR RESEARCH THAT FAST, YOUNG LADY.
MOM, DAD, YOU WOULDN'T BELIEVE WHAT JUST HAPPENED...

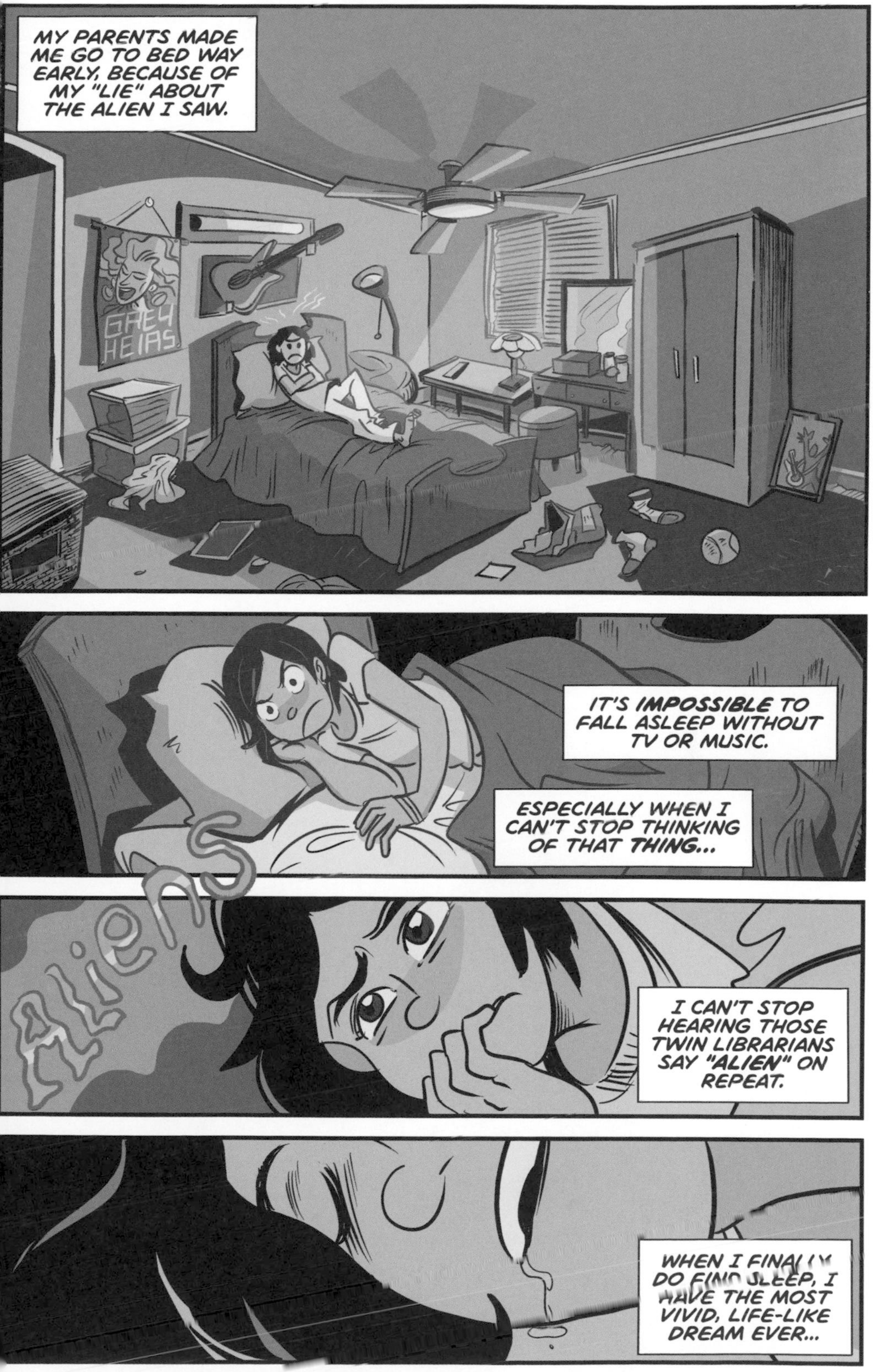
MY PARENTS MADE ME GO TO BED WAY EARLY, BECAUSE OF MY "LIE" ABOUT THE ALIEN I SAW.
IT'S **IMPOSSIBLE** TO FALL ASLEEP WITHOUT TV OR MUSIC.
ESPECIALLY WHEN I CAN'T STOP THINKING OF THAT **THING...**
Aliens
I CAN'T STOP HEARING THOSE TWIN LIBRARIANS SAY **"ALIEN"** ON REPEAT.
WHEN I FINALLY DO FIND SLEEP, I HAVE THE MOST VIVID, LIFE-LIKE DREAM EVER...

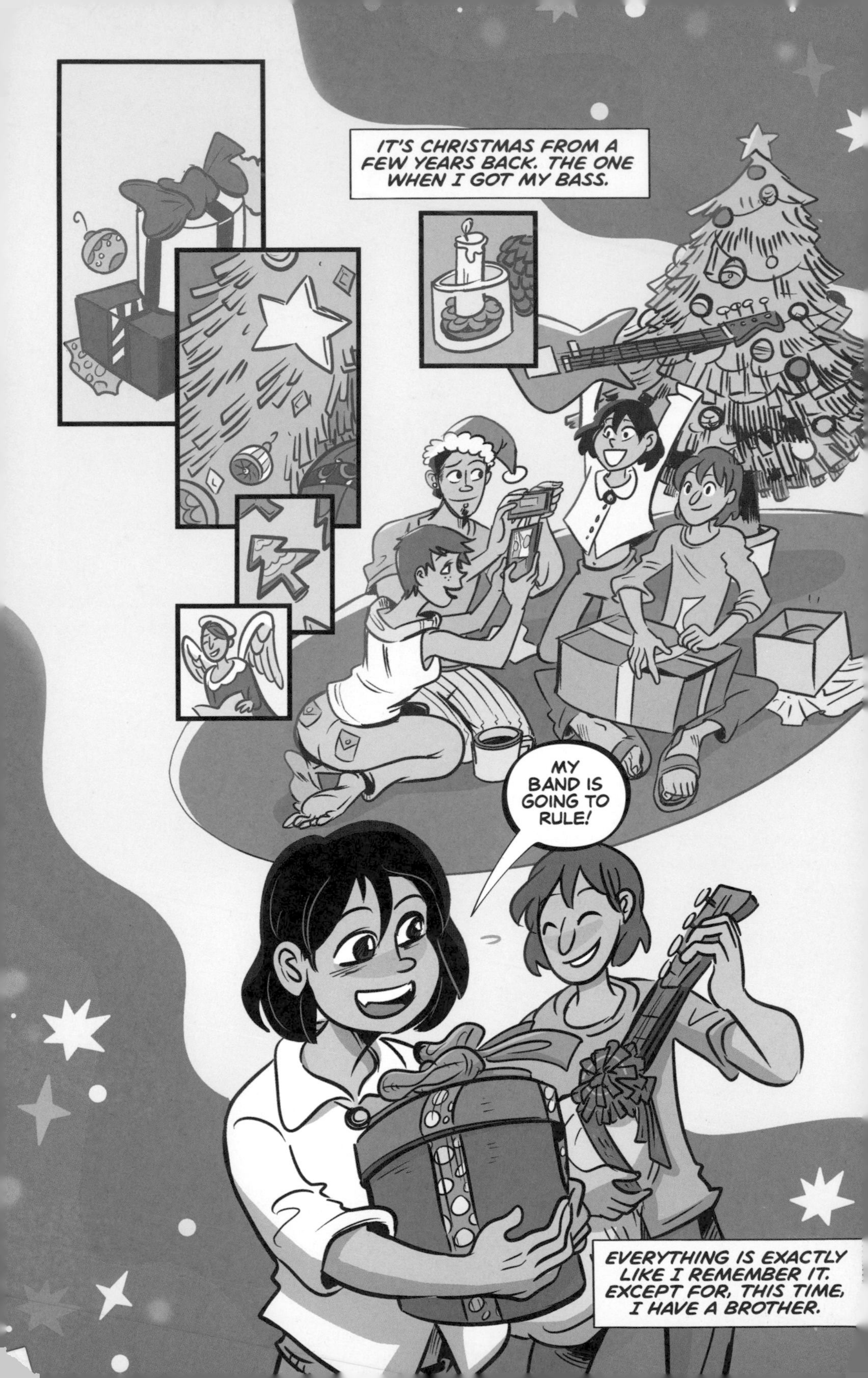
IT'S CHRISTMAS FROM A FEW YEARS BACK. THE ONE WHEN I GOT MY BASS.
MY BAND IS GOING TO RULE!
EVERYTHING IS EXACTLY LIKE I REMEMBER IT. EXCEPT FOR, THIS TIME, I HAVE A BROTHER.

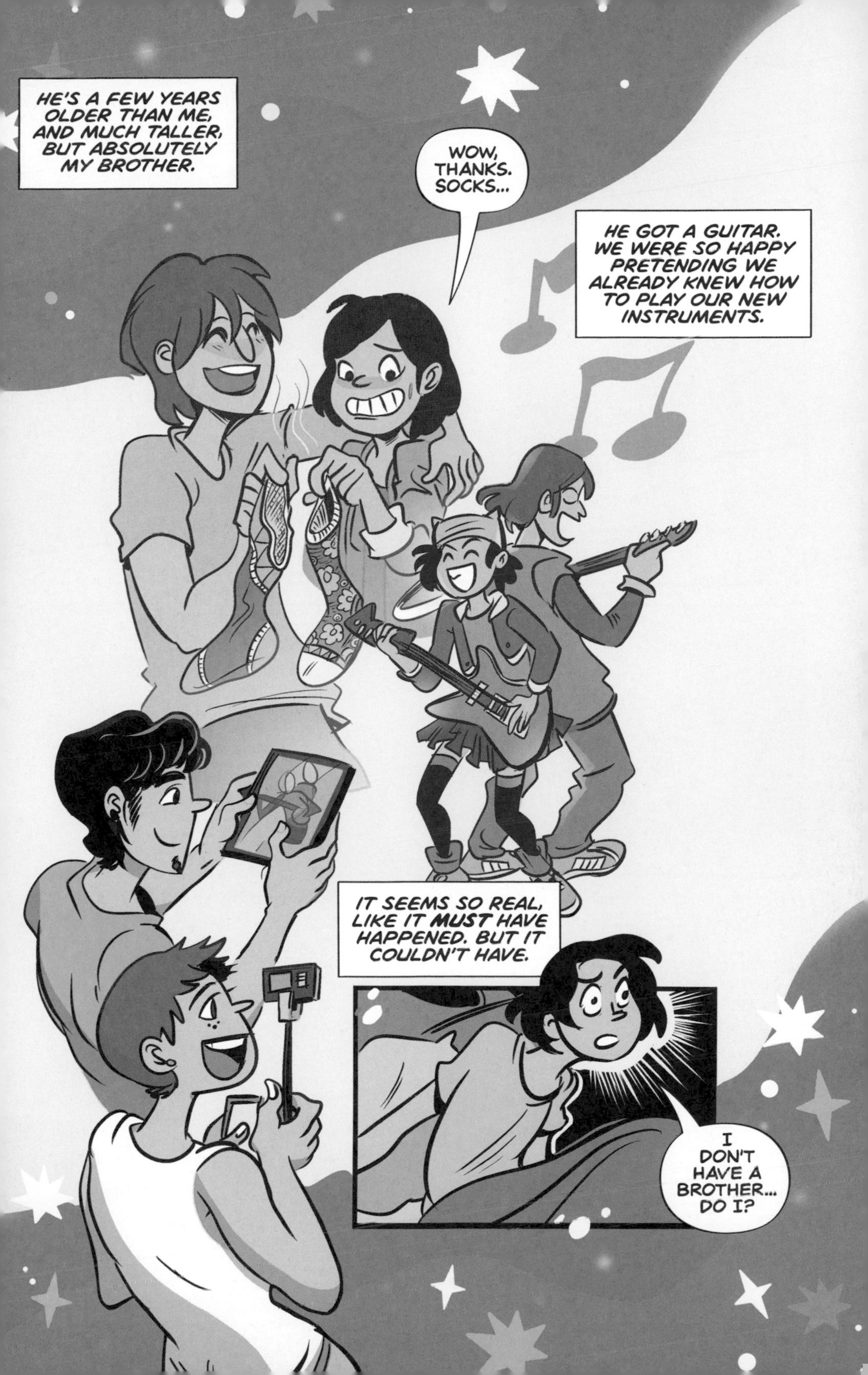
HE'S A FEW YEARS OLDER THAN ME, AND MUCH TALLER, BUT ABSOLUTELY MY BROTHER.
WOW, THANKS. SOCKS...
HE GOT A GUITAR. WE WERE SO HAPPY PRETENDING WE ALREADY KNEW HOW TO PLAY OUR NEW INSTRUMENTS.
IT SEEMS SO REAL, LIKE IT MUST HAVE HAPPENED. BUT IT COULDN'T HAVE.
I DON'T HAVE A BROTHER... DO I?

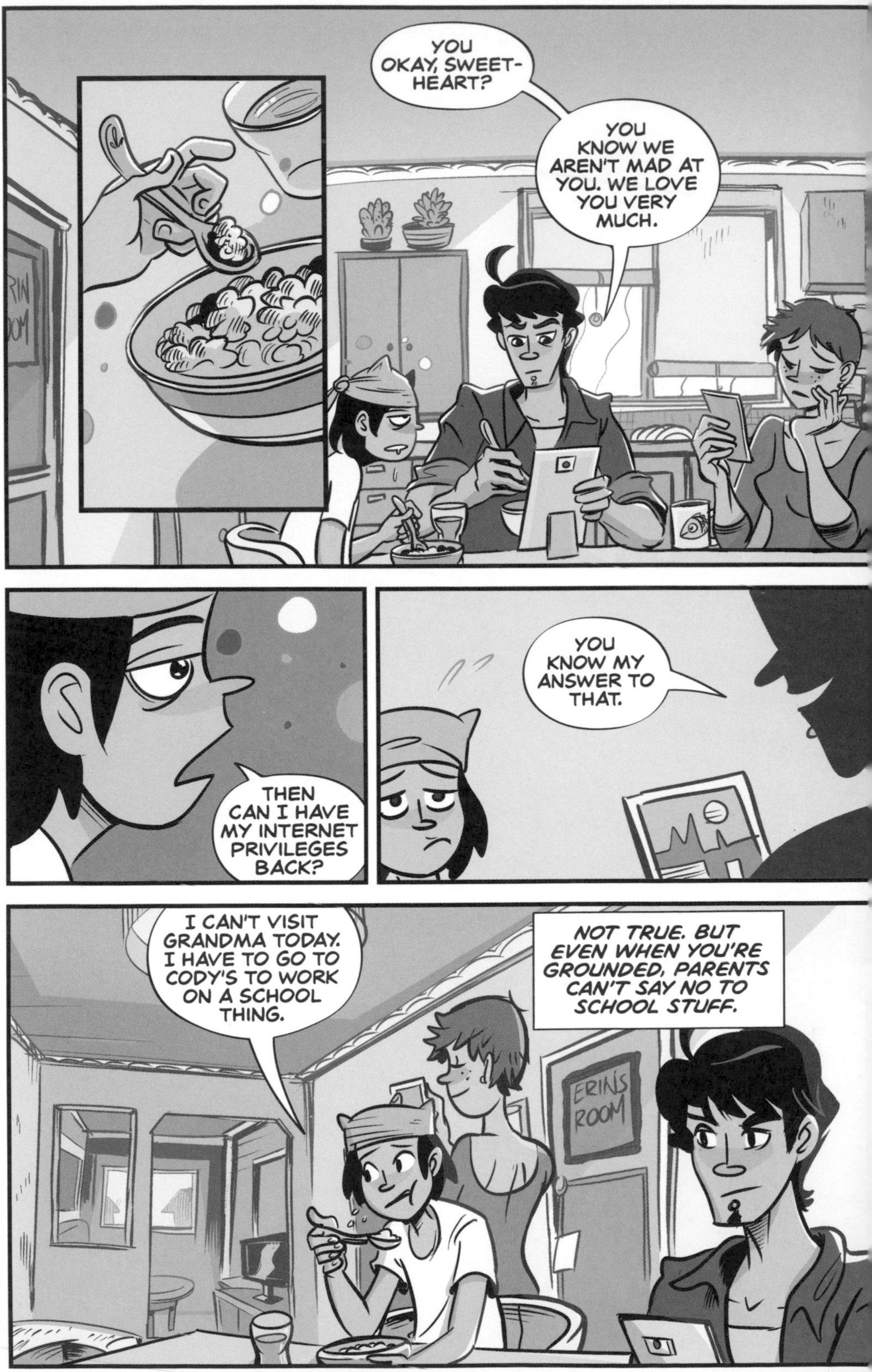
YOU OKAY, SWEET-HEART?
YOU KNOW WE AREN'T MAD AT YOU. WE LOVE YOU VERY MUCH.
ERIN ROOM
THEN CAN I HAVE MY INTERNET PRIVILEGES BACK?
YOU KNOW MY ANSWER TO THAT.
I CAN'T VISIT GRANDMA TODAY. I HAVE TO GO TO CODY'S TO WORK ON A SCHOOL THING.
NOT TRUE. BUT EVEN WHEN YOU'RE GROUNDED, PARENTS CAN'T SAY NO TO SCHOOL STUFF.
ERIN'S ROOM

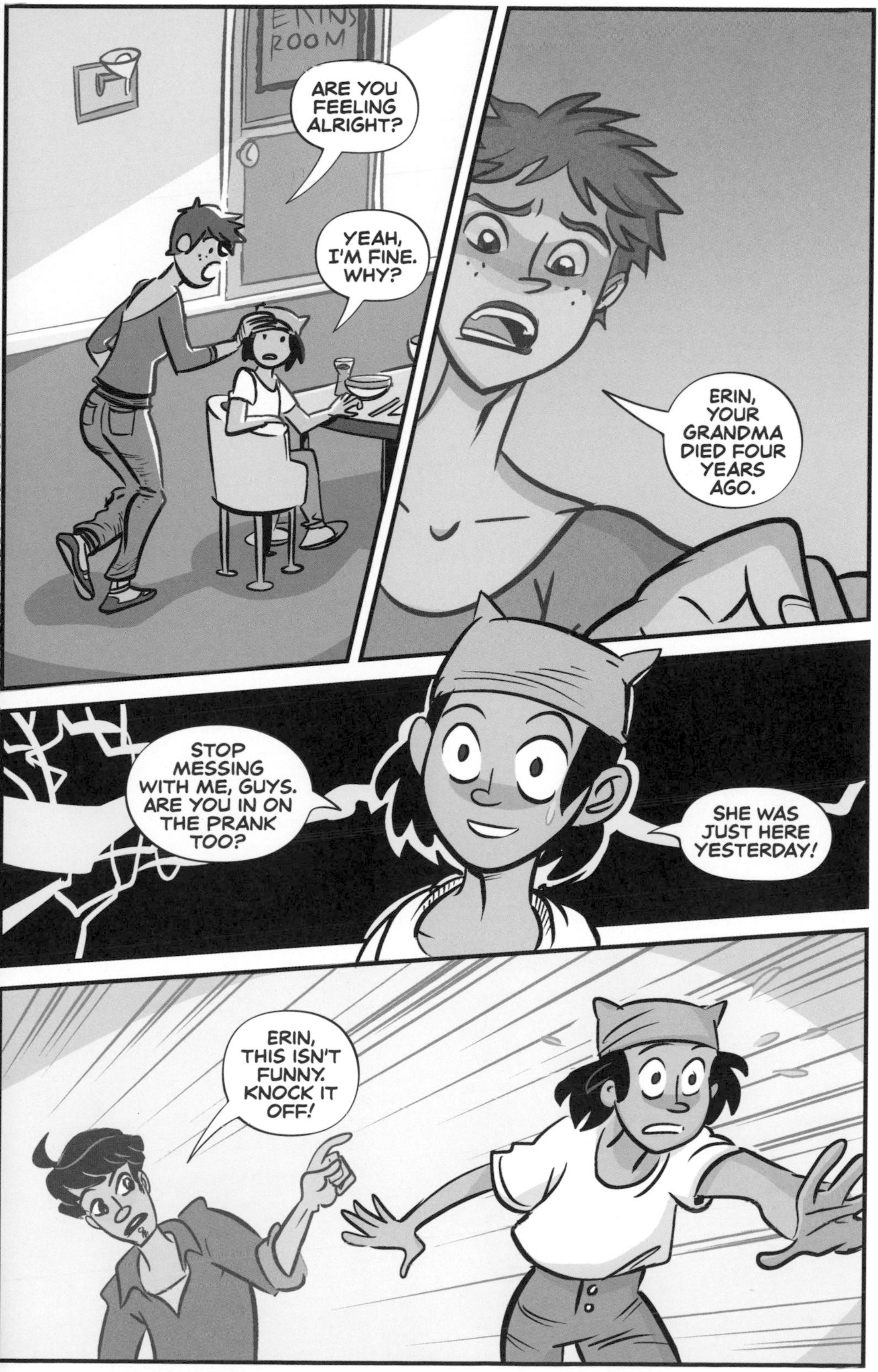
ARE YOU FEELING ALRIGHT?
YEAH, I'M FINE. WHY?
ERIN, YOUR GRANDMA DIED FOUR YEARS AGO.
STOP MESSING WITH ME, GUYS. ARE YOU IN ON THE PRANK TOO?
SHE WAS JUST HERE YESTERDAY!
ERIN, THIS ISN'T FUNNY. KNOCK IT OFF!

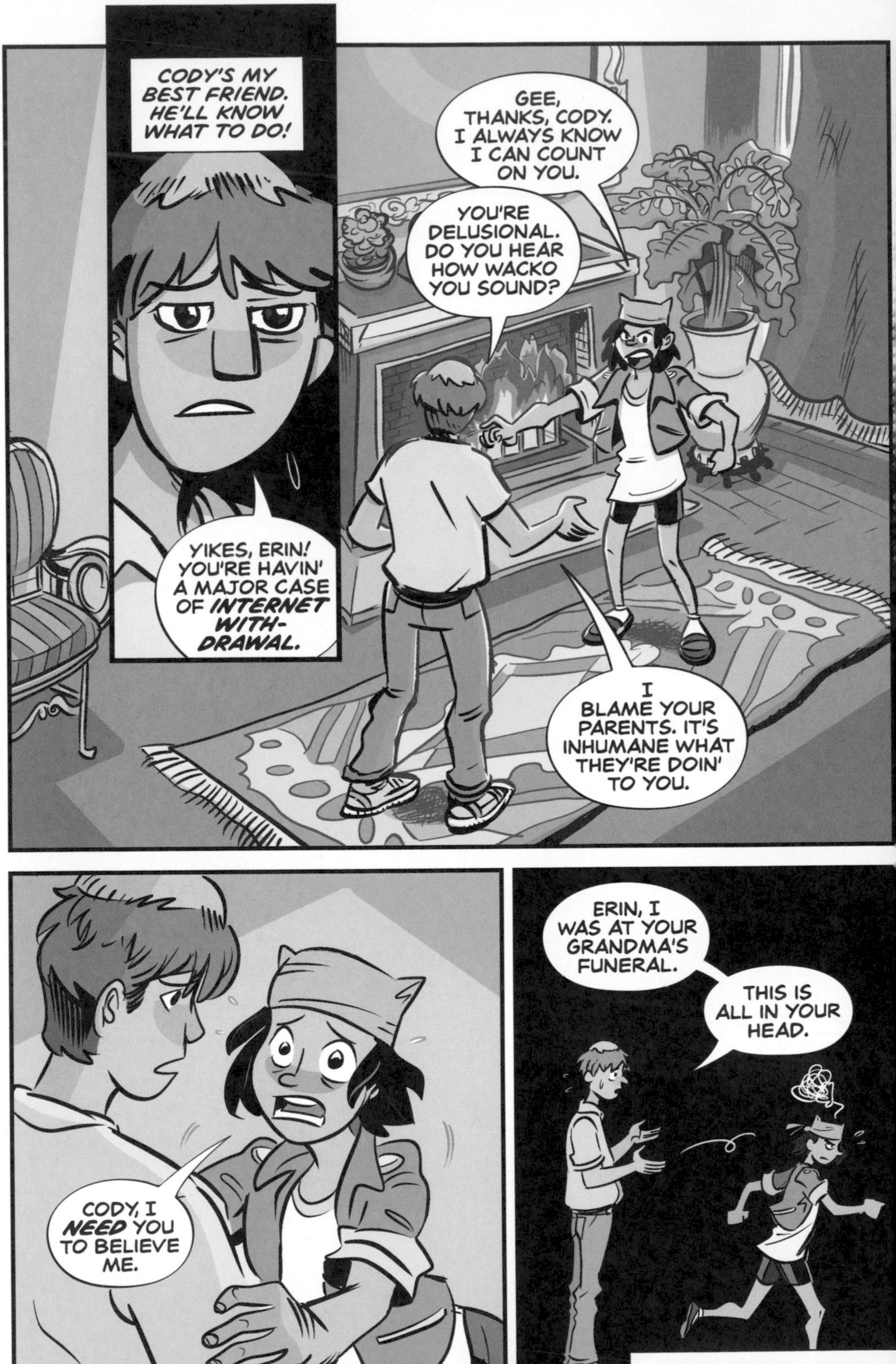
CODY'S MY BEST FRIEND. HE'LL KNOW WHAT TO DO!
YIKES, ERIN! YOU'RE HAVIN' A MAJOR CASE OF INTERNET WITH-DRAWAL.
YOU'RE DELUSIONAL. DO YOU HEAR HOW WACKO YOU SOUND?
GEE, THANKS, CODY. I ALWAYS KNOW I CAN COUNT ON YOU.
I BLAME YOUR PARENTS. IT'S INHUMANE WHAT THEY'RE DOIN' TO YOU.
CODY, I NEED YOU TO BELIEVE ME.
ERIN, I WAS AT YOUR GRANDMA'S FUNERAL.
THIS IS ALL IN YOUR HEAD.
OKAY, THINGS HAVE SHIFTED FROM SUPER STRANGE, TO SCARY...

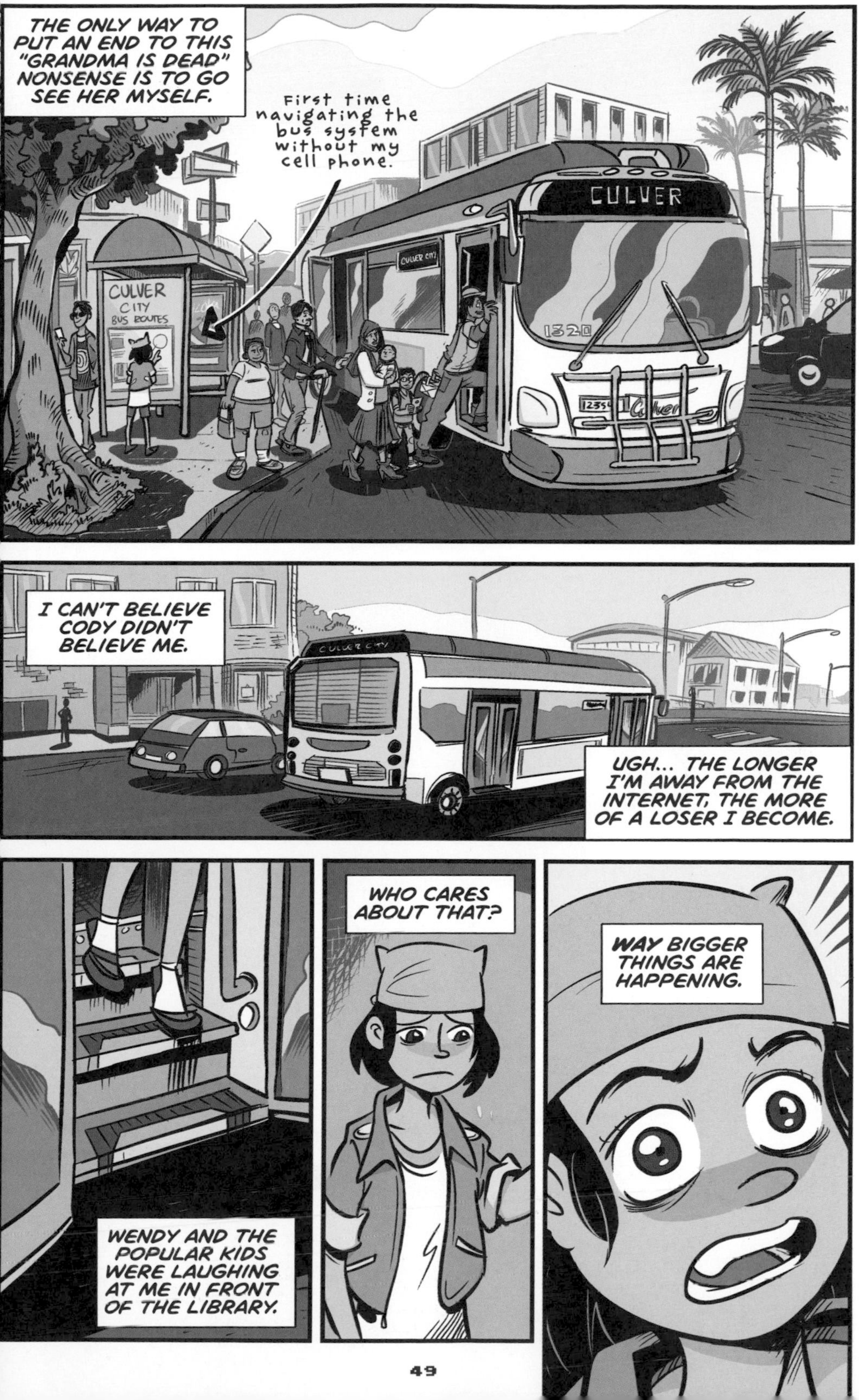
THE ONLY WAY TO PUT AN END TO THIS "GRANDMA IS DEAD" NONSENSE IS TO GO SEE HER MYSELF.
First time navigating the bus system without my cell phone.
CULVER CITY BUS ROUTES
CULVER
CULVER CITY
1320
Culver
I CAN'T BELIEVE CODY DIDN'T BELIEVE ME.
CULVER CITY
UGH... THE LONGER I'M AWAY FROM THE INTERNET, THE MORE OF A LOSER I BECOME.
WENDY AND THE POPULAR KIDS WERE LAUGHING AT ME IN FRONT OF THE LIBRARY.
WHO CARES ABOUT THAT?
WAY BIGGER THINGS ARE HAPPENING.

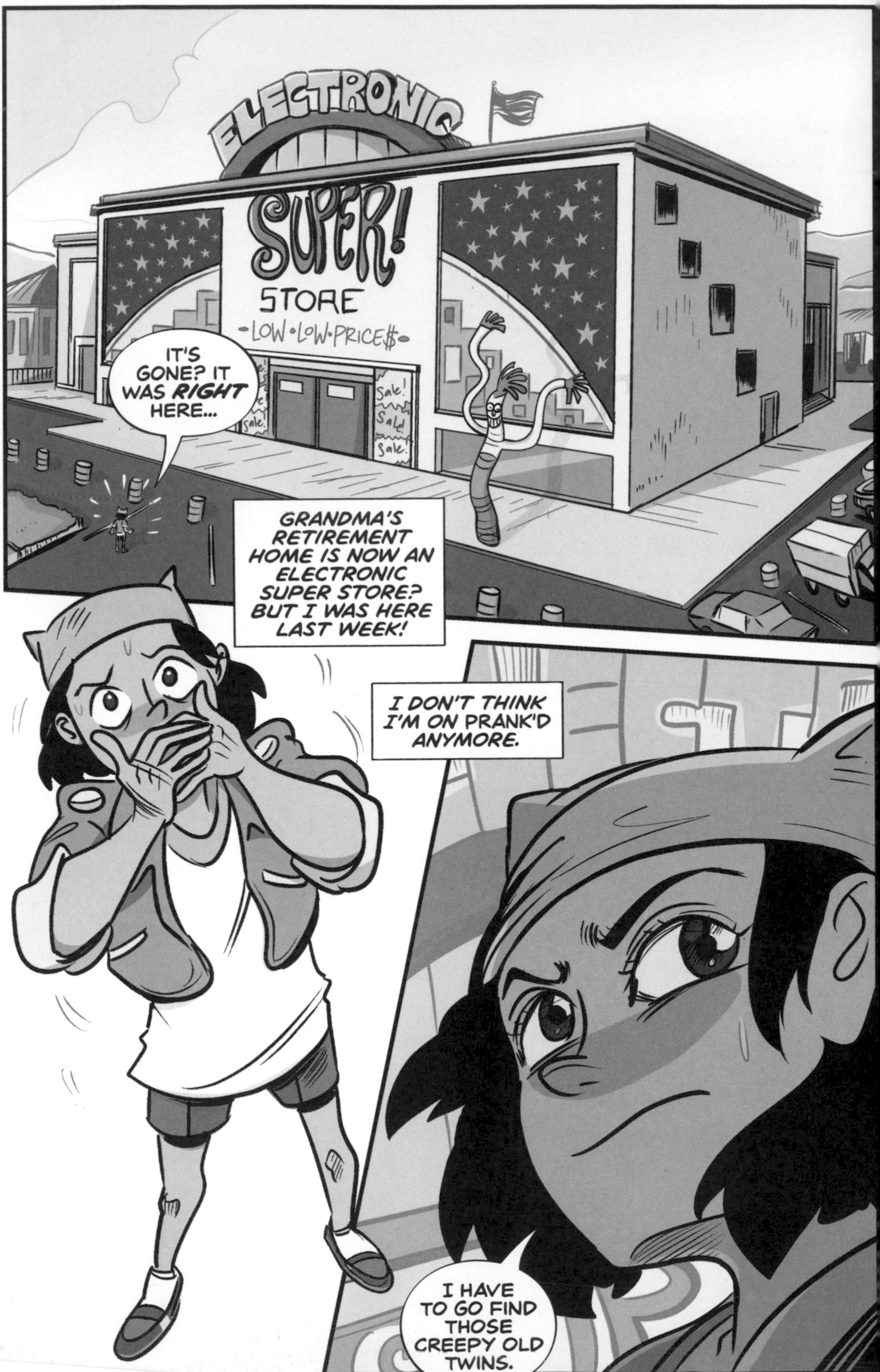
ELECTRONIC
SUPER!
STORE
LOW LOW PRICE$
Sale!
Sale!
Sale!
IT'S GONE? IT WAS *RIGHT* HERE...
GRANDMA'S RETIREMENT HOME IS NOW AN ELECTRONIC SUPER STORE? BUT I WAS HERE LAST WEEK!
I DON'T THINK I'M ON PRANK'D ANYMORE.
I HAVE TO GO FIND THOSE CREEPY OLD TWINS.

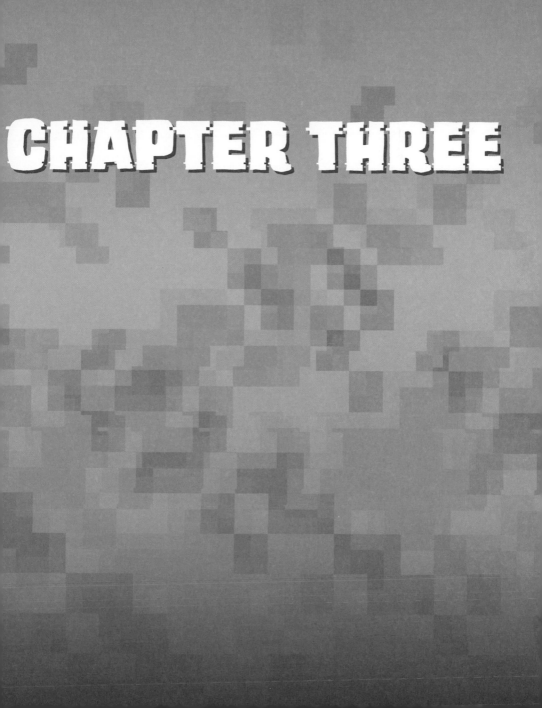

CHAPTER THREE

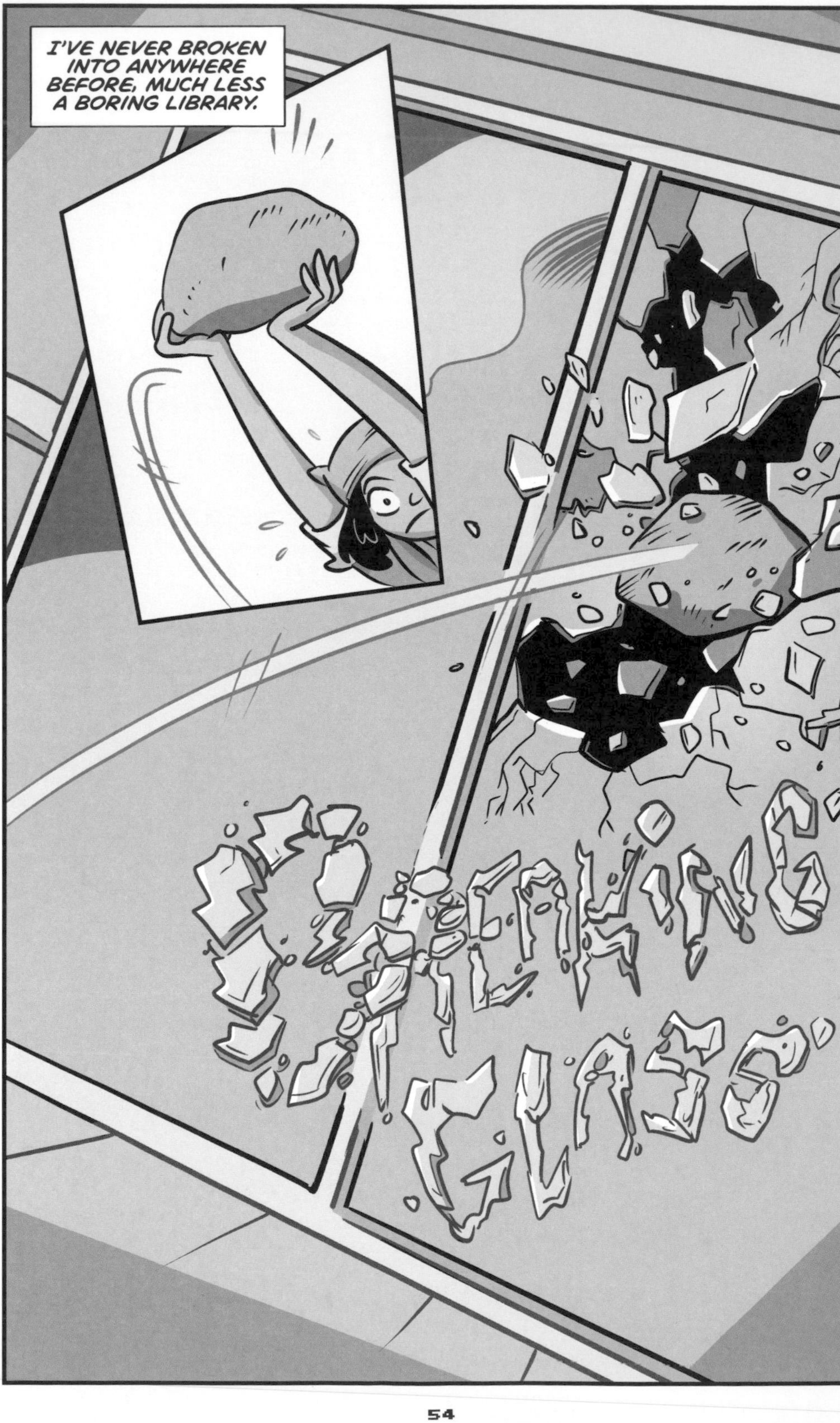
I'VE NEVER BROKEN INTO ANYWHERE BEFORE, MUCH LESS A BORING LIBRARY.
BREAKING GLASS

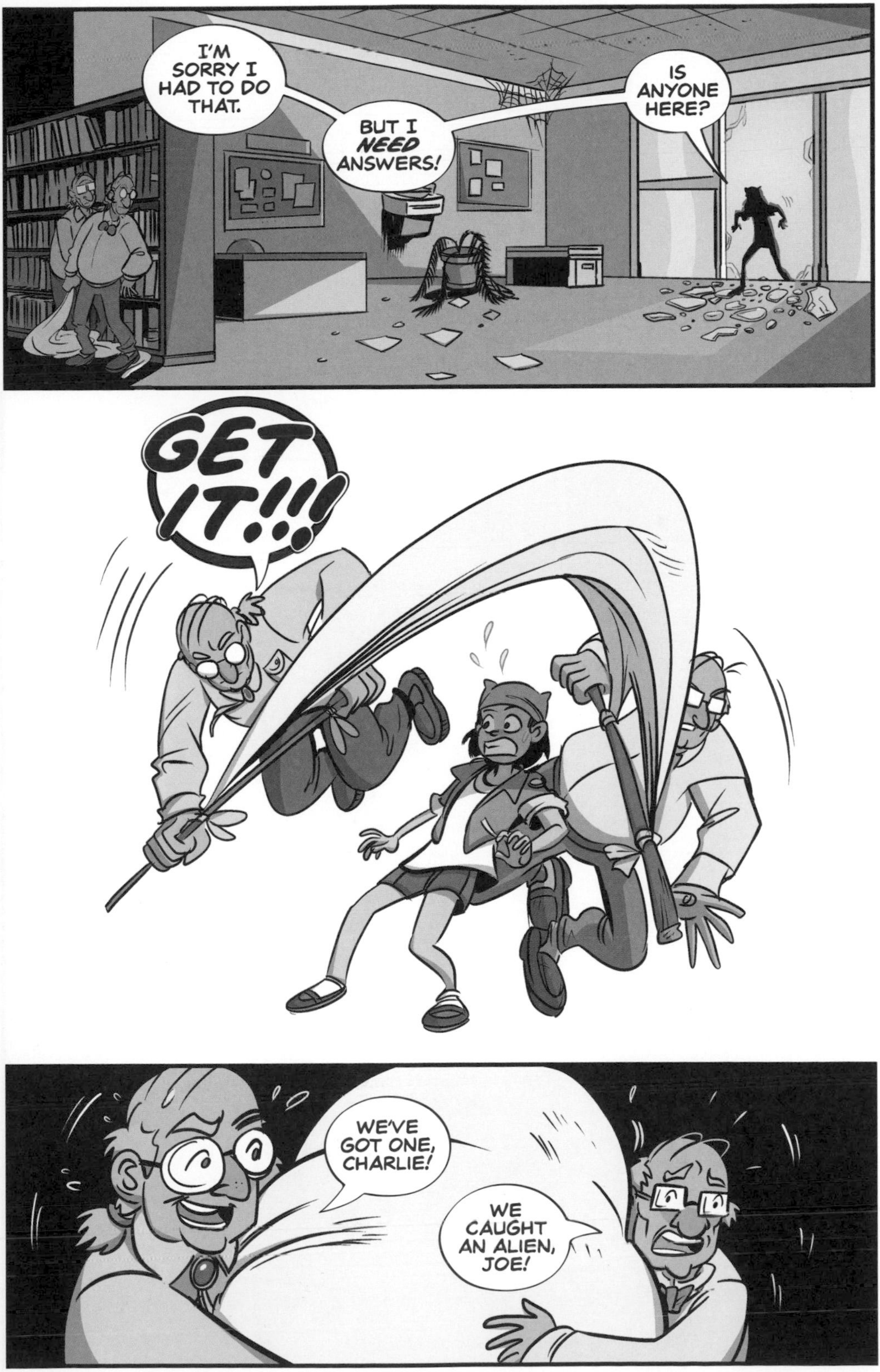
I'M SORRY I HAD TO DO THAT.
BUT I NEED ANSWERS!
IS ANYONE HERE?
GET IT!!!
WE'VE GOT ONE, CHARLIE!
WE CAUGHT AN ALIEN, JOE!

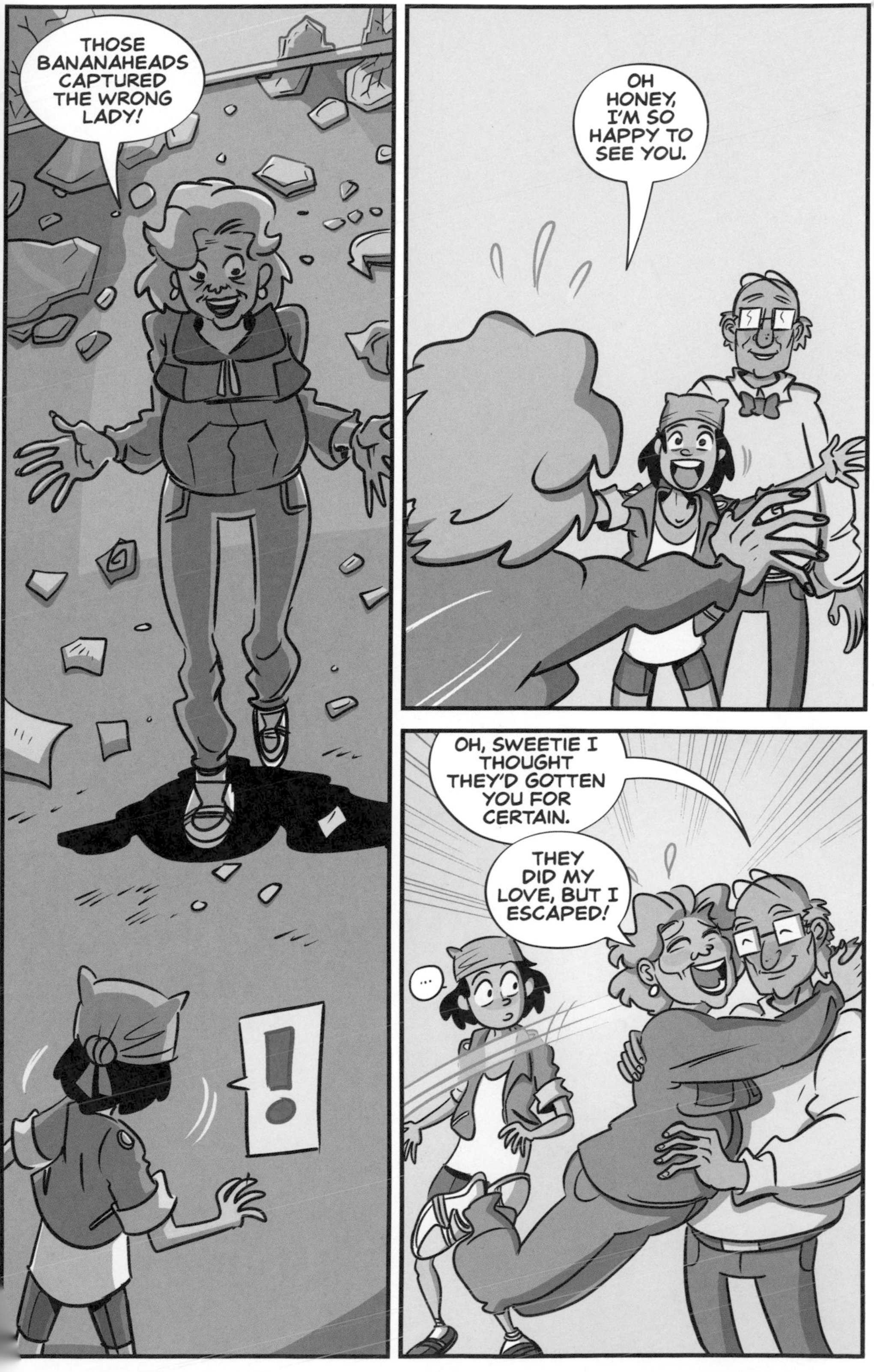
THOSE BANANAHEADS CAPTURED THE WRONG LADY!
!
OH HONEY, I'M SO HAPPY TO SEE YOU.
OH, SWEETIE I THOUGHT THEY'D GOTTEN YOU FOR CERTAIN.
THEY DID MY LOVE, BUT I ESCAPED!
...

63

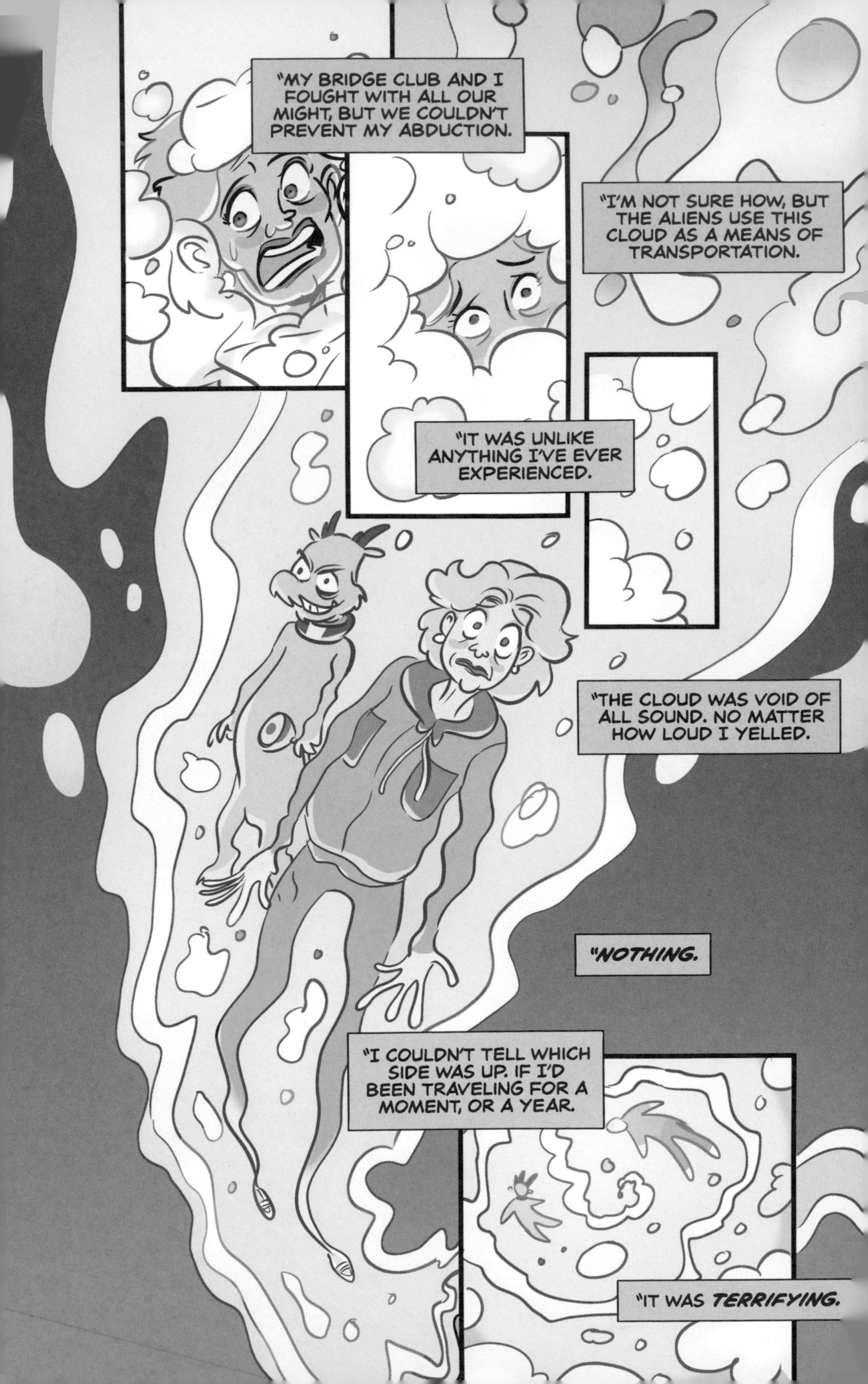
"MY BRIDGE CLUB AND I FOUGHT WITH ALL OUR MIGHT, BUT WE COULDN'T PREVENT MY ABDUCTION.
"I'M NOT SURE HOW, BUT THE ALIENS USE THIS CLOUD AS A MEANS OF TRANSPORTATION.
"IT WAS UNLIKE ANYTHING I'VE EVER EXPERIENCED.
"THE CLOUD WAS VOID OF ALL SOUND. NO MATTER HOW LOUD I YELLED.
"*NOTHING.*
"I COULDN'T TELL WHICH SIDE WAS UP. IF I'D BEEN TRAVELING FOR A MOMENT, OR A YEAR.
"IT WAS *TERRIFYING.*

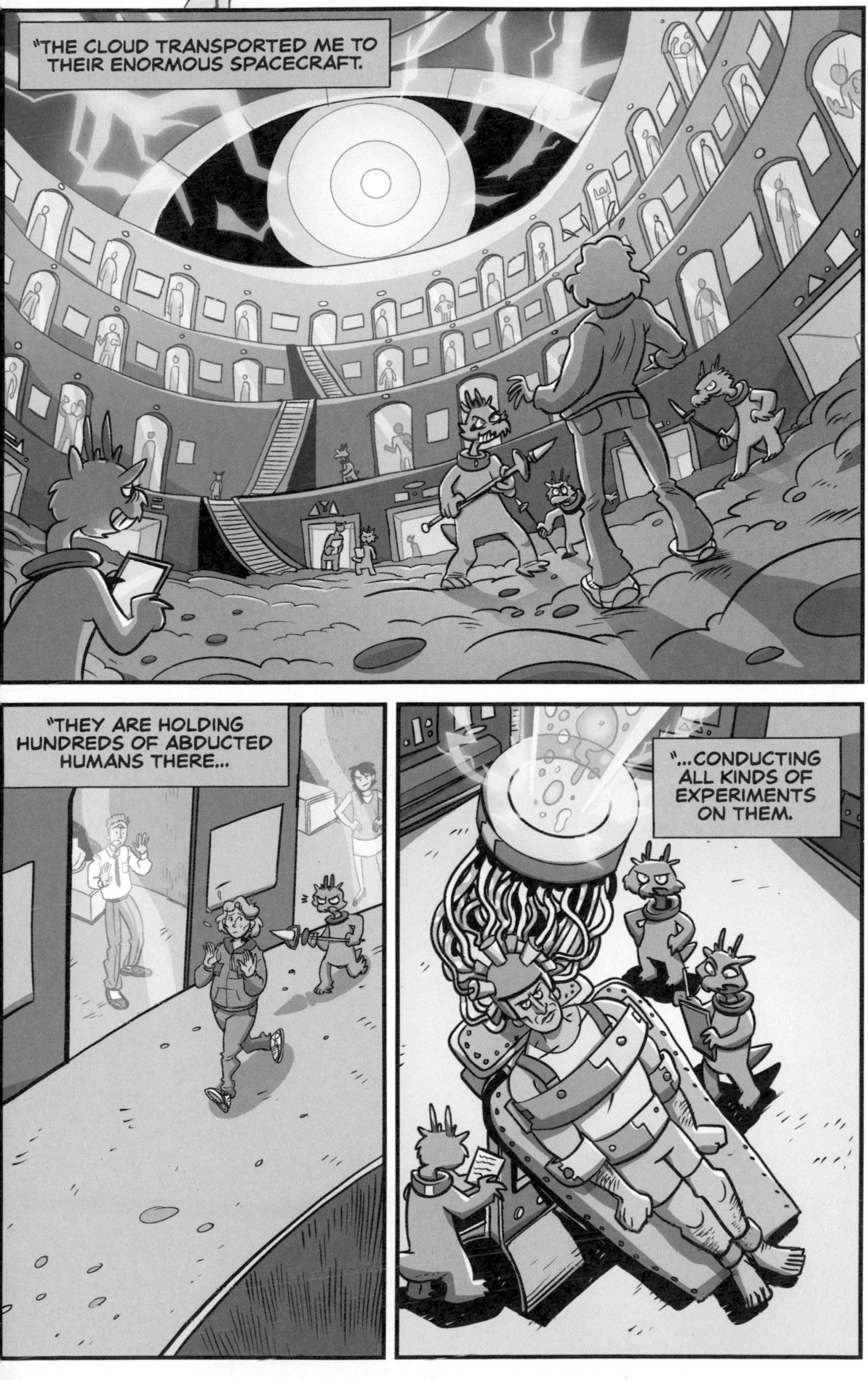
"THE CLOUD TRANSPORTED ME TO THEIR ENORMOUS SPACECRAFT.
"THEY ARE HOLDING HUNDREDS OF ABDUCTED HUMANS THERE...
"...CONDUCTING ALL KINDS OF EXPERIMENTS ON THEM.

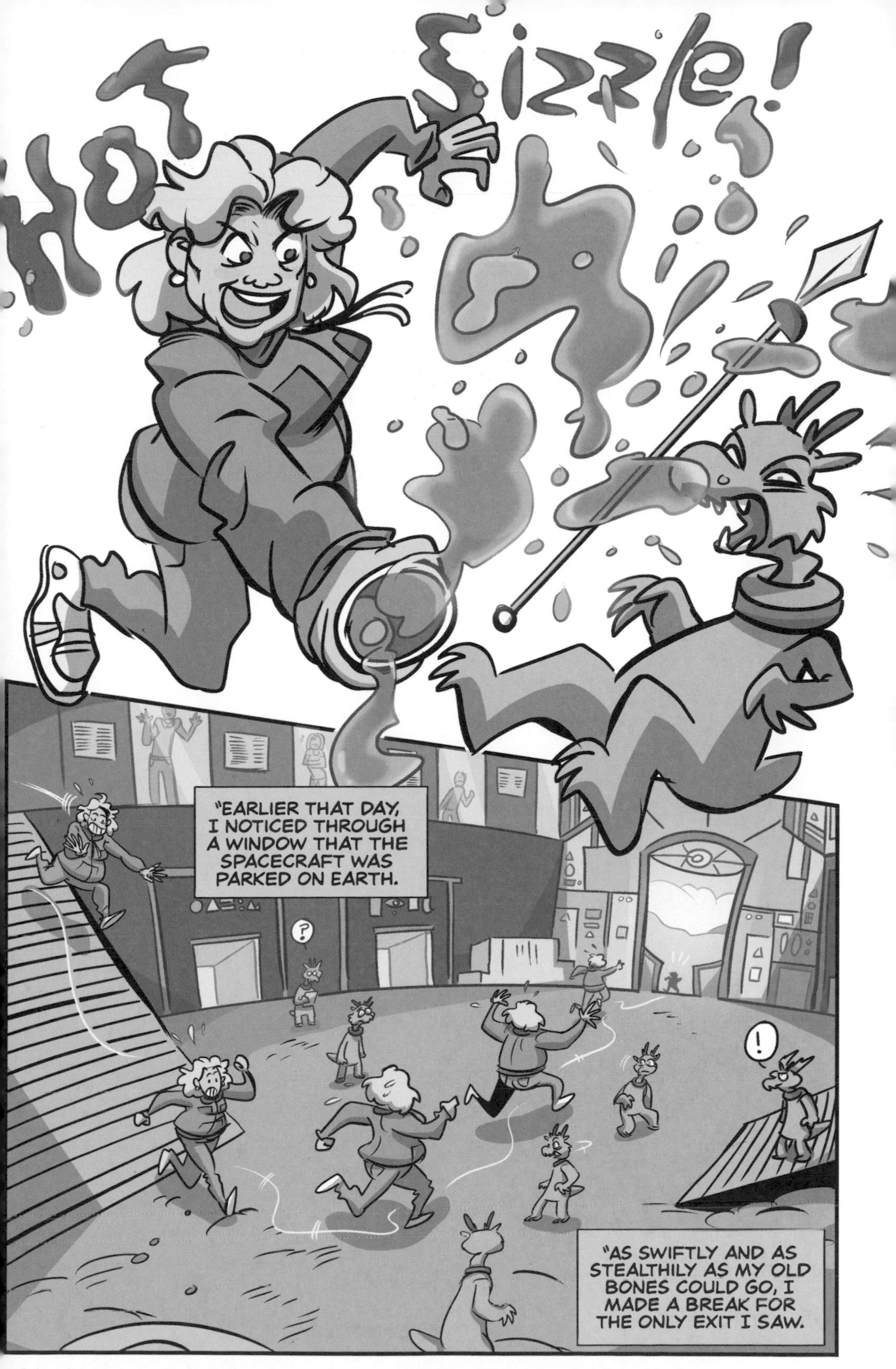
HOT SIZZLE!
"EARLIER THAT DAY, I NOTICED THROUGH A WINDOW THAT THE SPACECRAFT WAS PARKED ON EARTH.
?
!
"AS SWIFTLY AND AS STEALTHILY AS MY OLD BONES COULD GO, I MADE A BREAK FOR THE ONLY EXIT I SAW.

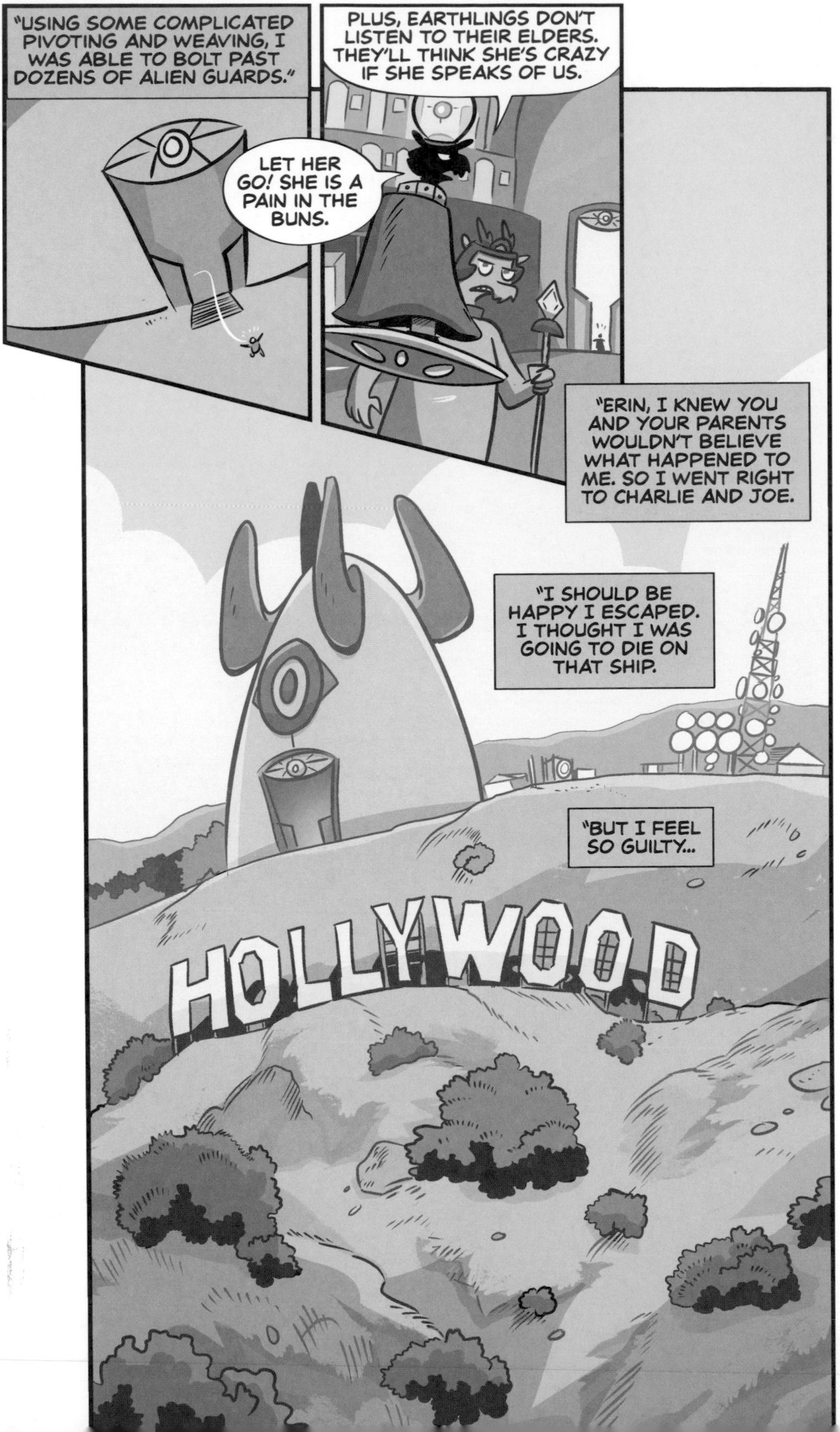
"USING SOME COMPLICATED PIVOTING AND WEAVING, I WAS ABLE TO BOLT PAST DOZENS OF ALIEN GUARDS."
PLUS, EARTHLINGS DON'T LISTEN TO THEIR ELDERS. THEY'LL THINK SHE'S CRAZY IF SHE SPEAKS OF US.
LET HER GO! SHE IS A PAIN IN THE BUNS.
"ERIN, I KNEW YOU AND YOUR PARENTS WOULDN'T BELIEVE WHAT HAPPENED TO ME. SO I WENT RIGHT TO CHARLIE AND JOE.
"I SHOULD BE HAPPY I ESCAPED. I THOUGHT I WAS GOING TO DIE ON THAT SHIP.
"BUT I FEEL SO GUILTY...
HOLLYWOOD

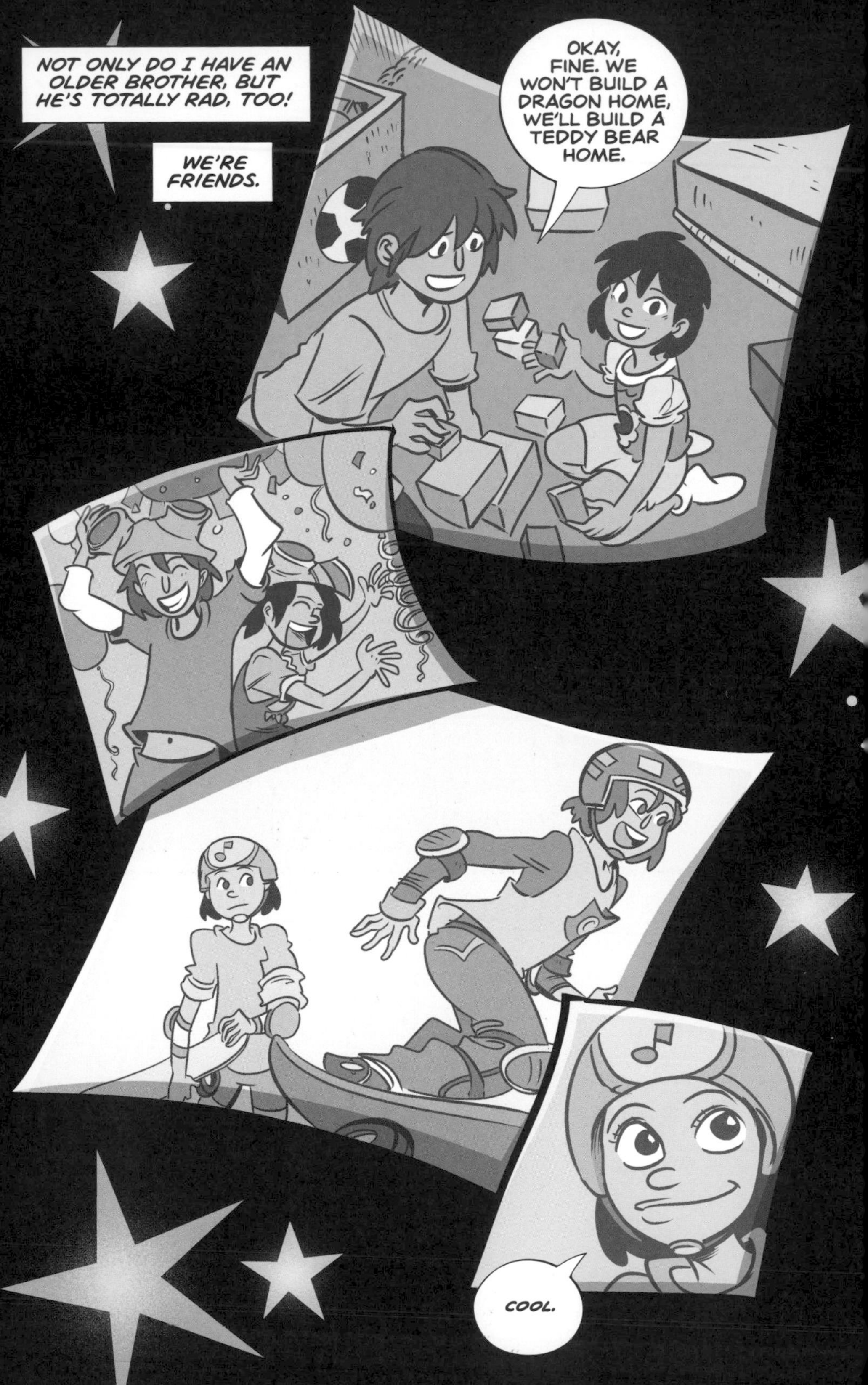
NOT ONLY DO I HAVE AN OLDER BROTHER, BUT HE'S TOTALLY RAD, TOO!
OKAY, FINE. WE WON'T BUILD A DRAGON HOME, WE'LL BUILD A TEDDY BEAR HOME.
WE'RE FRIENDS.
COOL.

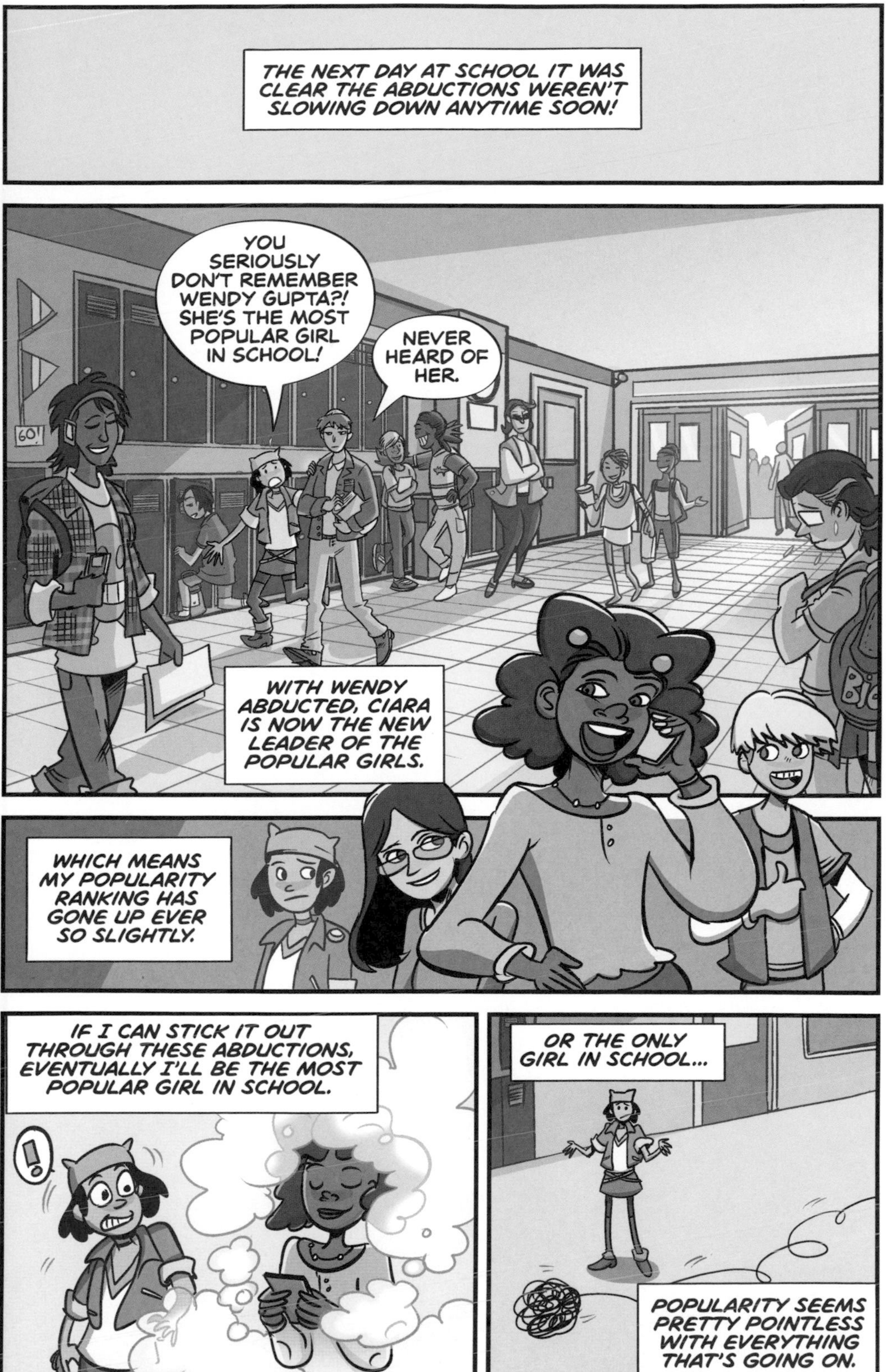

THE NEXT DAY AT SCHOOL IT WAS CLEAR THE ABDUCTIONS WEREN'T SLOWING DOWN ANYTIME SOON!
YOU SERIOUSLY DON'T REMEMBER WENDY GUPTA?! SHE'S THE MOST POPULAR GIRL IN SCHOOL!
NEVER HEARD OF HER.
GO!
WITH WENDY ABDUCTED, CIARA IS NOW THE NEW LEADER OF THE POPULAR GIRLS.
WHICH MEANS MY POPULARITY RANKING HAS GONE UP EVER SO SLIGHTLY.
IF I CAN STICK IT OUT THROUGH THESE ABDUCTIONS, EVENTUALLY I'LL BE THE MOST POPULAR GIRL IN SCHOOL.
!
OR THE ONLY GIRL IN SCHOOL...
POPULARITY SEEMS PRETTY POINTLESS WITH EVERYTHING THAT'S GOING ON.

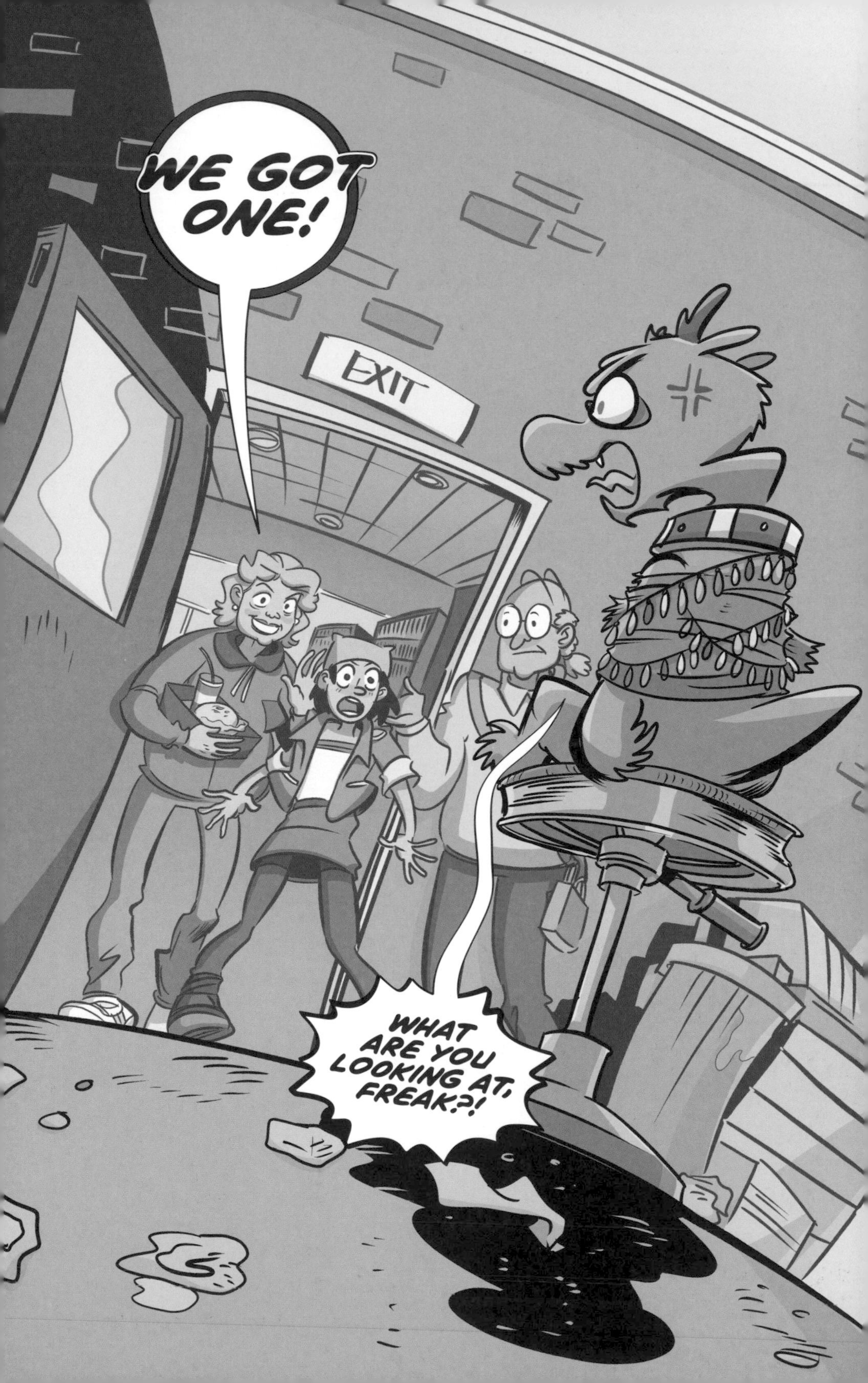
WE GOT ONE!
EXIT
WHAT ARE YOU LOOKING AT, FREAK?!

CHAPTER FOUR

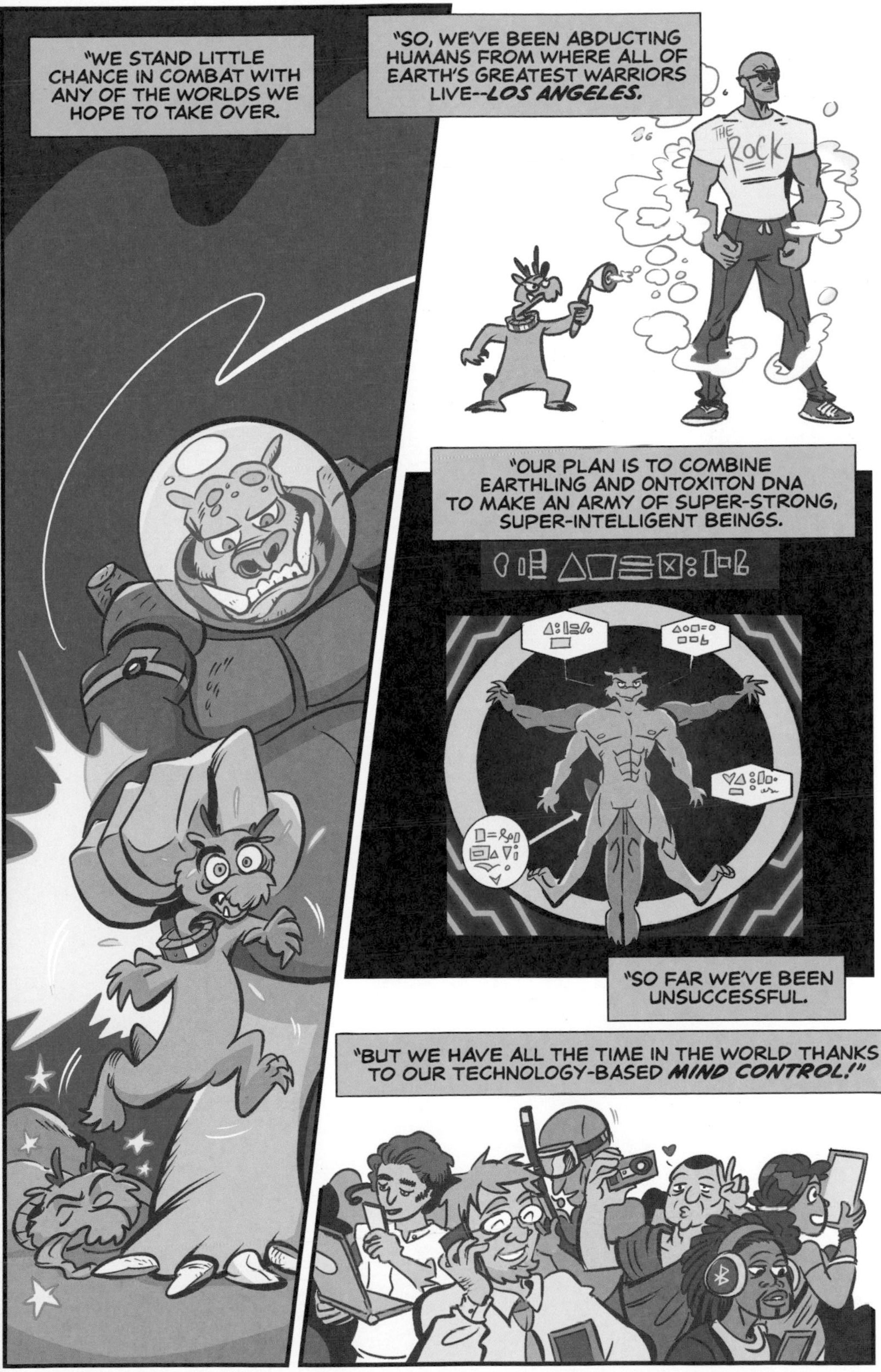
"WE STAND LITTLE CHANCE IN COMBAT WITH ANY OF THE WORLDS WE HOPE TO TAKE OVER.
"SO, WE'VE BEEN ABDUCTING HUMANS FROM WHERE ALL OF EARTH'S GREATEST WARRIORS LIVE--LOS ANGELES.
THE ROCK
"OUR PLAN IS TO COMBINE EARTHLING AND ONTOXITON DNA TO MAKE AN ARMY OF SUPER-STRONG, SUPER-INTELLIGENT BEINGS.
"SO FAR WE'VE BEEN UNSUCCESSFUL.
"BUT WE HAVE ALL THE TIME IN THE WORLD THANKS TO OUR TECHNOLOGY-BASED MIND CONTROL!"

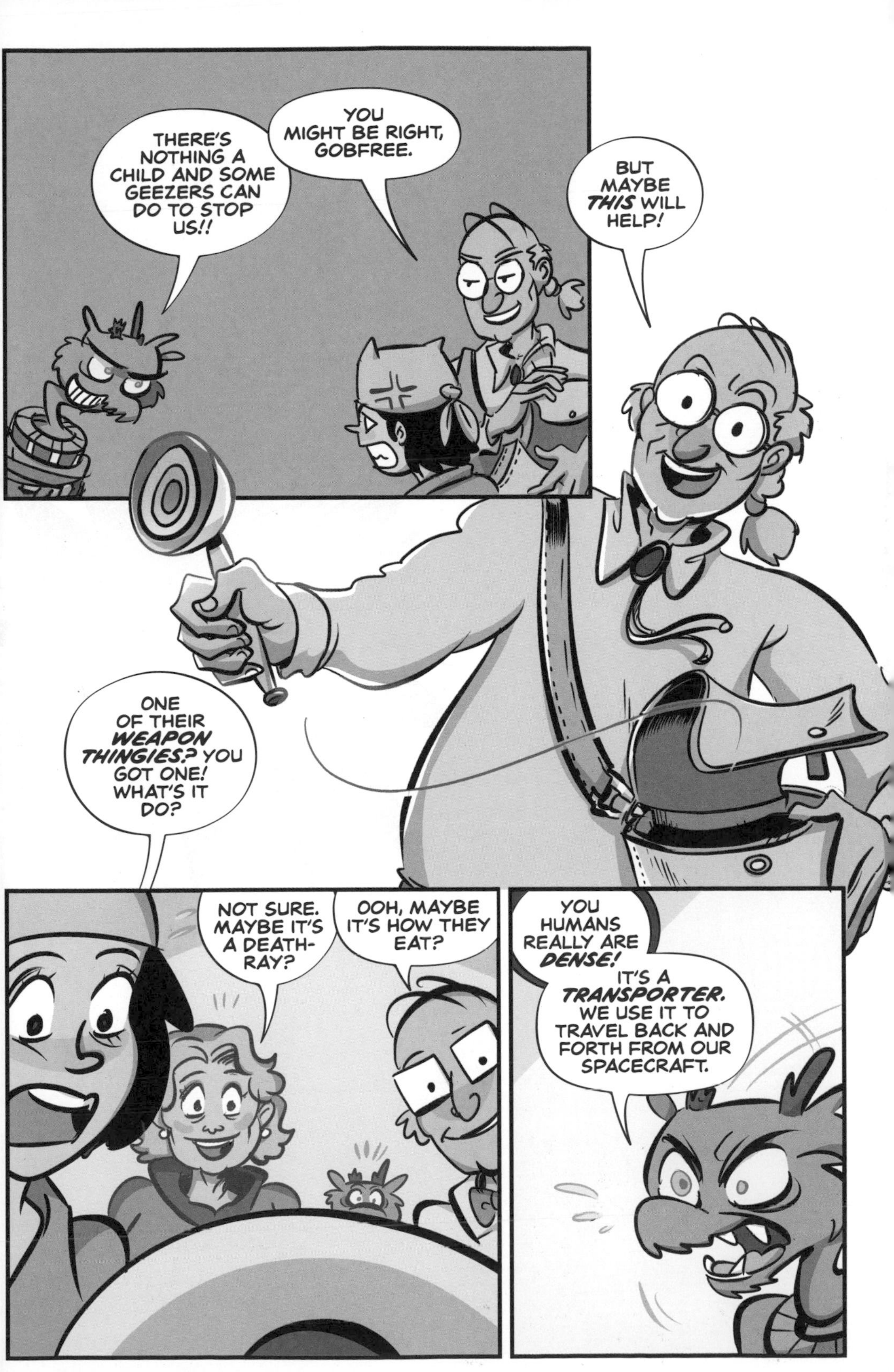
THERE'S NOTHING A CHILD AND SOME GEEZERS CAN DO TO STOP US!!
YOU MIGHT BE RIGHT, GOBFREE.
BUT MAYBE *THIS* WILL HELP!
ONE OF THEIR *WEAPON THINGIES?* YOU GOT ONE! WHAT'S IT DO?
NOT SURE. MAYBE IT'S A DEATH-RAY?
OOH, MAYBE IT'S HOW THEY EAT?
YOU HUMANS REALLY ARE *DENSE!*
IT'S A *TRANSPORTER.* WE USE IT TO TRAVEL BACK AND FORTH FROM OUR SPACECRAFT.

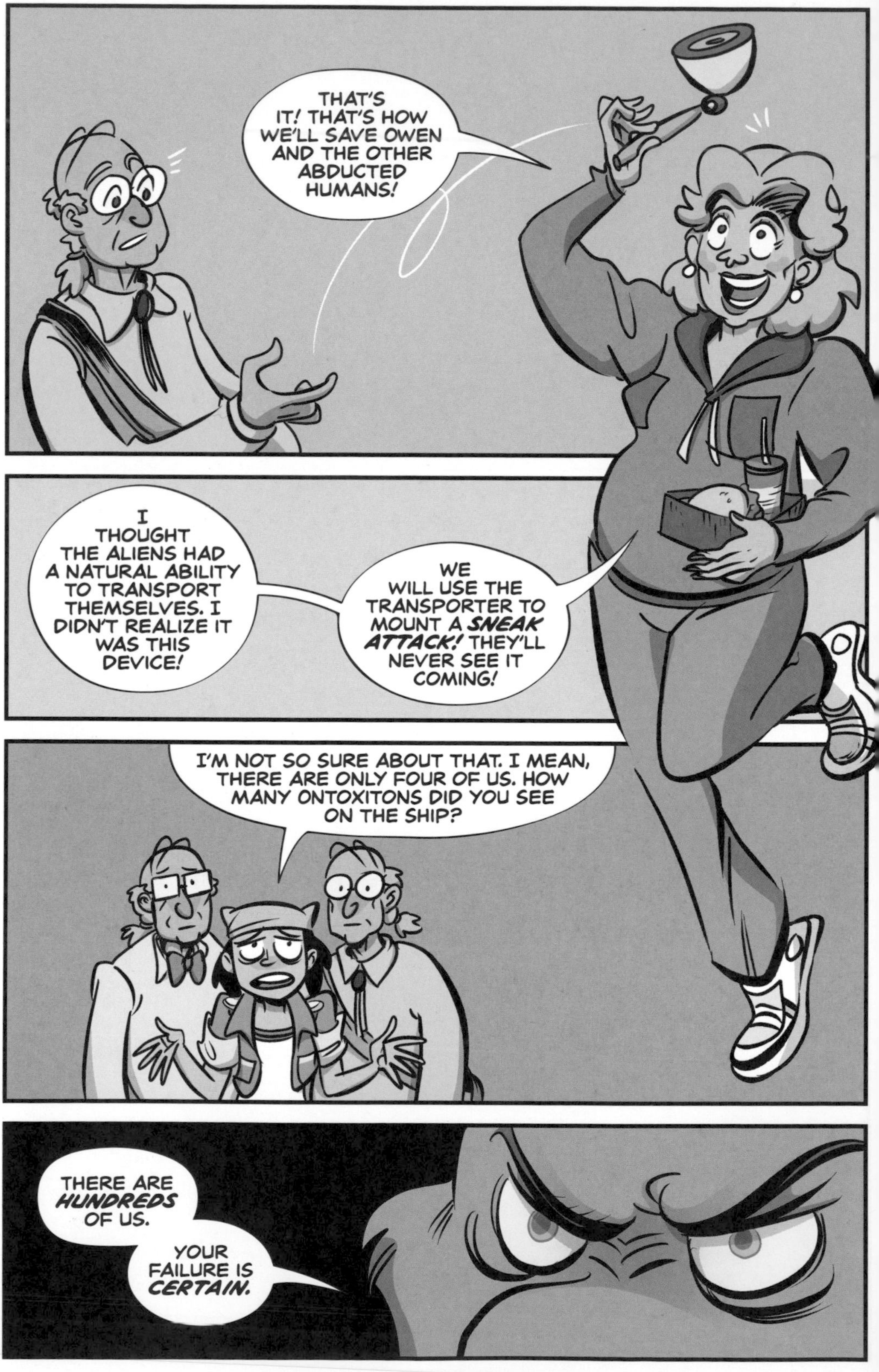
THAT'S IT! THAT'S HOW WE'LL SAVE OWEN AND THE OTHER ABDUCTED HUMANS!
I THOUGHT THE ALIENS HAD A NATURAL ABILITY TO TRANSPORT THEMSELVES. I DIDN'T REALIZE IT WAS THIS DEVICE!
WE WILL USE THE TRANSPORTER TO MOUNT A SNEAK ATTACK! THEY'LL NEVER SEE IT COMING!
I'M NOT SO SURE ABOUT THAT. I MEAN, THERE ARE ONLY FOUR OF US. HOW MANY ONTOXITONS DID YOU SEE ON THE SHIP?
THERE ARE HUNDREDS OF US.
YOUR FAILURE IS CERTAIN.

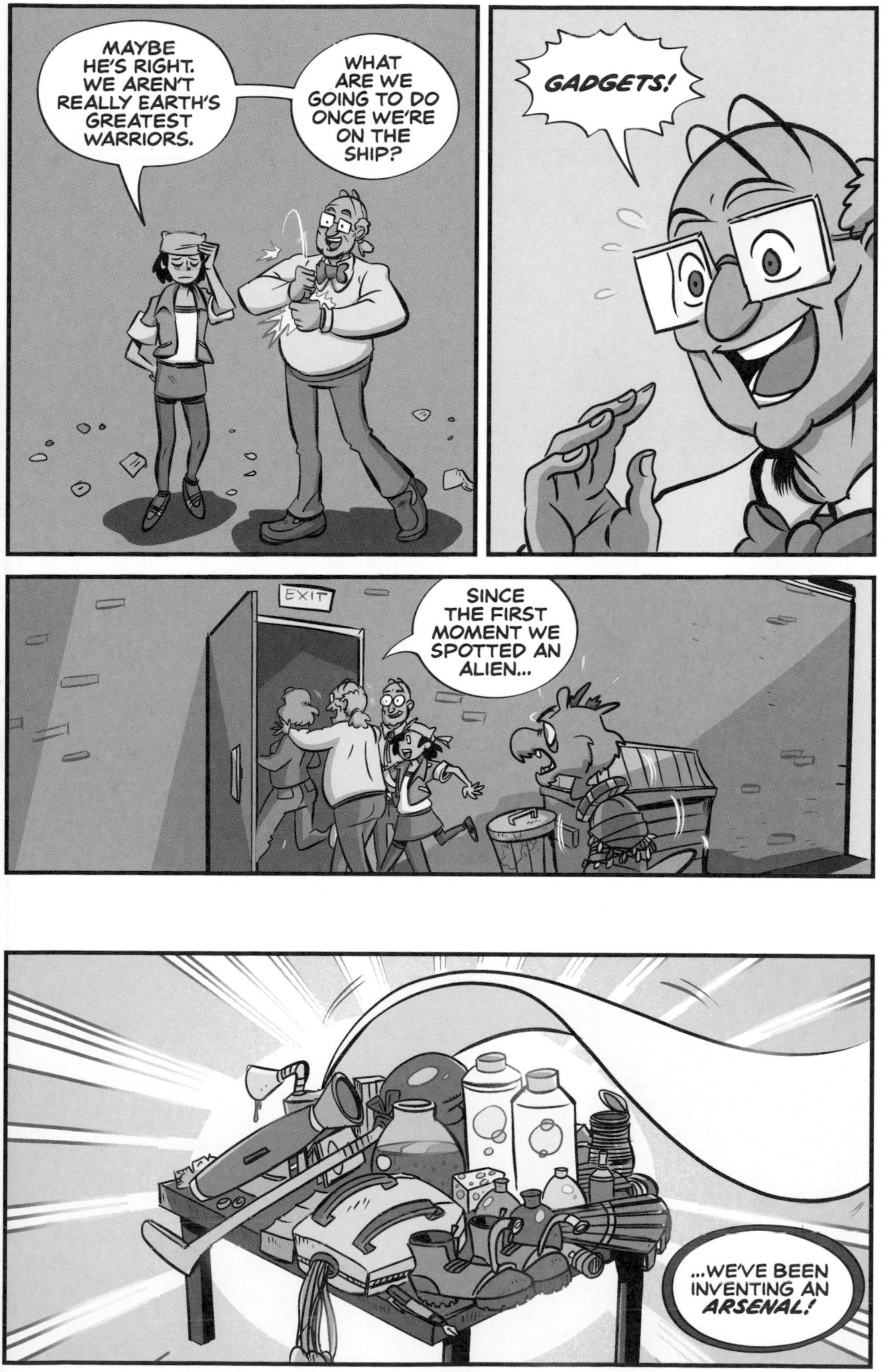
MAYBE HE'S RIGHT. WE AREN'T REALLY EARTH'S GREATEST WARRIORS.
WHAT ARE WE GOING TO DO ONCE WE'RE ON THE SHIP?
GADGETS!
EXIT
SINCE THE FIRST MOMENT WE SPOTTED AN ALIEN...
...WE'VE BEEN INVENTING AN *ARSENAL!*

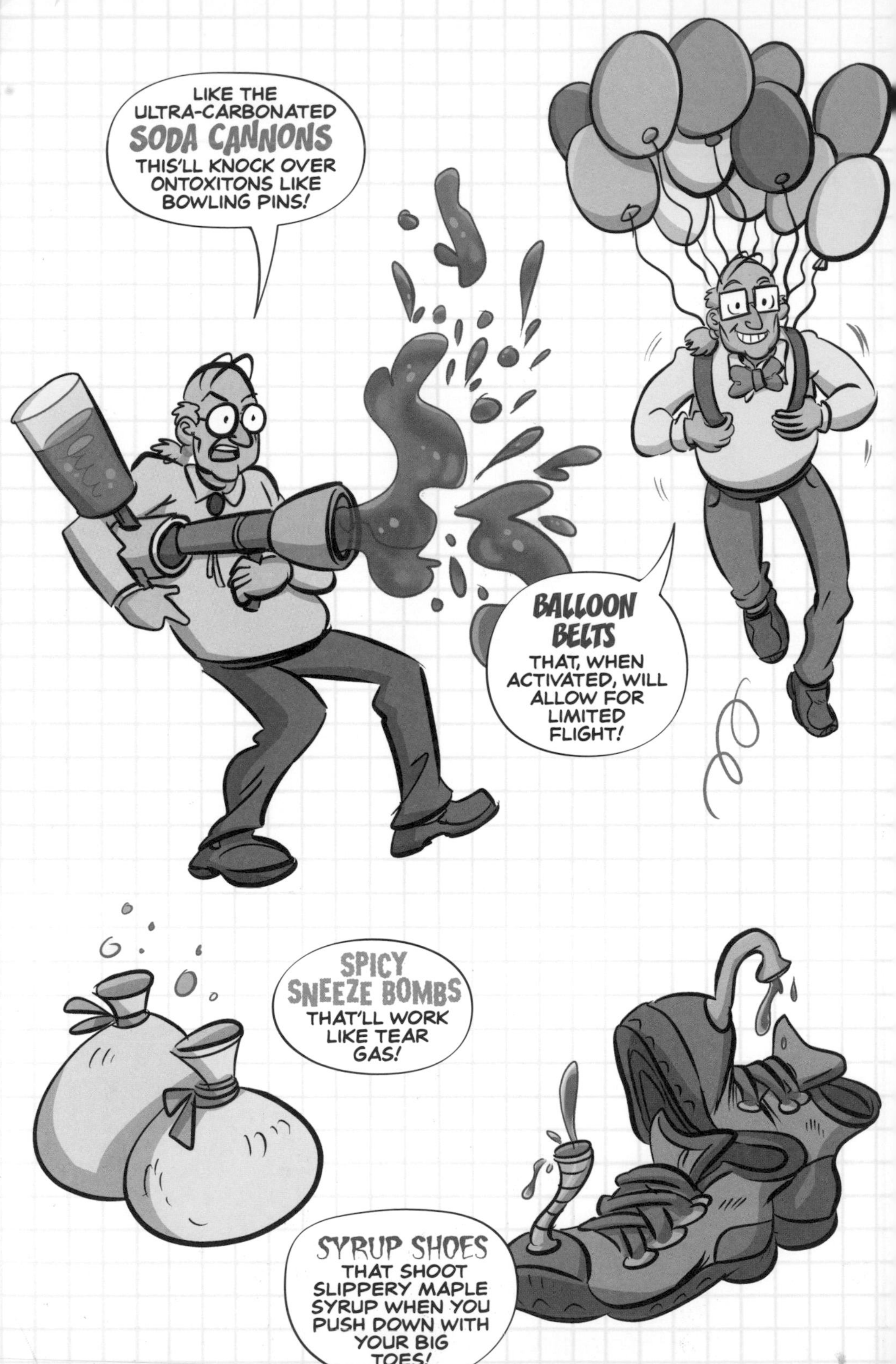
LIKE THE ULTRA-CARBONATED SODA CANNONS THIS'LL KNOCK OVER ONTOXITONS LIKE BOWLING PINS!
BALLOON BELTS THAT, WHEN ACTIVATED, WILL ALLOW FOR LIMITED FLIGHT!
SPICY SNEEZE BOMBS THAT'LL WORK LIKE TEAR GAS!
SYRUP SHOES THAT SHOOT SLIPPERY MAPLE SYRUP WHEN YOU PUSH DOWN WITH YOUR BIG TOES!

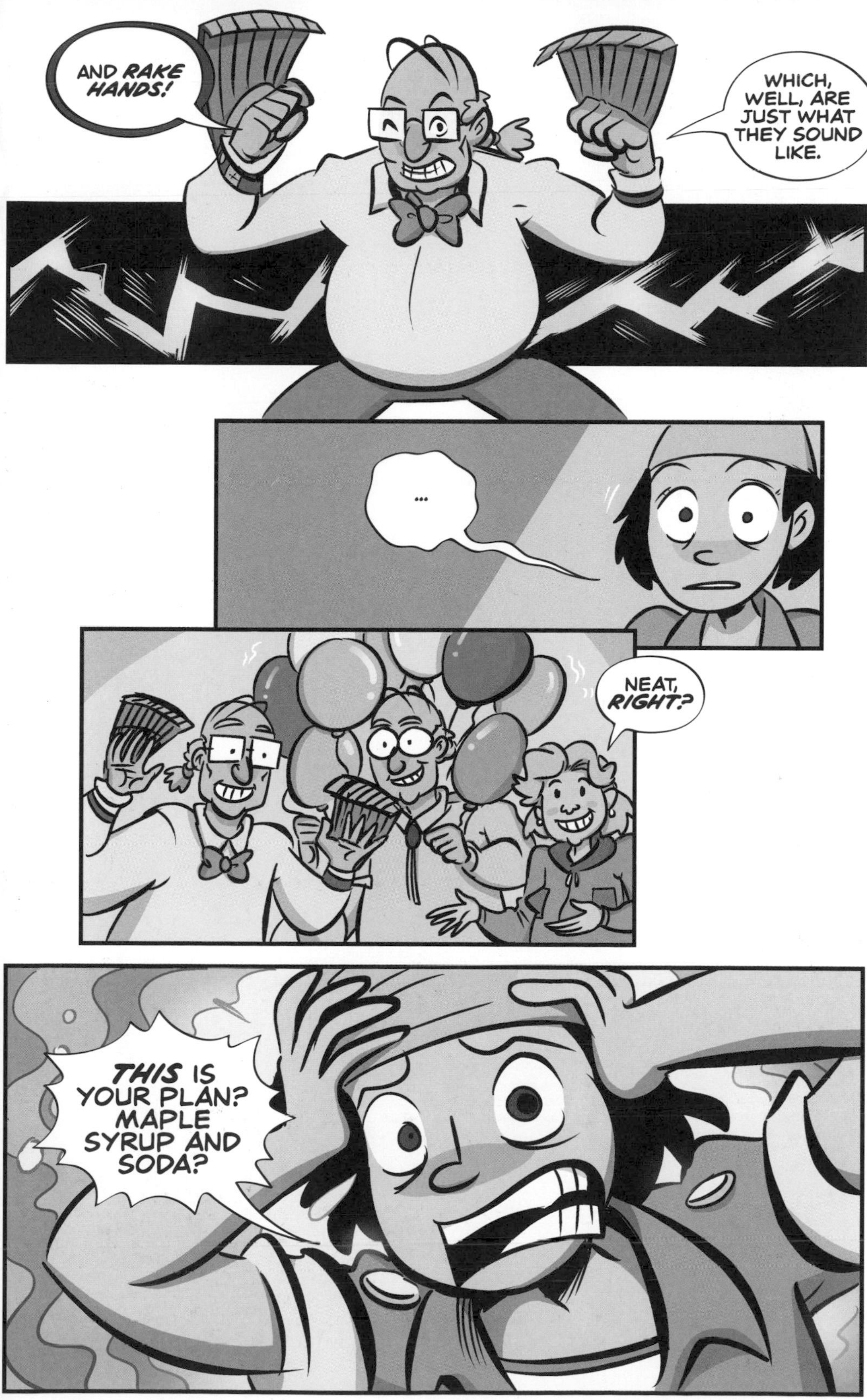
AND *RAKE HANDS!*
WHICH, WELL, ARE JUST WHAT THEY SOUND LIKE.
...
NEAT, *RIGHT?*
THIS IS YOUR PLAN? MAPLE SYRUP AND SODA?

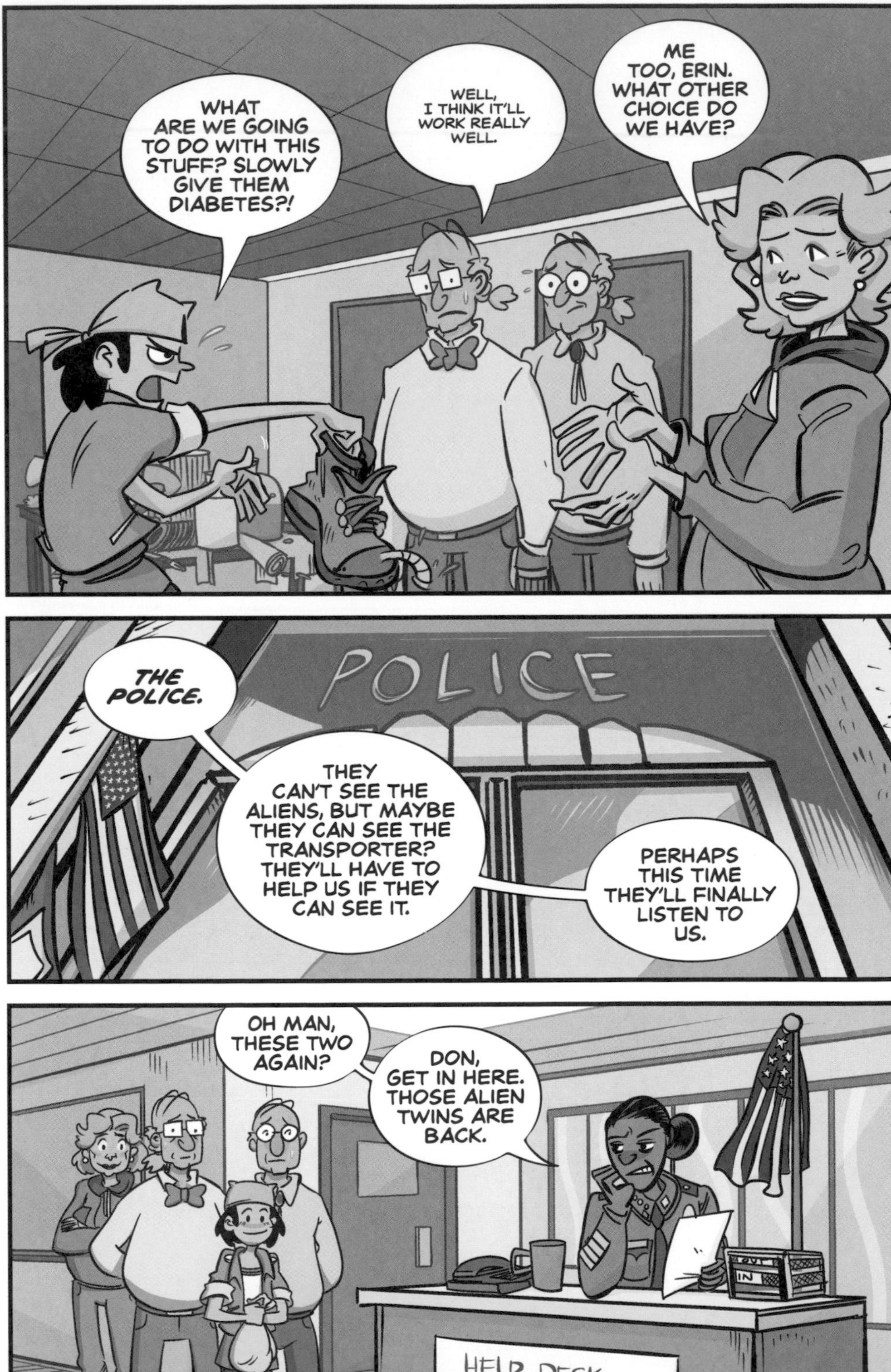
WHAT ARE WE GOING TO DO WITH THIS STUFF? SLOWLY GIVE THEM DIABETES?!
WELL, I THINK IT'LL WORK REALLY WELL.
ME TOO, ERIN. WHAT OTHER CHOICE DO WE HAVE?
POLICE
THE POLICE.
THEY CAN'T SEE THE ALIENS, BUT MAYBE THEY CAN SEE THE TRANSPORTER? THEY'LL HAVE TO HELP US IF THEY CAN SEE IT.
PERHAPS THIS TIME THEY'LL FINALLY LISTEN TO US.
OH MAN, THESE TWO AGAIN?
DON, GET IN HERE. THOSE ALIEN TWINS ARE BACK.
OUT
IN
HELP DESK

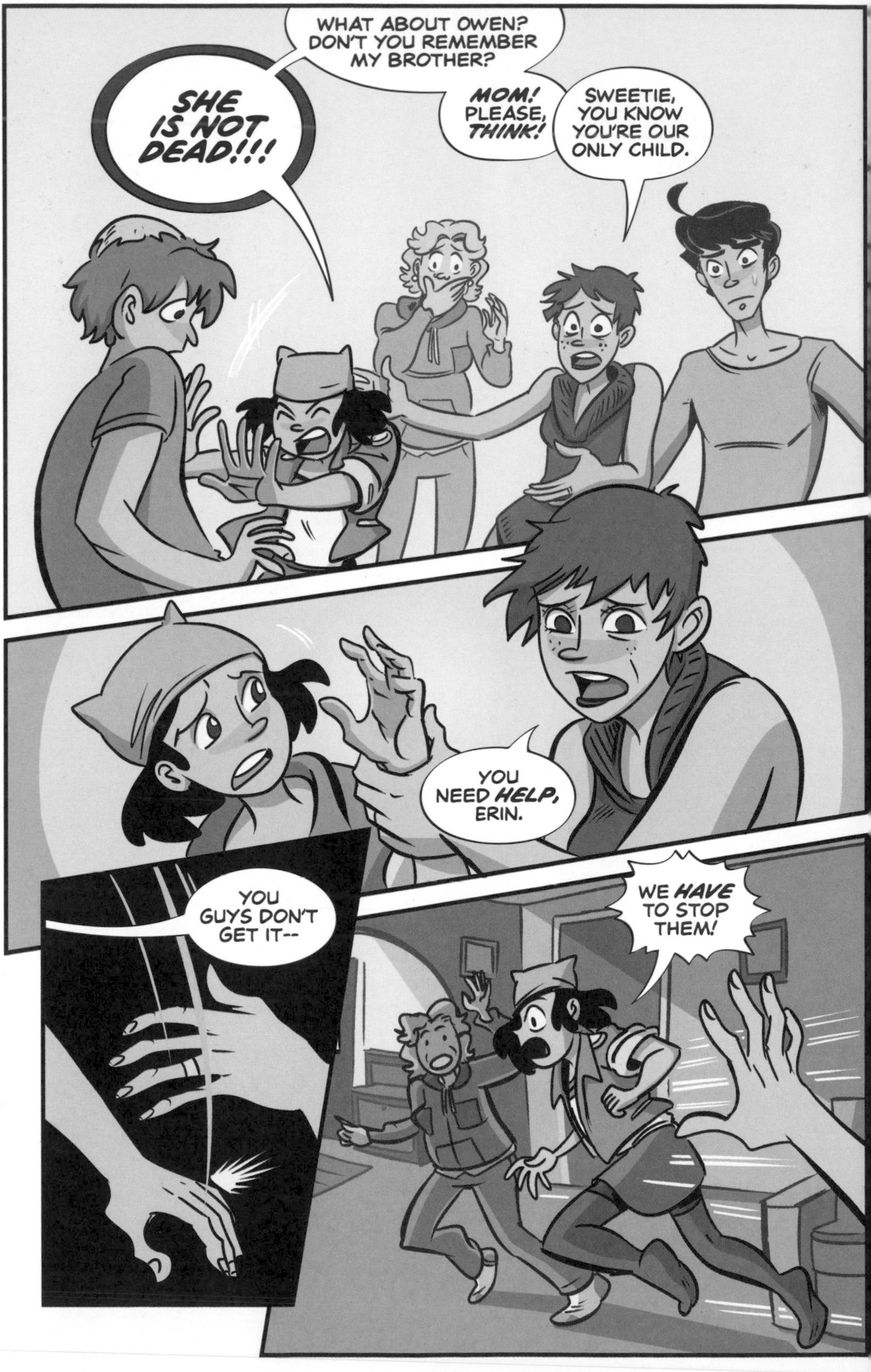
SHE IS NOT DEAD!!!
WHAT ABOUT OWEN? DON'T YOU REMEMBER MY BROTHER?
MOM! PLEASE, THINK!
SWEETIE, YOU KNOW YOU'RE OUR ONLY CHILD.
YOU NEED HELP, ERIN.
YOU GUYS DON'T GET IT--
WE HAVE TO STOP THEM!

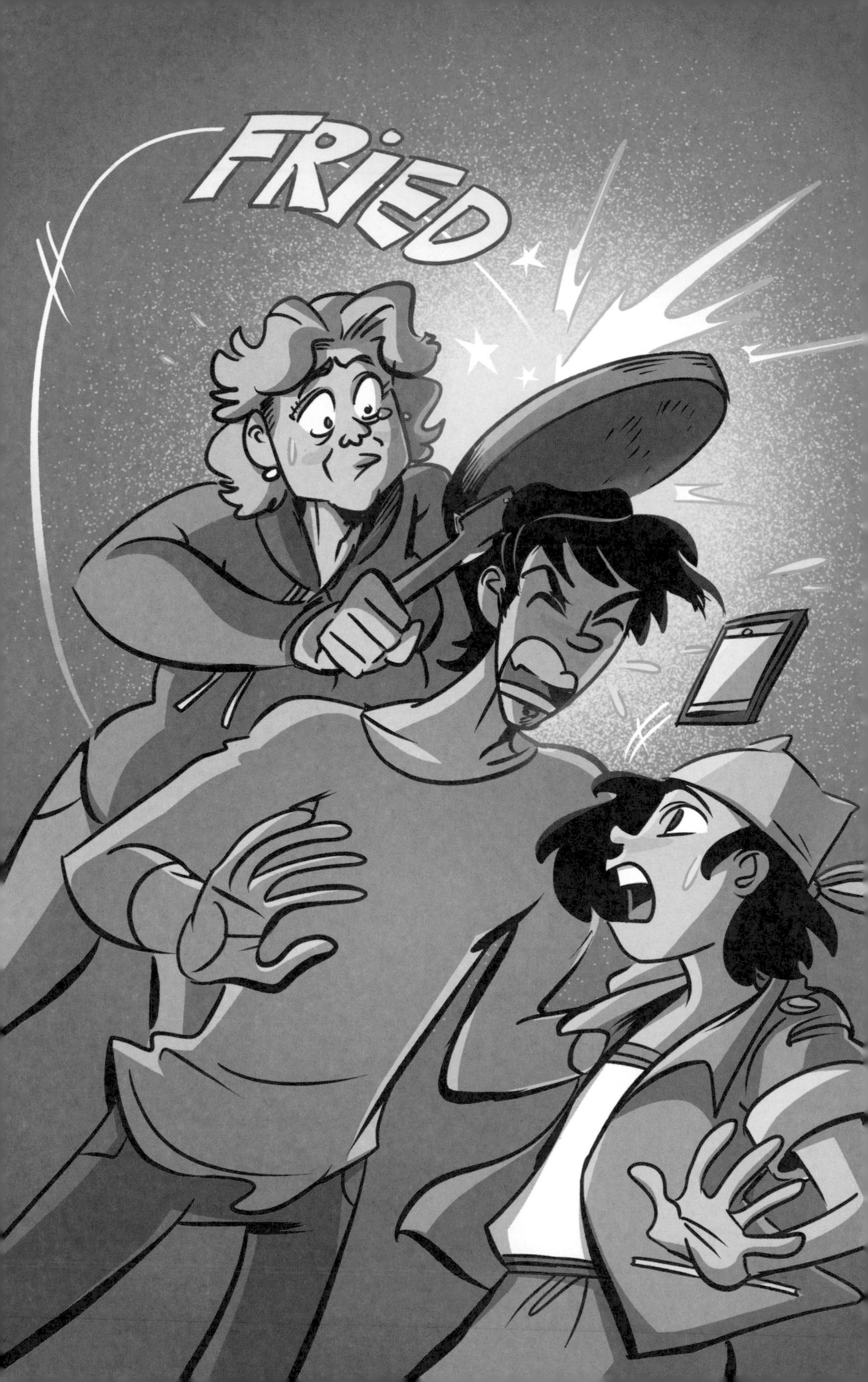
FRIED

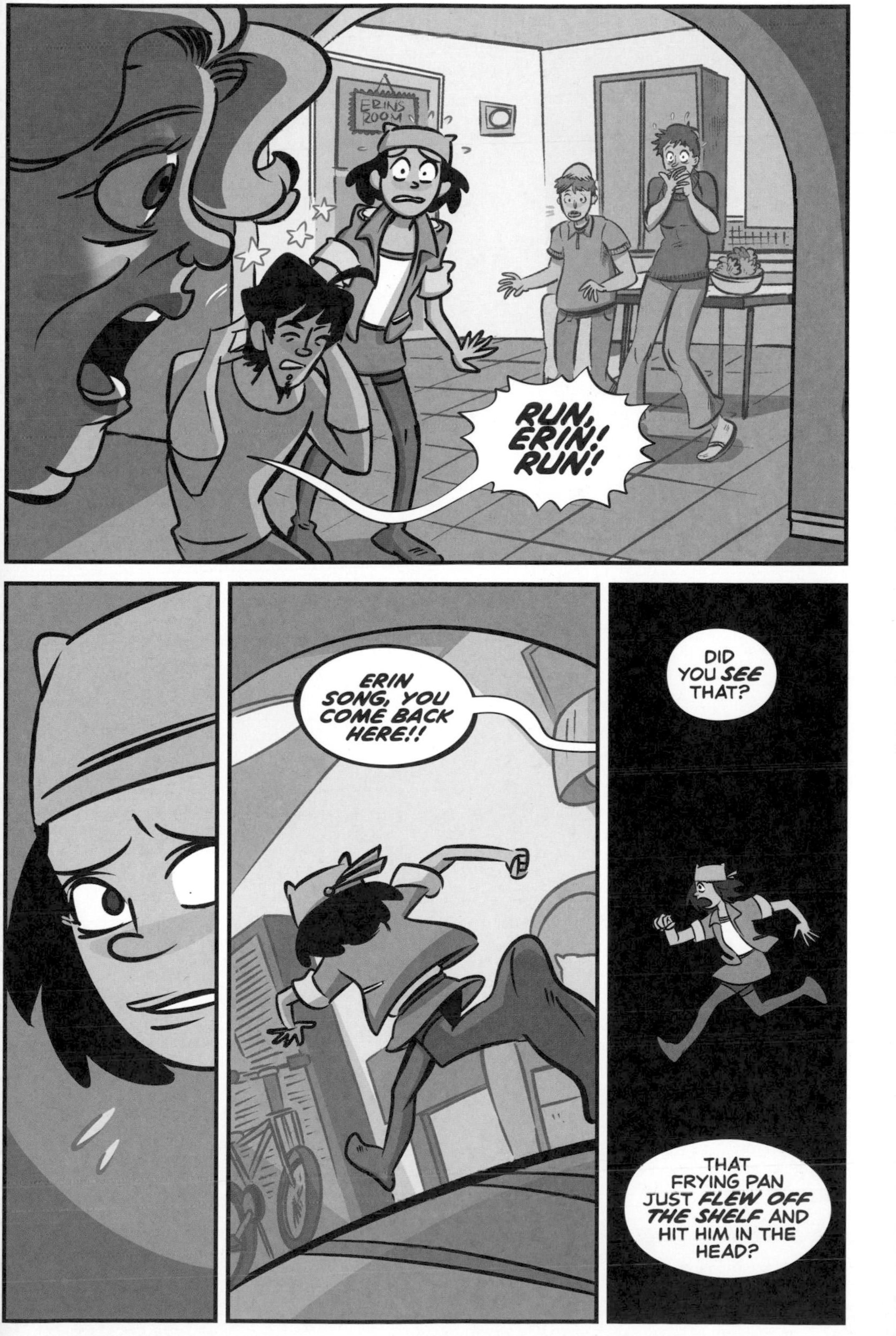
ERIN'S ROOM
RUN, ERIN! RUN!
ERIN SONG, YOU COME BACK HERE!!
DID YOU SEE THAT?
THAT FRYING PAN JUST FLEW OFF THE SHELF AND HIT HIM IN THE HEAD?

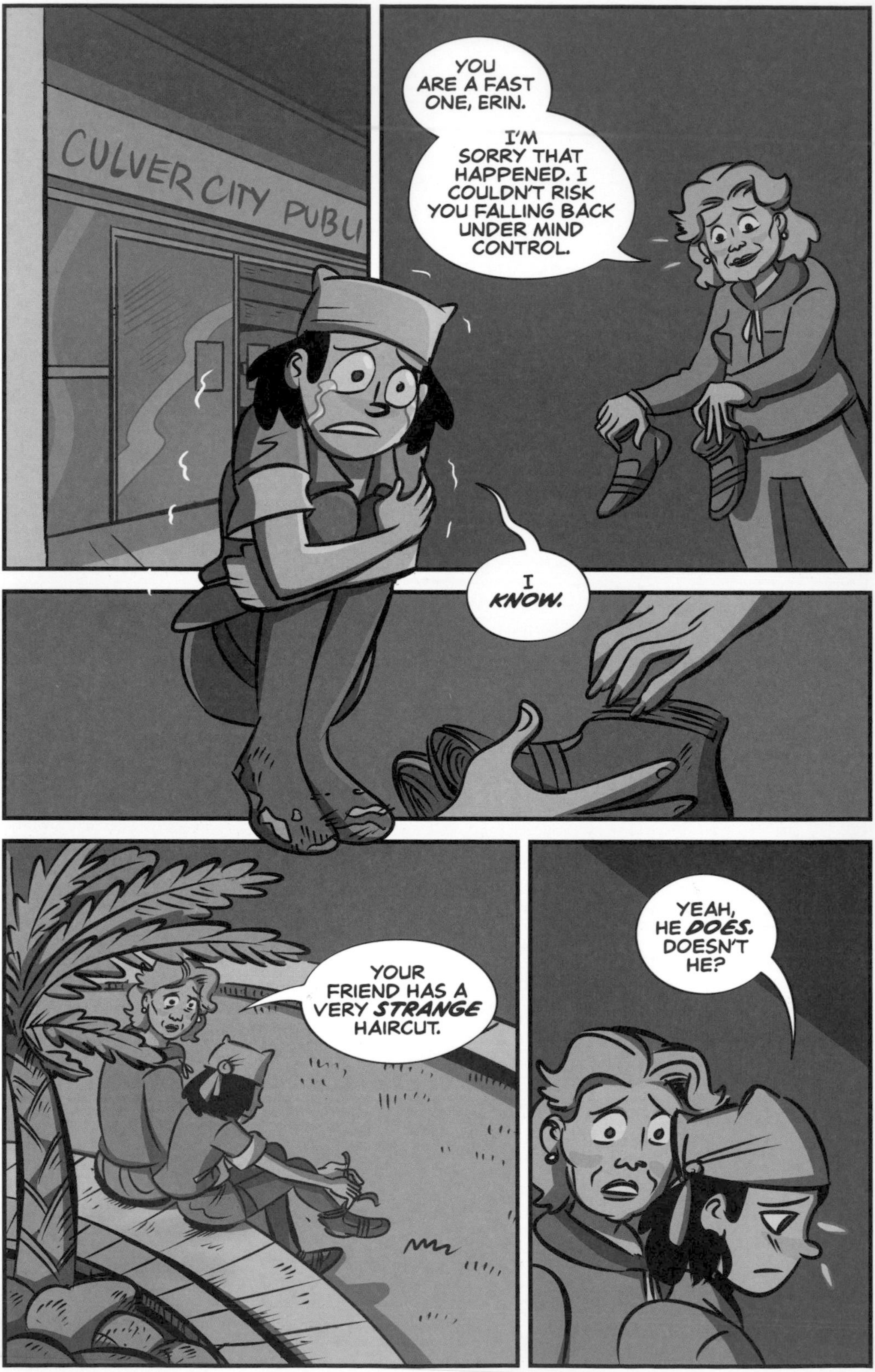
CULVER CITY PUBLI
YOU ARE A FAST ONE, ERIN.
I'M SORRY THAT HAPPENED. I COULDN'T RISK YOU FALLING BACK UNDER MIND CONTROL.
I *KNOW.*
YOUR FRIEND HAS A VERY ***STRANGE*** HAIRCUT.
YEAH, HE ***DOES.*** DOESN'T HE?

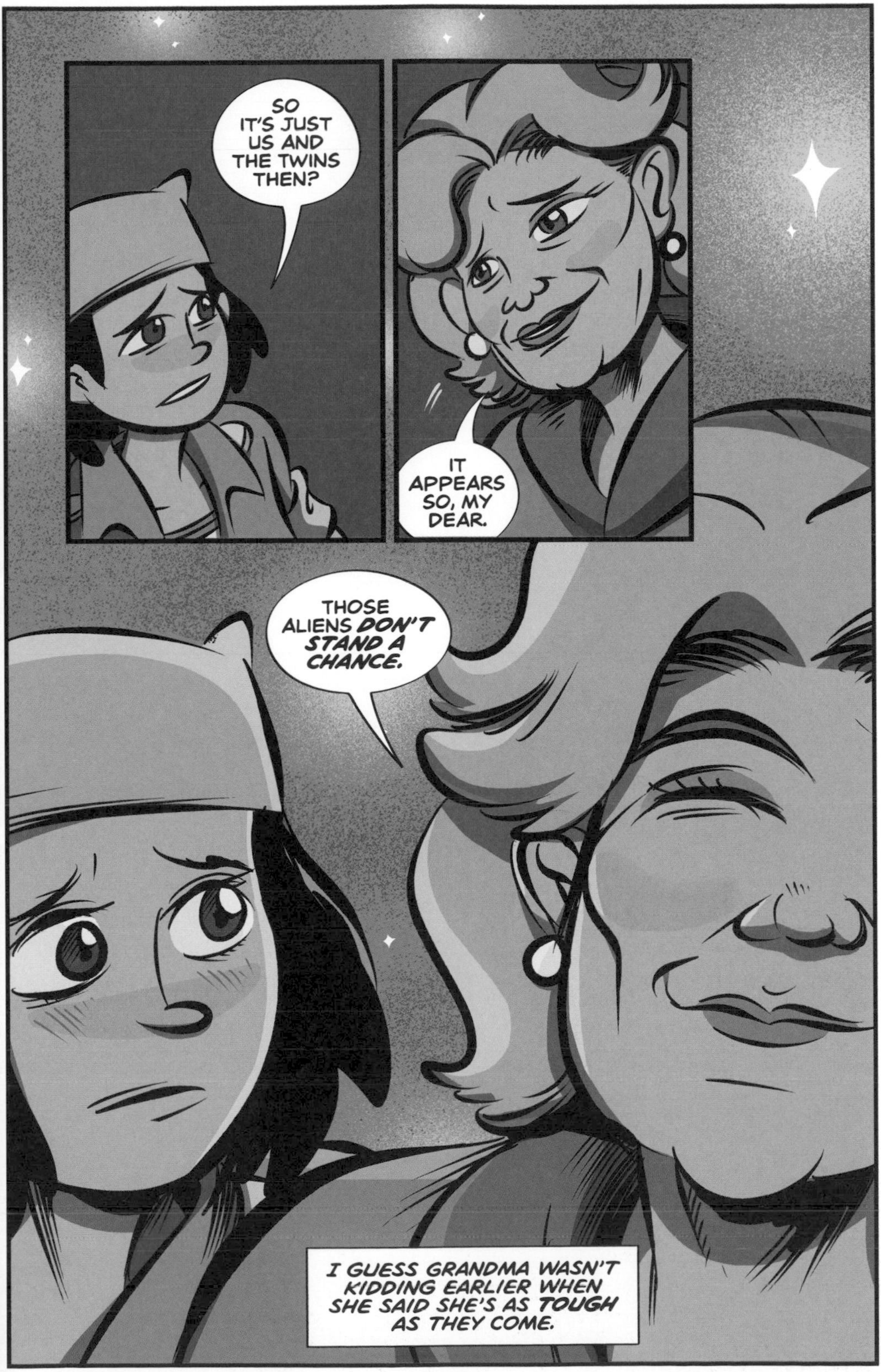
SO IT'S JUST US AND THE TWINS THEN?
IT APPEARS SO, MY DEAR.
THOSE ALIENS DON'T STAND A CHANCE.
I GUESS GRANDMA WASN'T KIDDING EARLIER WHEN SHE SAID SHE'S AS TOUGH AS THEY COME.

CHAPTER FIVE

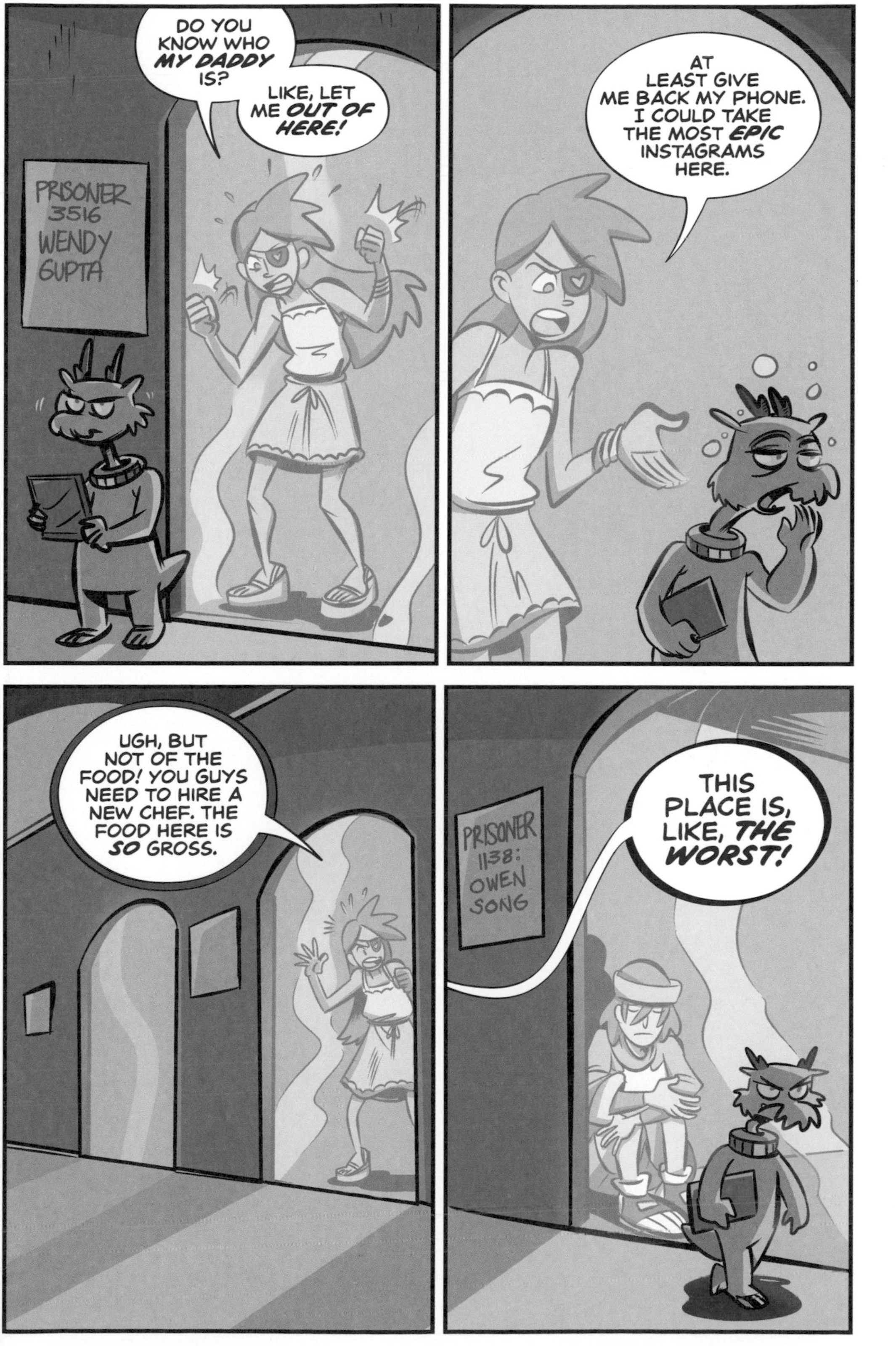
DO YOU KNOW WHO MY DADDY IS?
LIKE, LET ME OUT OF HERE!
PRISONER 3516 WENDY GUPTA
AT LEAST GIVE ME BACK MY PHONE. I COULD TAKE THE MOST EPIC INSTAGRAMS HERE.
UGH, BUT NOT OF THE FOOD! YOU GUYS NEED TO HIRE A NEW CHEF. THE FOOD HERE IS SO GROSS.
PRISONER 1138: OWEN SONG
THIS PLACE IS, LIKE, THE WORST!

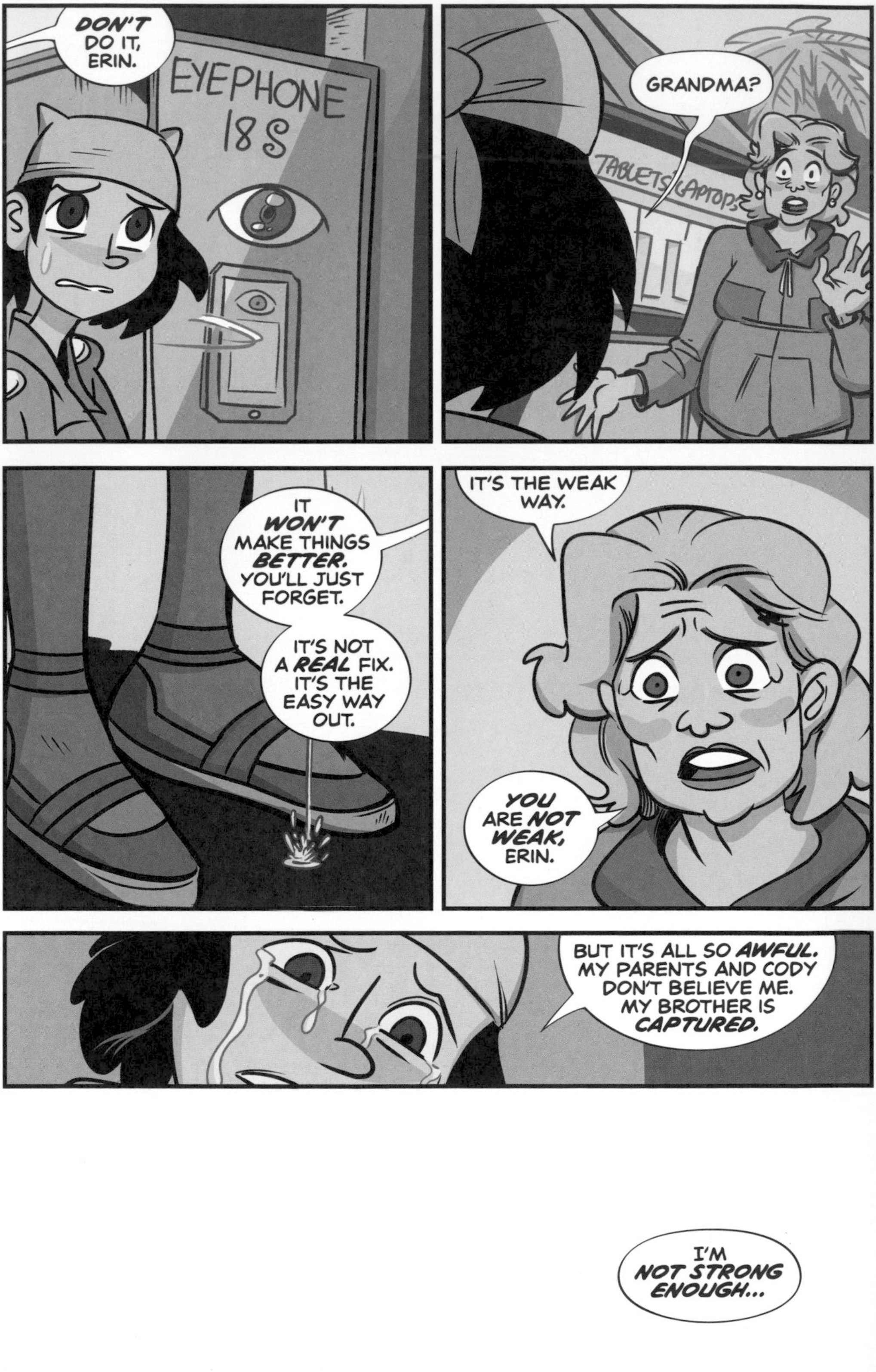
DON'T DO IT, ERIN.
EYEPHONE 18S
GRANDMA?
TABLETS LAPTOPS
IT WON'T MAKE THINGS BETTER. YOU'LL JUST FORGET.
IT'S NOT A REAL FIX. IT'S THE EASY WAY OUT.
IT'S THE WEAK WAY.
YOU ARE NOT WEAK, ERIN.
BUT IT'S ALL SO AWFUL. MY PARENTS AND CODY DON'T BELIEVE ME. MY BROTHER IS CAPTURED.
I'M NOT STRONG ENOUGH...

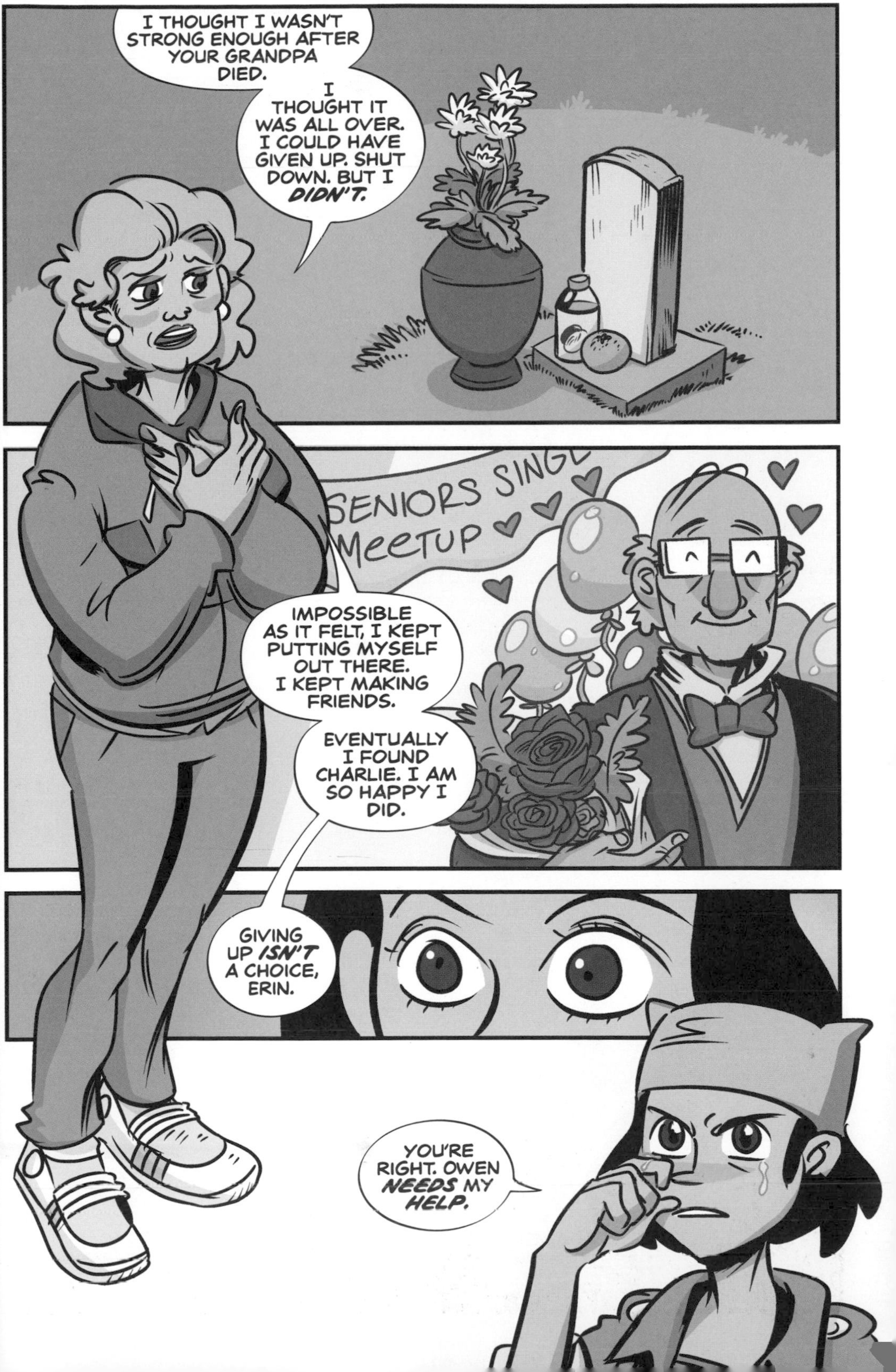
I THOUGHT I WASN'T STRONG ENOUGH AFTER YOUR GRANDPA DIED.
I THOUGHT IT WAS ALL OVER. I COULD HAVE GIVEN UP. SHUT DOWN. BUT I *DIDN'T.*
SENIORS SINGL
MEETUP
IMPOSSIBLE AS IT FELT, I KEPT PUTTING MYSELF OUT THERE. I KEPT MAKING FRIENDS.
EVENTUALLY I FOUND CHARLIE. I AM SO HAPPY I DID.
GIVING UP *ISN'T* A CHOICE, ERIN.
YOU'RE RIGHT. OWEN *NEEDS* MY *HELP.*

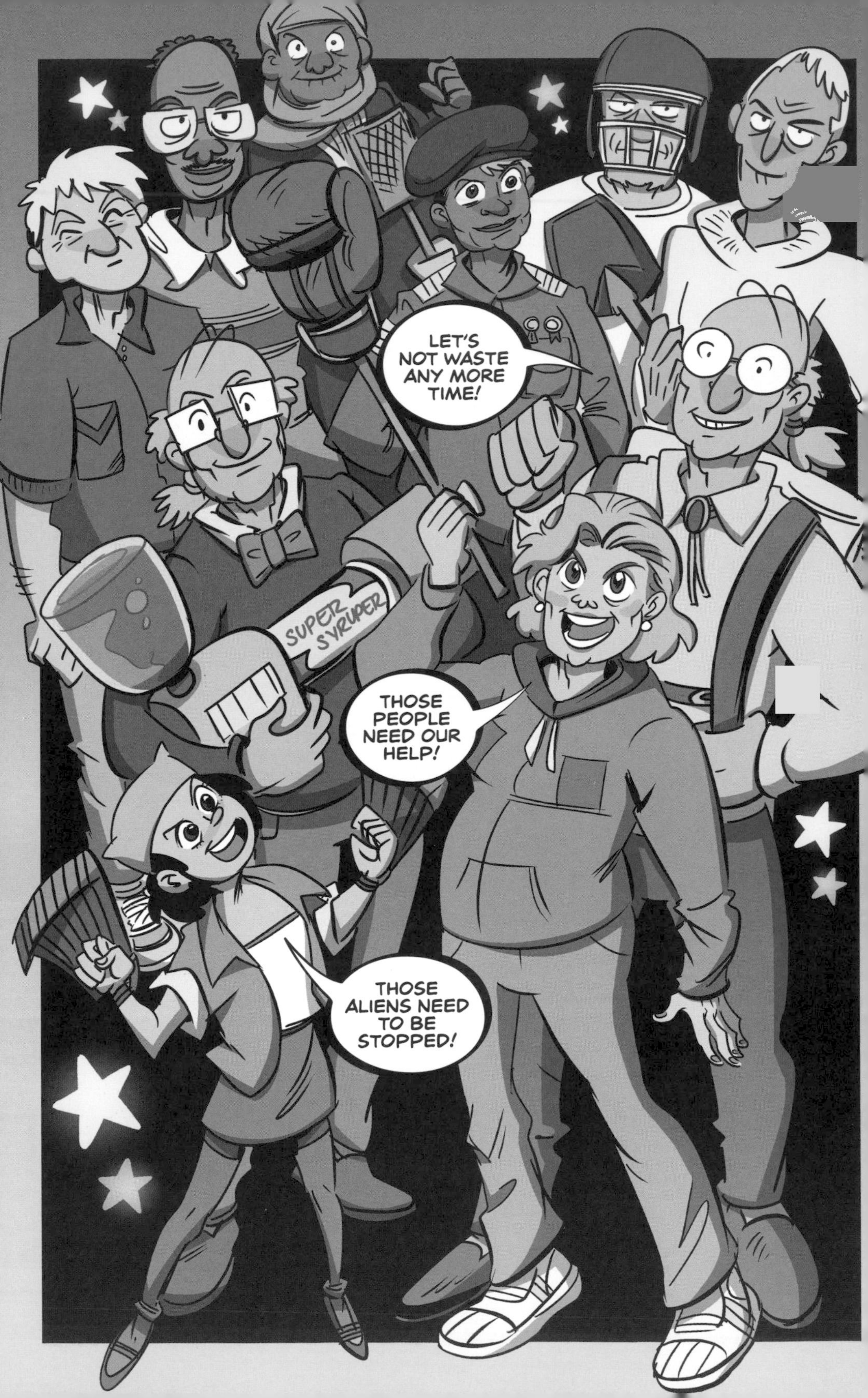
LET'S NOT WASTE ANY MORE TIME!
SUPER SYRUPER
THOSE PEOPLE NEED OUR HELP!
THOSE ALIENS NEED TO BE STOPPED!

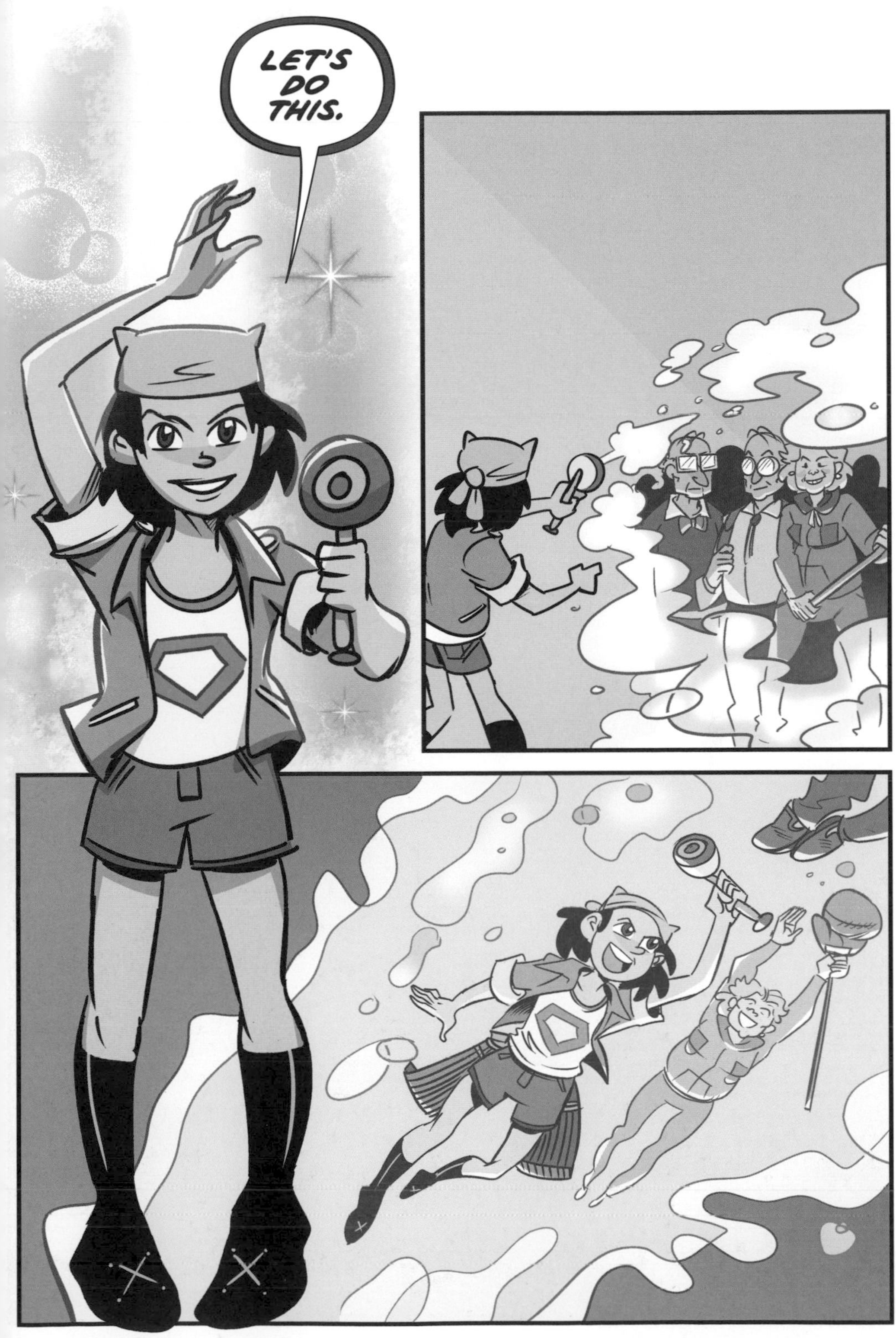
LET'S DO THIS.

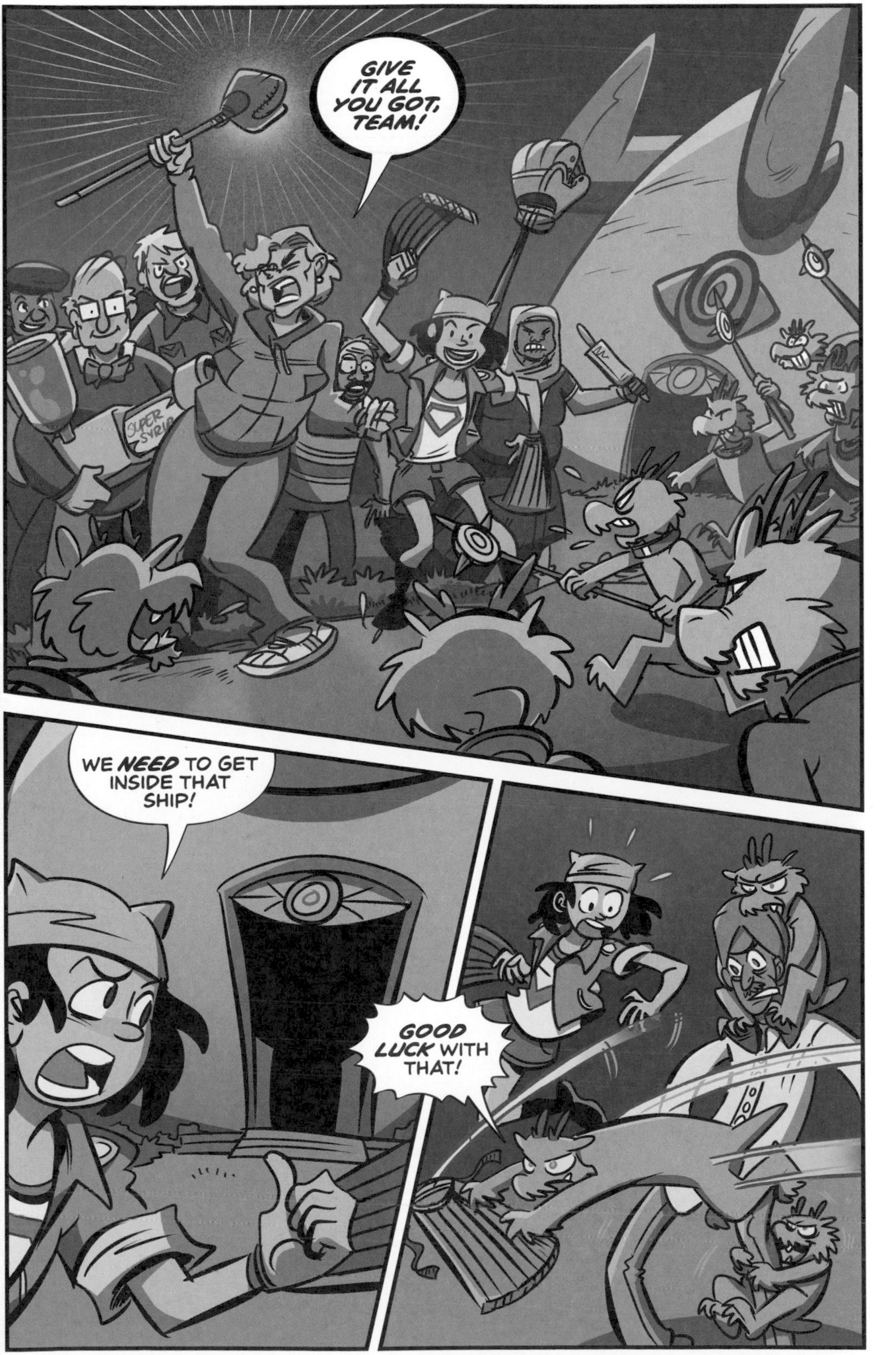
GIVE IT ALL YOU GOT, TEAM!
SUPER SYRUP
WE NEED TO GET INSIDE THAT SHIP!
GOOD LUCK WITH THAT!

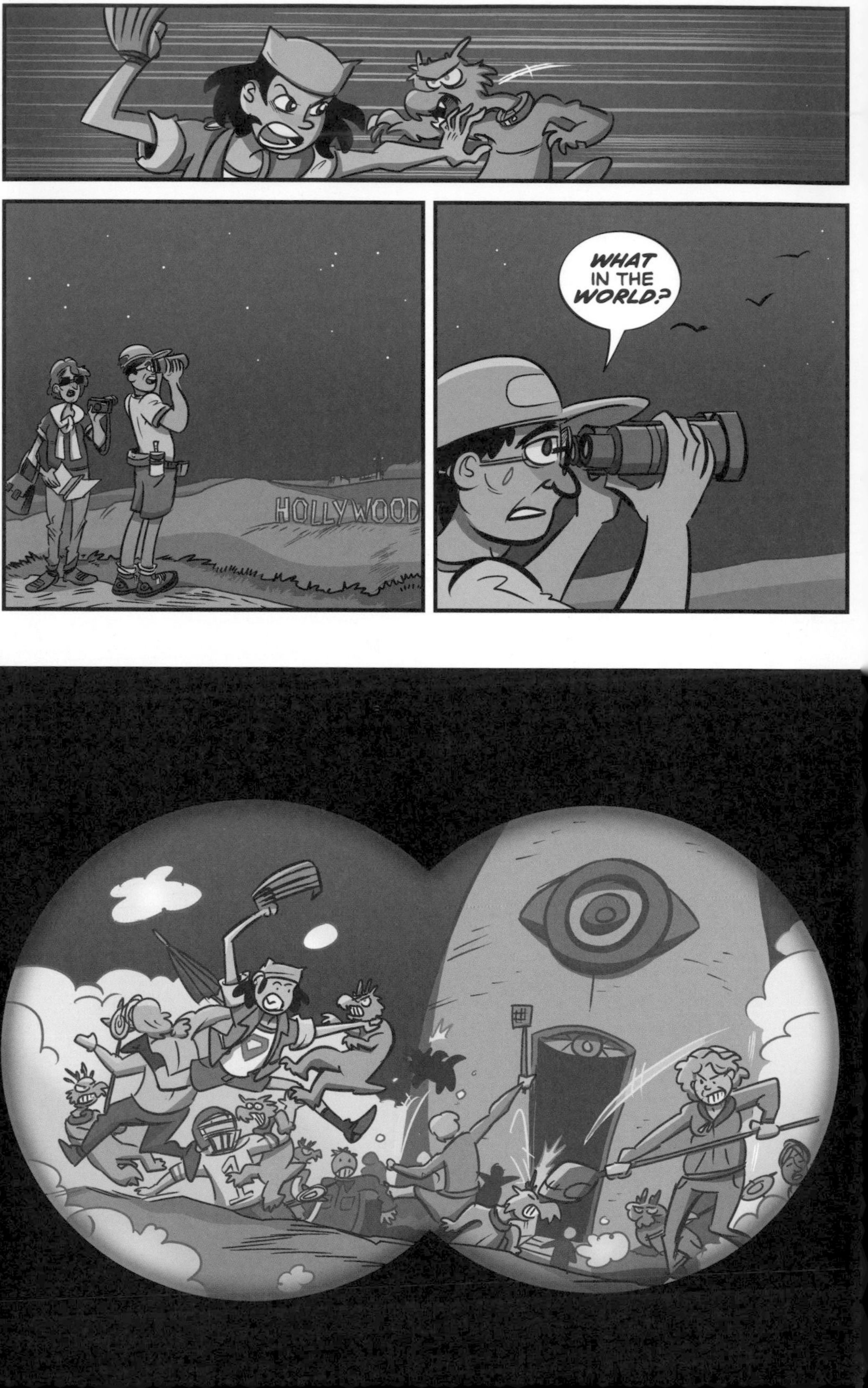
HOLLYWOOD
WHAT IN THE WORLD?

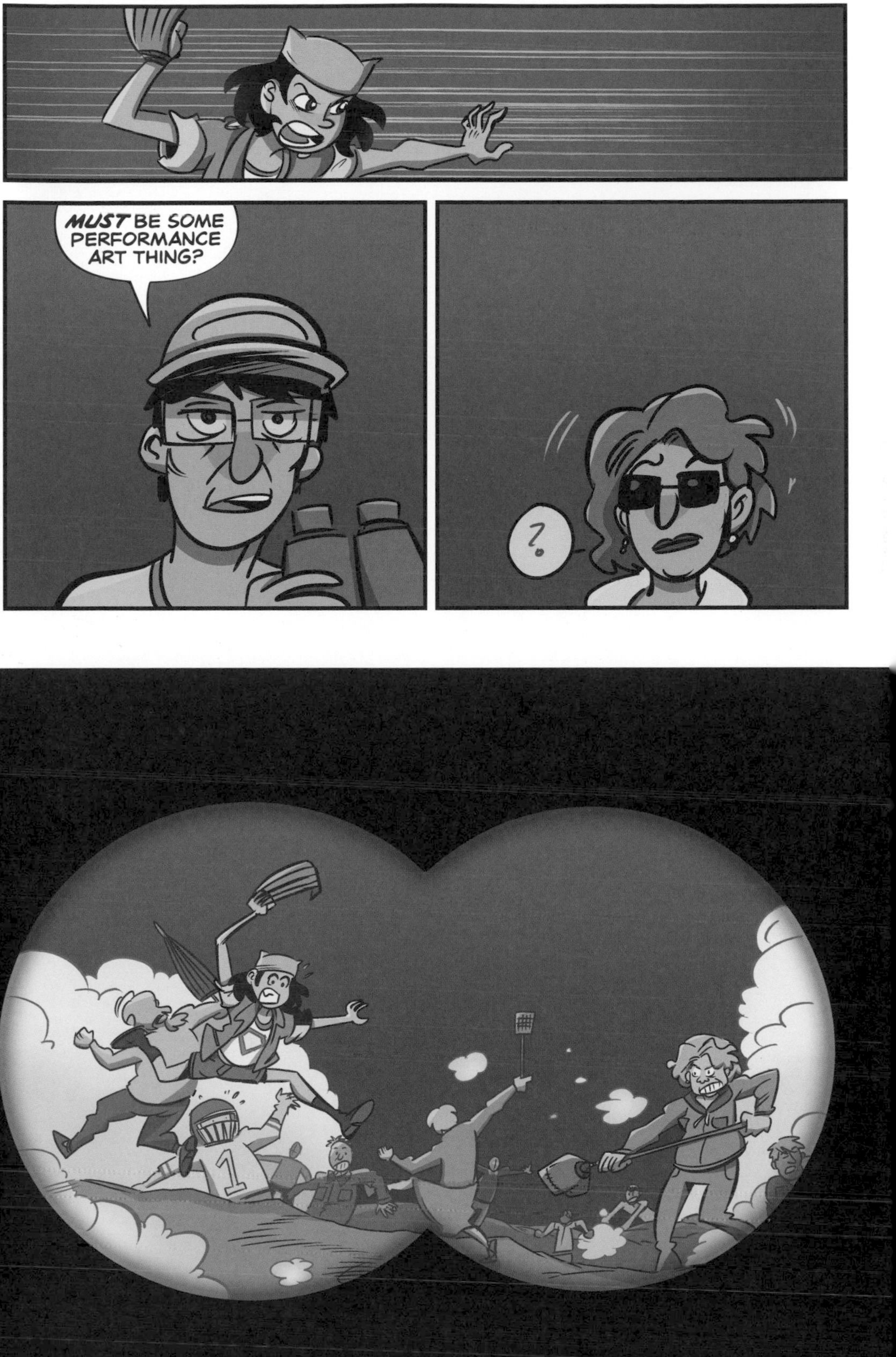
MUST BE SOME PERFORMANCE ART THING?
?

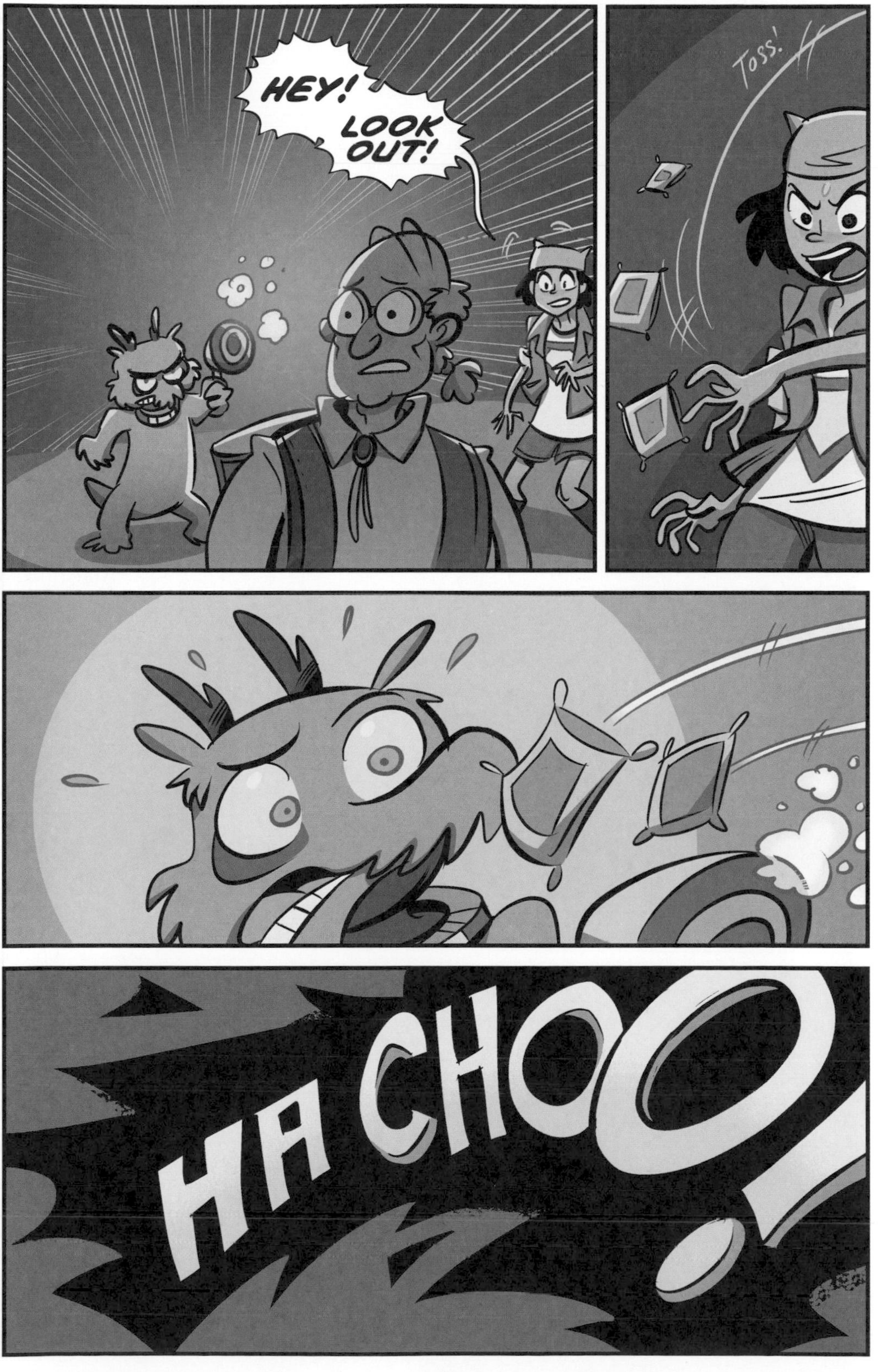
HEY!
LOOK OUT!
TOSS!
HA CHOO!

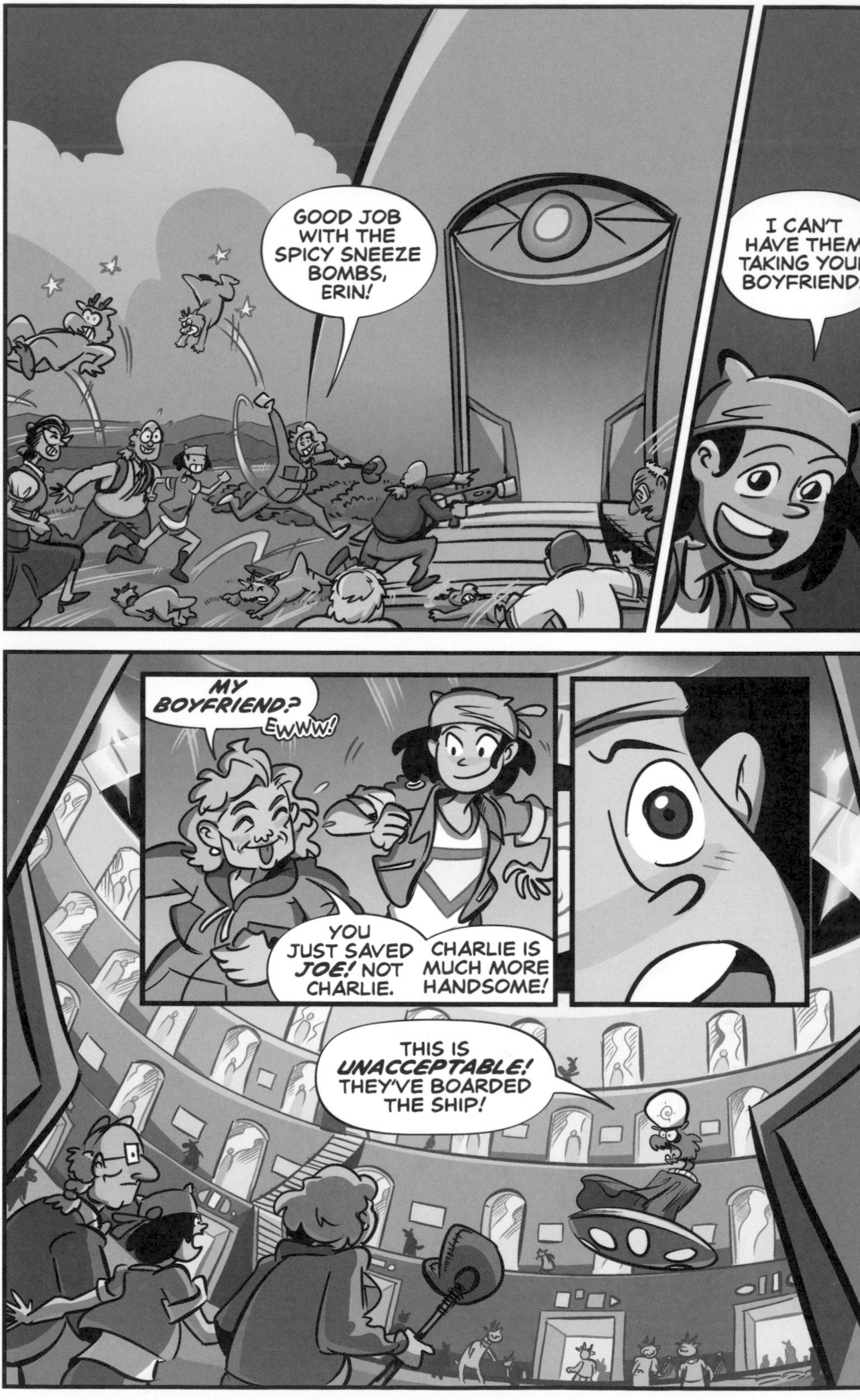
GOOD JOB WITH THE SPICY SNEEZE BOMBS, ERIN!
I CAN'T HAVE THEM TAKING YOUR BOYFRIEND!
MY BOYFRIEND? EWWW!
YOU JUST SAVED JOE! NOT CHARLIE.
CHARLIE IS MUCH MORE HANDSOME!
THIS IS UNACCEPTABLE! THEY'VE BOARDED THE SHIP!

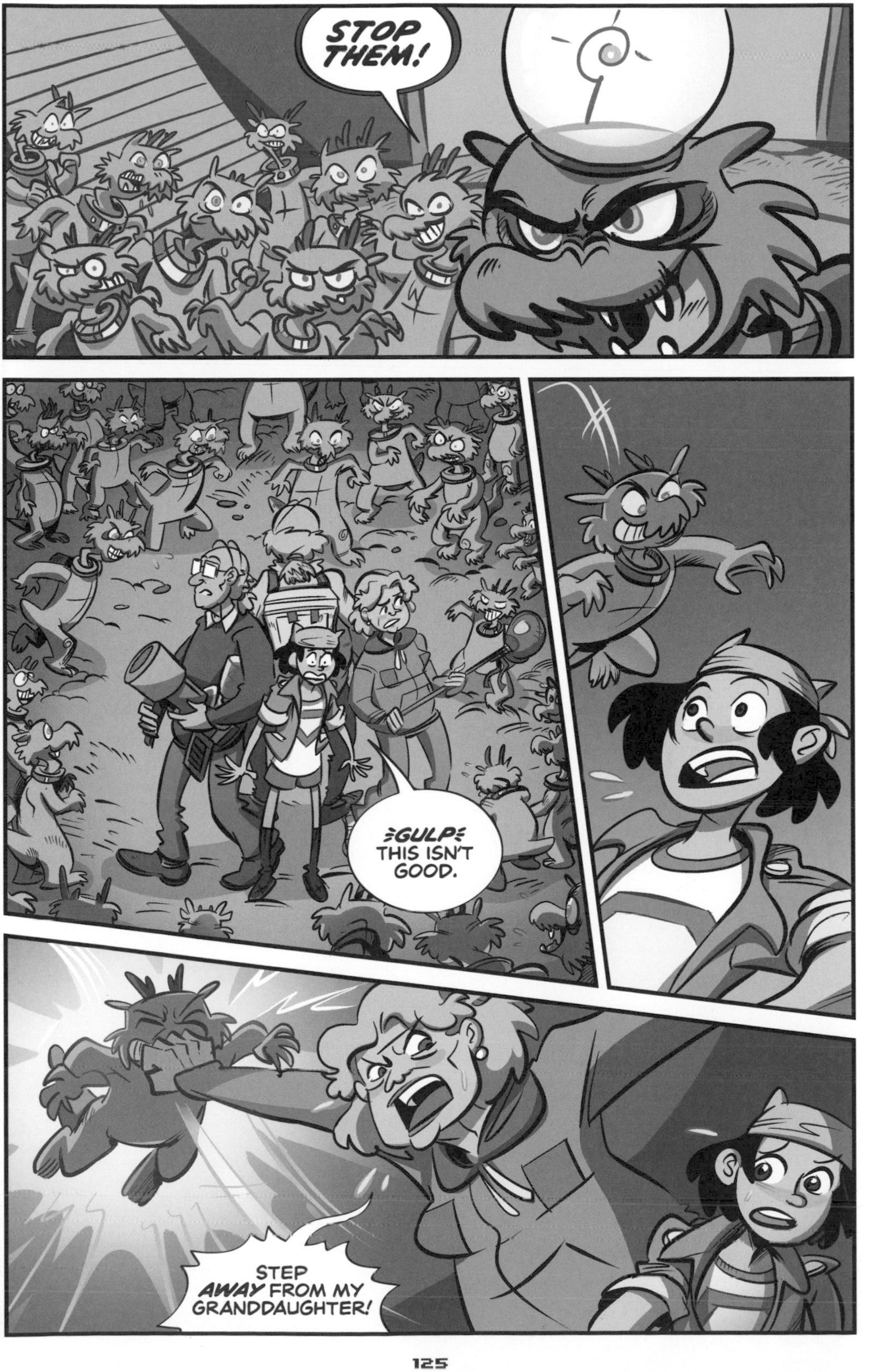
STOP THEM!
≶GULP≶ THIS ISN'T GOOD.
STEP AWAY FROM MY GRANDDAUGHTER!

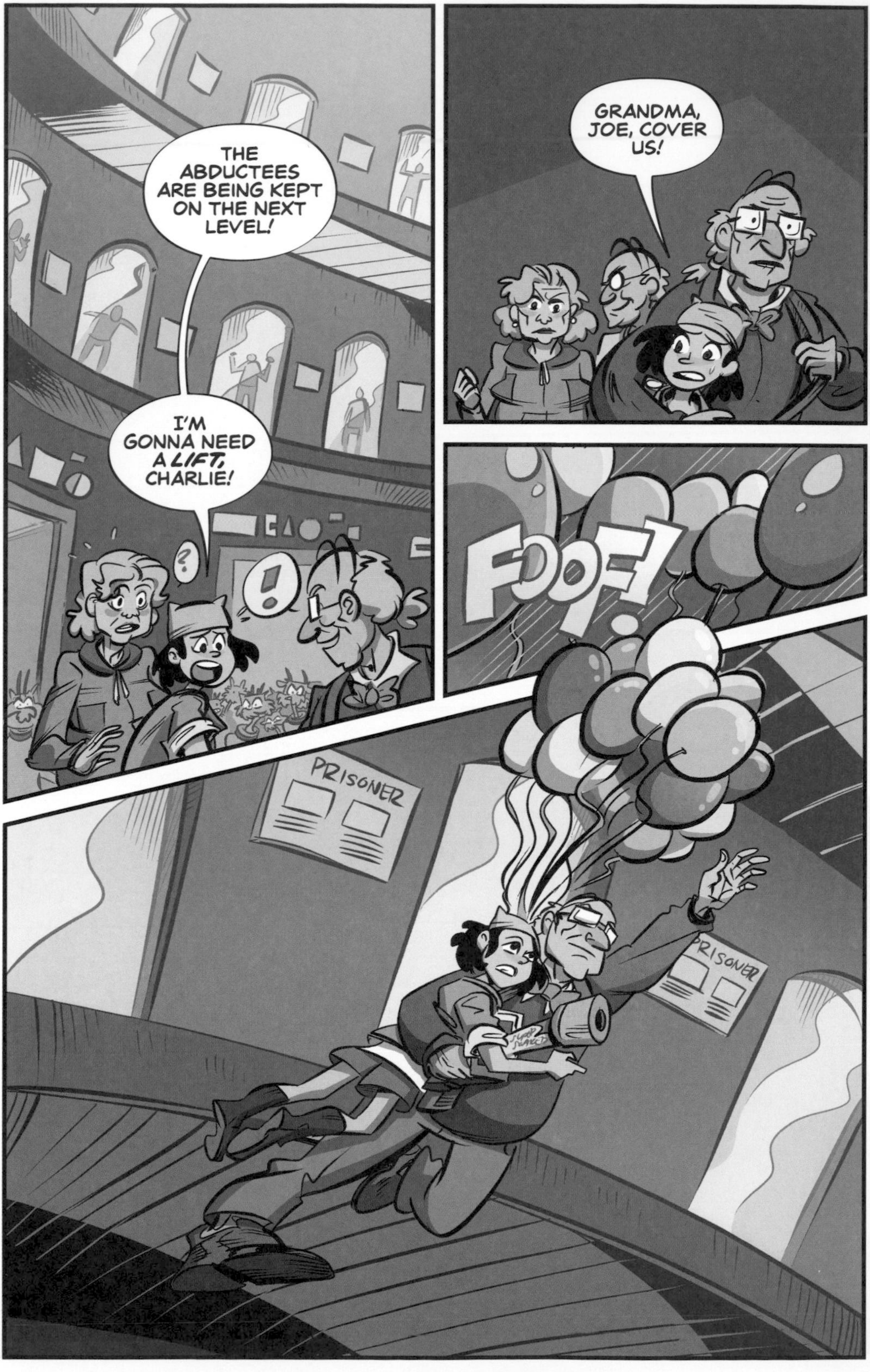
THE ABDUCTEES ARE BEING KEPT ON THE NEXT LEVEL!
I'M GONNA NEED A *LIFT,* CHARLIE!
?
!
GRANDMA, JOE, COVER US!
FOOF!
PRISONER
PRISONER

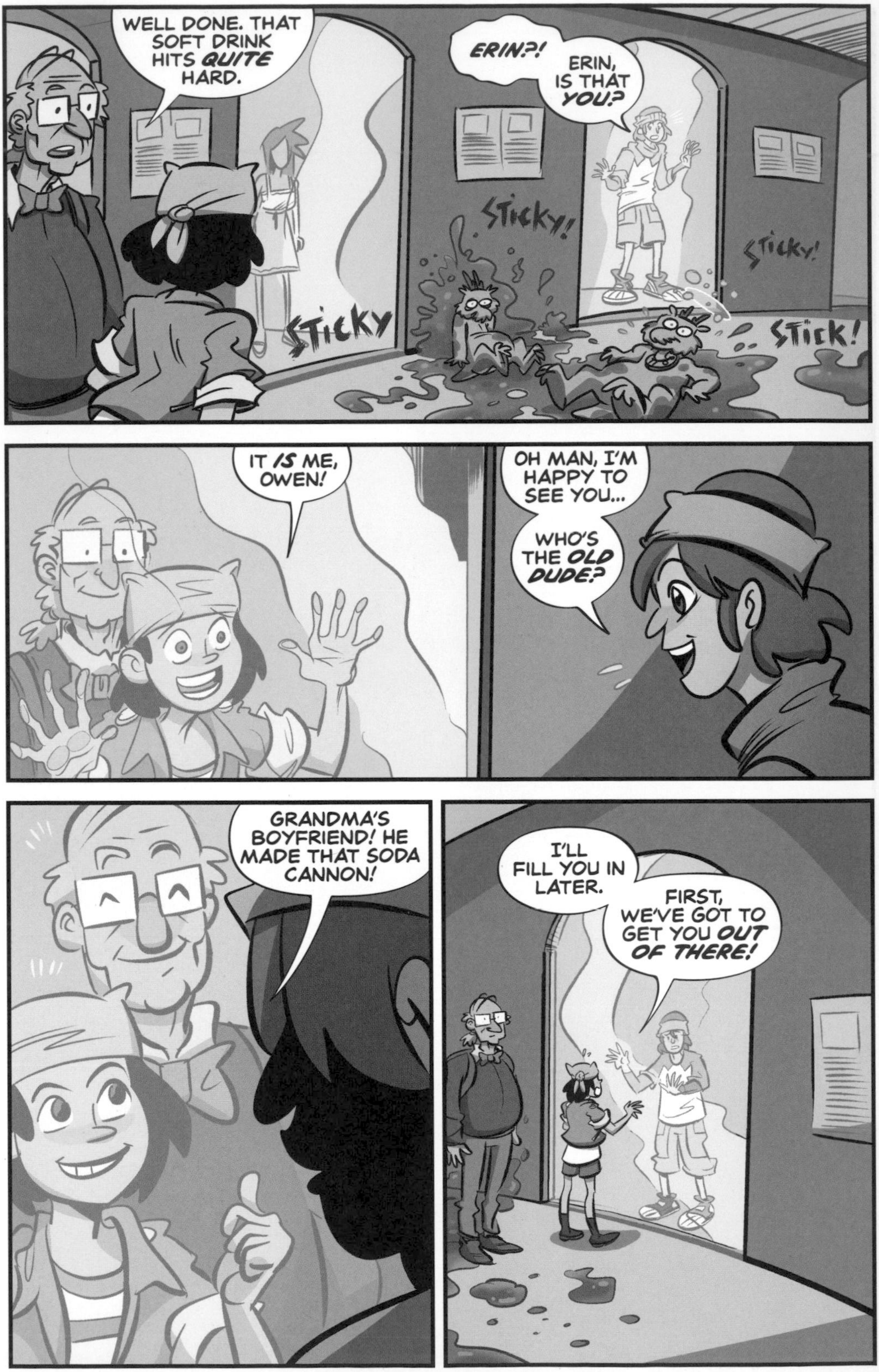
WELL DONE. THAT SOFT DRINK HITS QUITE HARD.
ERIN?!
ERIN, IS THAT YOU?
STICKY
STICKY!
STICKY!
STICK!
IT IS ME, OWEN!
OH MAN, I'M HAPPY TO SEE YOU...
WHO'S THE OLD DUDE?
GRANDMA'S BOYFRIEND! HE MADE THAT SODA CANNON!
I'LL FILL YOU IN LATER.
FIRST, WE'VE GOT TO GET YOU OUT OF THERE!

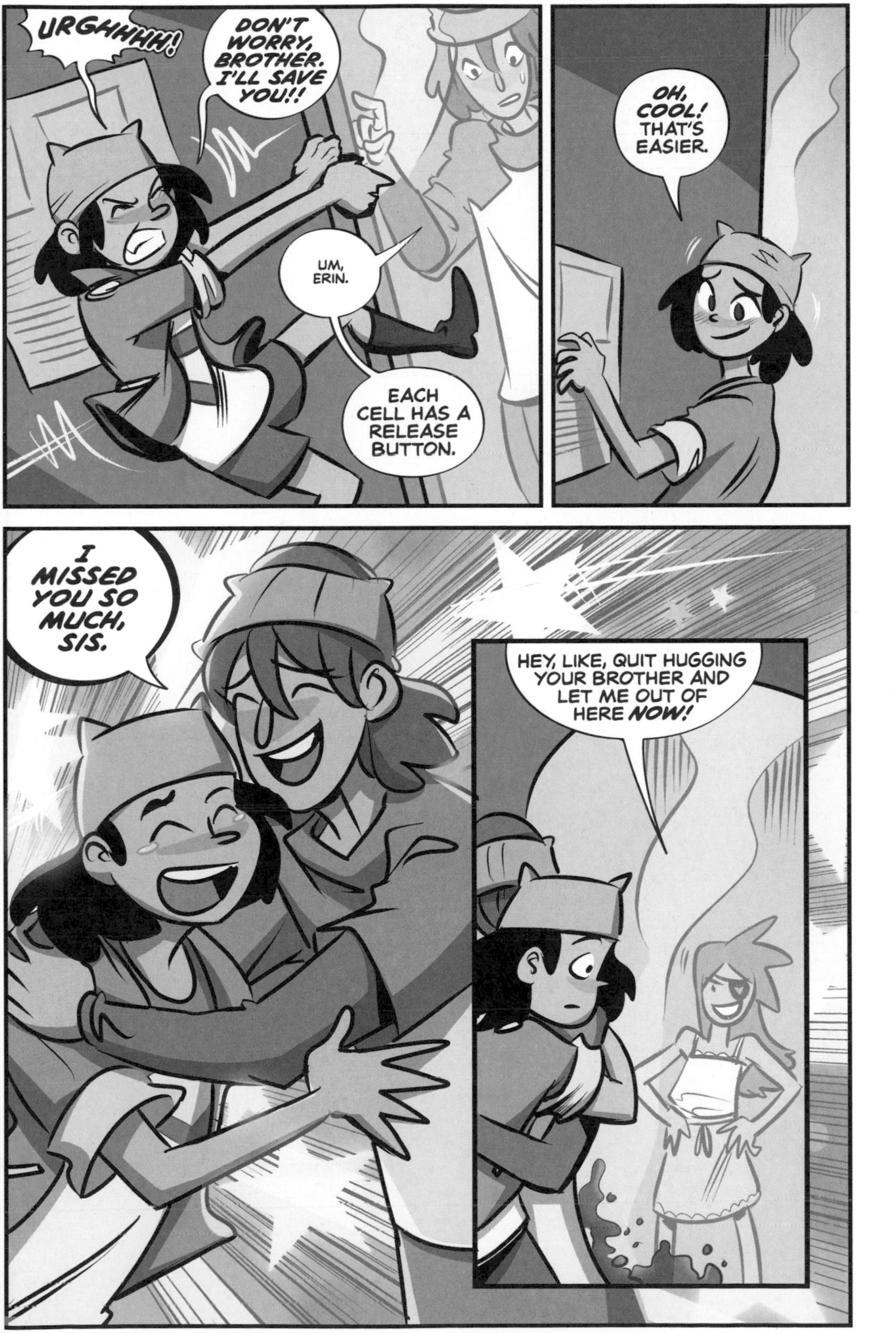
URGHHHH!
DON'T WORRY, BROTHER. I'LL SAVE YOU!!
UM, ERIN.
EACH CELL HAS A RELEASE BUTTON.
OH, COOL! THAT'S EASIER.
I MISSED YOU SO MUCH, SIS.
HEY, LIKE, QUIT HUGGING YOUR BROTHER AND LET ME OUT OF HERE NOW!

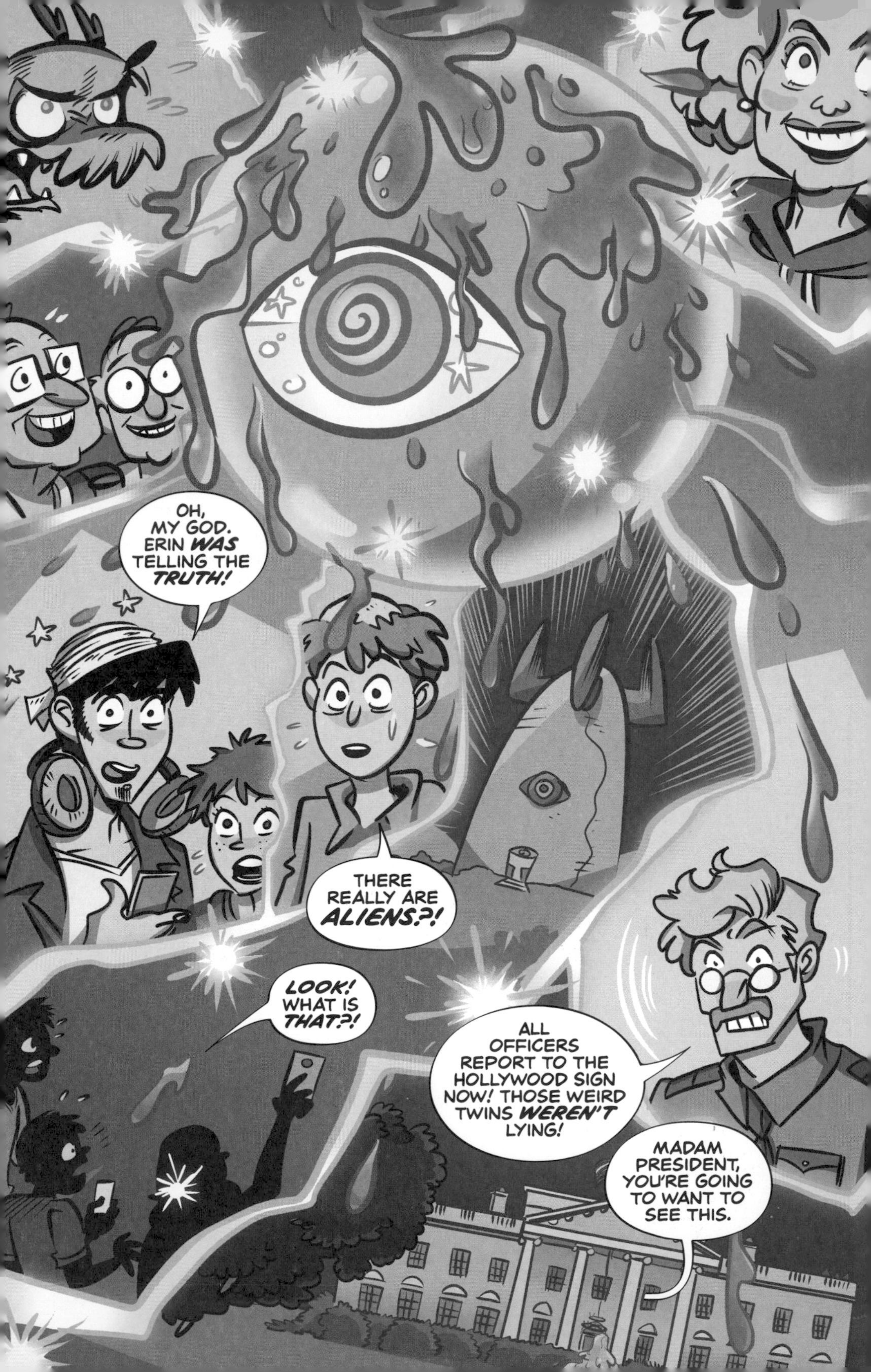
OH, MY GOD. ERIN *WAS* TELLING THE *TRUTH!*
THERE REALLY ARE *ALIENS?!*
LOOK! WHAT IS *THAT?!*
ALL OFFICERS REPORT TO THE HOLLYWOOD SIGN NOW! THOSE WEIRD TWINS *WEREN'T* LYING!
MADAM PRESIDENT, YOU'RE GOING TO WANT TO SEE THIS.

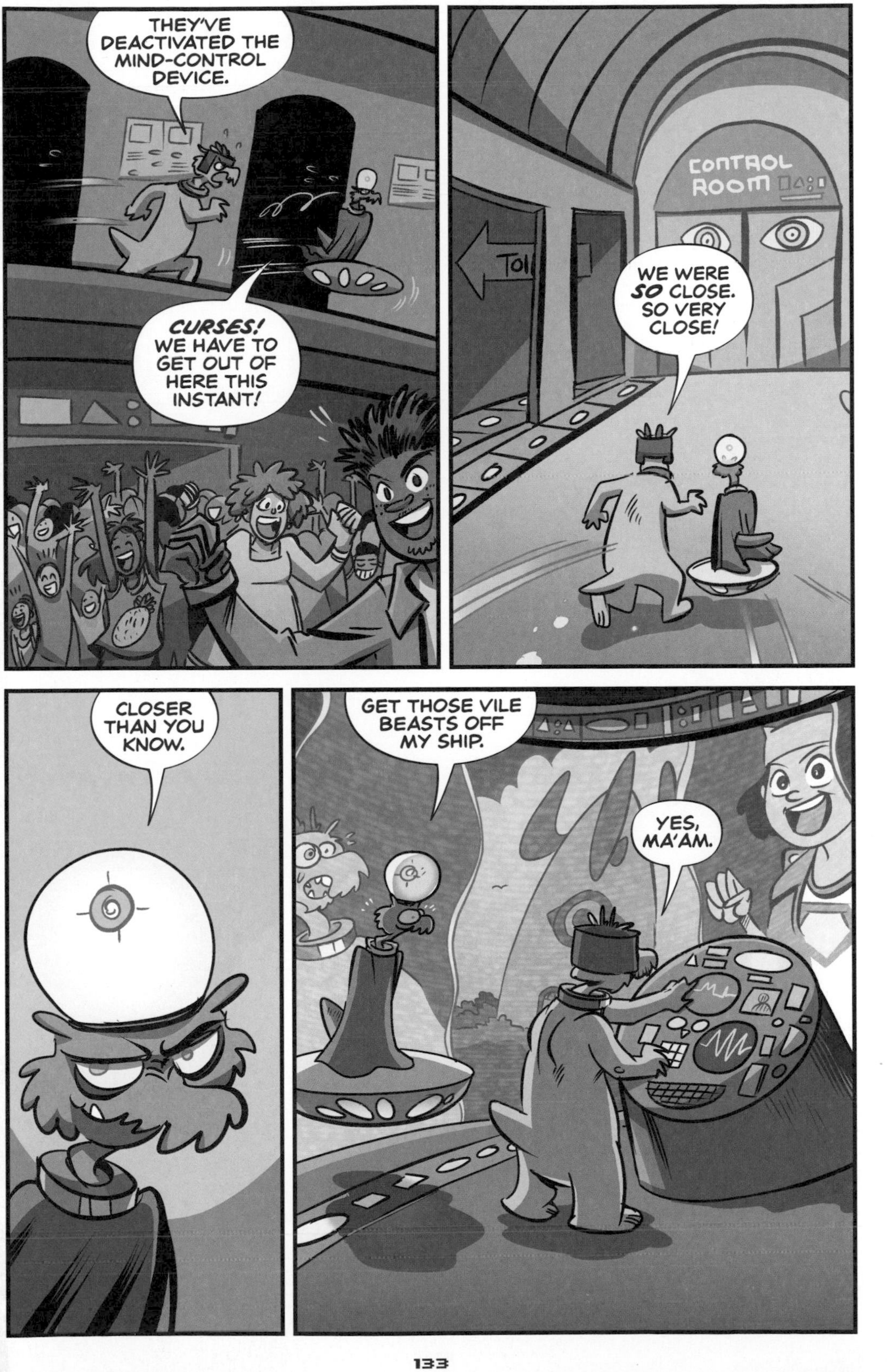
THEY'VE DEACTIVATED THE MIND-CONTROL DEVICE.
CURSES! WE HAVE TO GET OUT OF HERE THIS INSTANT!
CONTROL ROOM
WE WERE SO CLOSE. SO VERY CLOSE!
CLOSER THAN YOU KNOW.
GET THOSE VILE BEASTS OFF MY SHIP.
YES, MA'AM.

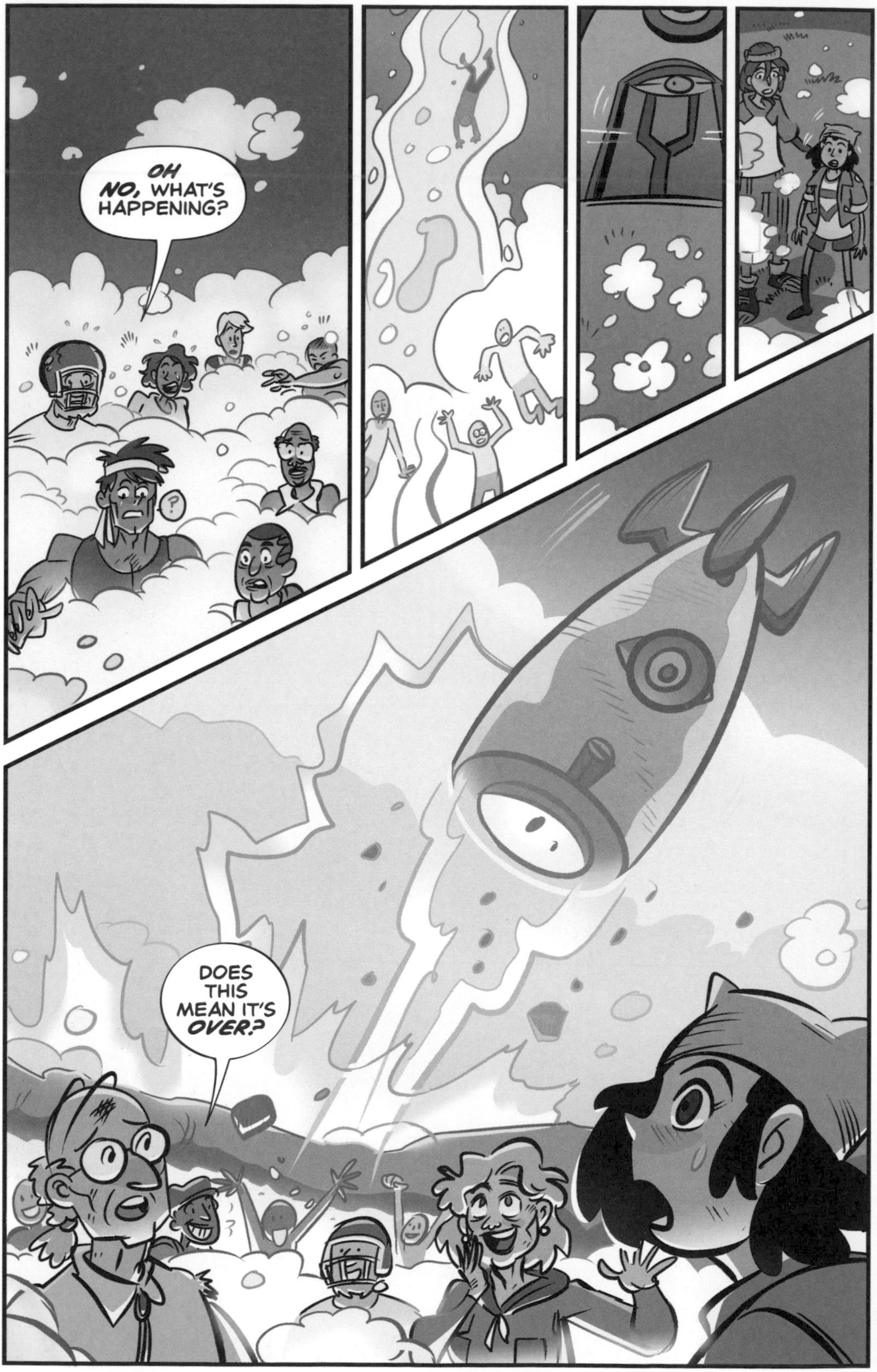
OH NO, WHAT'S HAPPENING?
?
DOES THIS MEAN IT'S OVER?

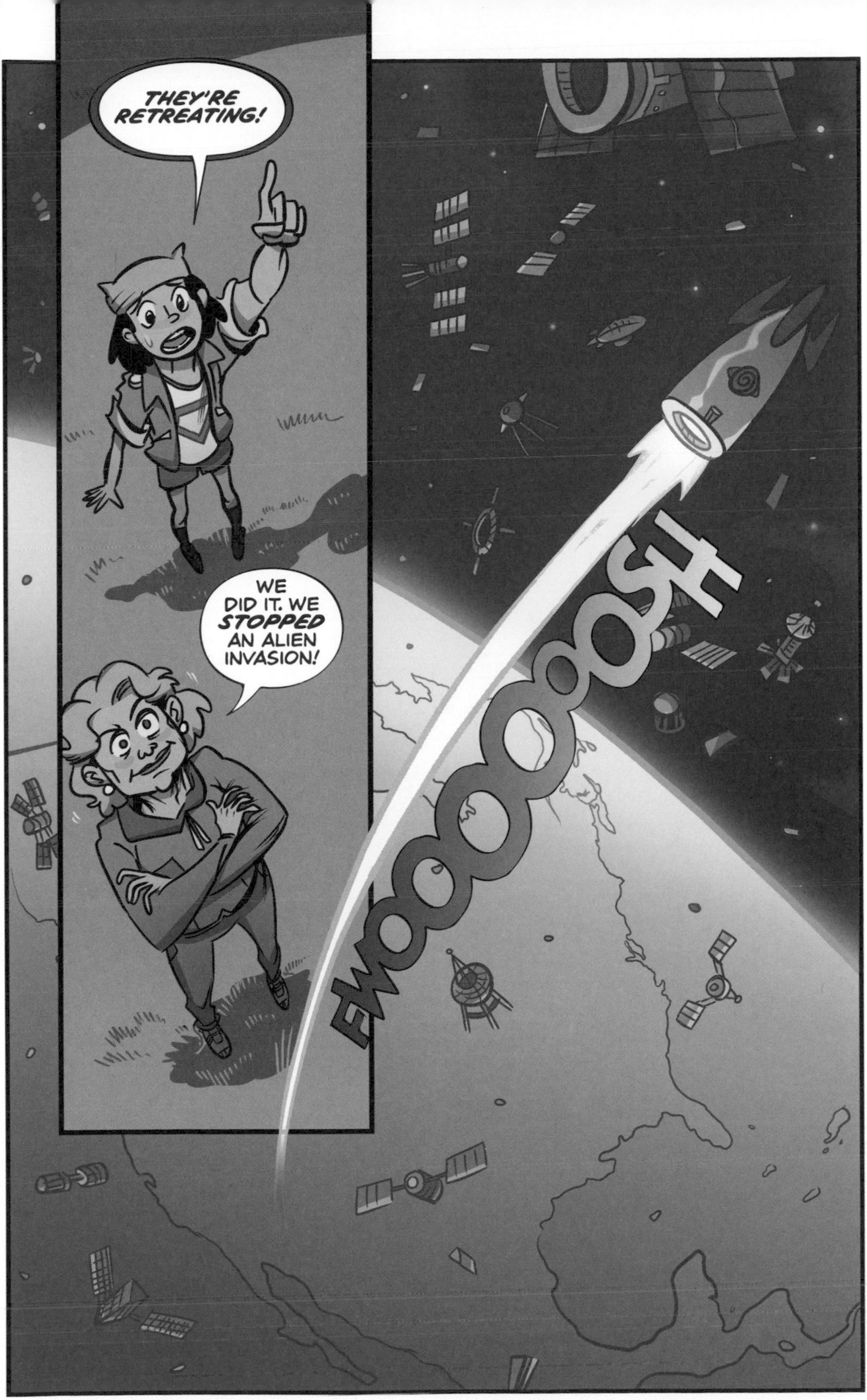
THEY'RE RETREATING!
WE DID IT. WE STOPPED AN ALIEN INVASION!
FWOOOOOOOSH

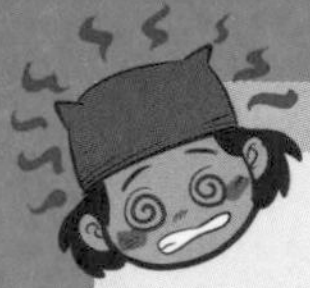

TOP TEN REASONS TO UNPLUG!

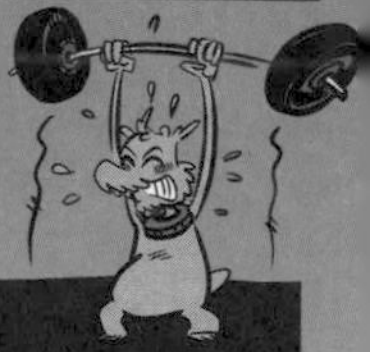

X

Obviously you can't unplug all of the time—the world runs on technology. But sometimes it can be beneficial to unplug for a little bit. Here are ten reasons why.

10. IT'S GOOD FOR YOUR EYES!

Some screens, like from computers and phones, give off blue light. What is blue light? Think of the visible color spectrum as a rainbow. Colors like red, yellow, and orange have long wavelengths and low energy. Colors on the other end of the spectrum, blues and purples, have short wavelengths and high energy. Research is still ongoing about whether these higher energy lights are harmful to human eyes over longer exposure. Do your eyes ever hurt after staring at a computer or a phone for a long time? Focusing on something else for a bit could help!

9. SOME THINGS ARE BETTER IN REAL LIFE

Which would you rather see, a video of a cute tiger sitting in a tree, or an actual tiger sitting in a tree right outside of your house? Okay, bad example—the real tiger is much more dangerous. But there is a difference between seeing something on a screen and seeing it IRL. For one thing, a screen only involves two of your five senses: hearing and sight. Viewing something in real life, you can also utilize touch, taste, and smell! Okay, maybe don't lick or touch the tiger. But you get the idea: the internet is a great way to get a lot of information—just not always the best way!

8. GET USED TO DELAYED GRATIFICATION

Being online is all about instant gratification. With higher wifi speeds and tons of websites to explore, it's nearly impossible to be bored on the internet. Real life isn't the same way, though—there are definitely things in life you'll have to wait for, like checking out at the grocery store or traveling to a new destination. These things take time, and it's good to get used to not getting things in an instant.

7. SOME THINGS CAN'T BE DONE ON A SCREEN

There are great drawing programs available for artists. In fact, Tintin Pantoja, the artist of this book, drew most of it digitally, instead of using ink and paper. But there are some aspects of art that haven't been perfected digitally yet, like painting with oil paints, or creating pottery. (You still gotta use your hands for those!) There are many experiences that can't be replicated on screens, so give them a try! You might find something new to love.

6. BECOME MORE AWARE OF YOUR SURROUNDINGS

Have you ever "lost" an hour because you were so engrossed in what was on your screen that the time seemed to pass very quickly? Or, have you ever been so engrossed in what was on your screen that day turned to night without you realizing? Unplugging for a bit can refamiliarize you with your surroundings and what is happening around you.

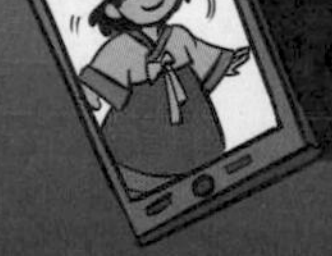

5. GET SOME MUCH-NEEDED EXERCISE

The benefits of regular exercise are well documented. What most people might not know is that any amount of exercise is good. You don't need to be running three miles, or even one mile, or even half a mile. Walking is exercise too, after all! Find a physical activity that works with your level of physical ability.

4. PRACTICAL EXPERIENCE

Sure, a YouTube video can teach you how to make your own soap, but until you put those teachings into practice, you still won't have soap. And even with the video, you may mess up the first time... or the second... or the twelfth.... So you've got to keep at it!

3. SAVE ENERGY

If you're looking for ways to decrease your carbon footprint, unplugging is a great (and, let's face it, small) way to help. You probably already turn off lights in rooms you aren't using or shut the refrigerator door instead of standing there, gazing into it, like some kind of energy-wasting doofus. Go for the gold and unplug for a bit!

2. LET YOUR BRAIN REST FOR A BIT

Sometimes when you're on your phone or computer, looking up information or watching video after video, your brain can start to feel... overwhelmed. Of course it's great to learn, but hey, sometimes your brain doesn't like being in school all day either! That's why there's breaks at school—recess, lunch, etc. Make sure you give your brain a recess if you're spending too much time on screens.

1. MAYBE EVERYONE AROUND YOU IS ACTUALLY BEING MIND-CONTROLLED BY ALIENS AND THE ONLY WAY TO STOP THEIR INFLUENCE IS TO TURN OFF ALL SCREENS

Hey, it could happen.

X

NEED SUGGESTIONS?

The Unplugged and Unpopular team share their favorite unplugging activities below.

MAT HEAGERTY

Sweet nature walk adventures with my family, drawing rad stuff (like a surfing Pig-Dragon), going to the dog park, going to the human park, relaxing on the beach, letting my mind wander and enjoying silence

TINTIN PANTOJA

Chugging cups of gasoline-strength coffee, doodling with my fountain pens, petting one (or more) of our four dogs. If I'm unplugged, I'm probably at the country farm. There's no internet or cell signal!

MIKE AMANTE

Going on an out-of-town trip with your loved ones every once in a while, going out for a swim at the local swimming pool, playing the piano

HASSAN OTSMANE-ELHAOU

Cuddling my dog, getting lost in the countryside, eating as much food as possible, reading as many comics as possible

MAT HEAGERTY

is a chipper bartender and comic book writer who currently has multiple projects in the works. The height of his internet popularity was being retweeted once by MC Hammer. Mat lives in the Bay Area where he happily orbits around his daughter, wife, and black lab. If you haven't lost your internet privileges, you can find him on Twitter (@matheagerty) or on his website (matheagerty.com).

TINTIN PANTOJA

has previously illustrated graphic novels such as *Who Is AC?* (written by Hope Larson) and the *Manga Math Mysteries* series (by Melinda Thielbar). She enjoys journaling, fountain pens, and fine chocolates. *Unplugged and Unpopular* is her first all-digitally-inked book, which means she'd be the first one brainwashed! She also loves bad puns and window shopping. Tintin lives in Manila, Philippines with four dogs and 1/2 cat.

MIKE AMANTE

is a freelance children's book illustrator who has worked on the *Shahnameh for Kids* series and on OMF Literature books such as *Dyaran! Ang Kambal Na Hebigat! (Tada! The Heavyweight Twins!)* and *Ang Allowance Na Hindi Bitin*. He loves to drink tea, listen to lo-fi music, and read comics. He thinks aliens are cool so he made a bunch of minicomics about them. Mike currently resides in Laguna, Philippines along with his family and their overly energetic poodle.

HASSAN OTSMANE-ELHAOU

was recently diagnosed with a severe Twitter addiction. In between tweets, he has lettered comics like *Dream Daddy*, *Shanghai Red*, *Peter Cannon*, *Red Sonja*, and more. He's also the editor behind Eisner-nominated *PanelxPanel*, and the host of the *Strip Panel Naked* YouTube series. You can usually find him explaining that comics are totally a real job to his parents.